The Girl

"The Girl"

Constructions of the Girl in Contemporary Fiction by Women

Edited by Ruth O. Saxton

St. Martin's Press
New York

THE GIRL: CONSTRUCTIONS OF THE GIRL IN CONTEMPORARY FICTION BY WOMEN

St. Martin's Press, 175 Fifth Avenue, New York, N.Y. 10010.

ISBN 0-312-17353-9

Library of Congress Cataloging-in-Publication Data

The girl : constructions of the girl in contemporary fiction by women / edited by Ruth O. Saxton.

p. cm.

Includes bibliographical references and index.

ISBN 0-312-17353-9

1. American fiction—Women authors—History and criticism. 2. Girls in literature. 3. Women and literature—United States--History—20th century. 4. Women and literature—Great Britain--History—20th century. 5. English fiction—Women authors—History and criticism. 6. American fiction—20th century—History and criticism. I. Saxton, Ruth.

PS374.G55G57 1998 98-3849
813'.540992827'082—dc21 CIP

Design by Acme Art, Inc.
First edition: September 1998
10 9 8 7 6 5 4 3 2

For
Katherine Blair Saxton

Contents

Acknowledgments

This collection of essays originated with Maura Burnett, who first saw the possibility of a book in my call for papers for a special session on "The Girl" for the 1996 Modern Language Asssociation Convention, and I would like to thank her for her enthusiasm and practical encouragement. Thanks also to the contributors in this volume, who met deadlines promptly and graciously and whose work is the life of the book. A Faculty Research Summer grant as well as Quigley Women's Studies support from Mills College made possible the assistance of Emily Anderson whose early research helped me discover what already existed in print on the subject of girls in general and girls in contemporary literature by women. Jessica Mason and Shamira Gratch assisted in every step of the production and editing work of assembling this volume, created the index, and buoyed my spirits when multiple tasks of teaching and administration threatened to derail the project.

Kirsten Saxton, my daughter, colleague, and most rigorous editor, read every word as she always does, and Katherine Saxton, my daughter and sounding board, helped keep me honest about the lives of living, breathing girls of her generation as she went from soccer practice to cross country championships, filed college applications, chose her prom dress, and still found time to talk with me about books around the edges. Paul, my partner for thirty-five years, David Saxton, my son, and Karl Garcia, my son-in-law, continued to believe the book would see its way to print, and collectively helped keep me balanced by doing what they do so well—listening and shoring up the foundations of daily life.

Finally, thank you to Mom and Dad, who were there from the beginning, opening me to the world of language as Dad read aloud daily and Mom penned stories and poetry.

Introduction

RUTH O. SAXTON

This book investigates the legacies of expectation, competing cultural ideologies, and multiplicities of growing up female in British, American, and postcolonial societies at the end of the twentieth century as portrayed in contemporary fictions by women.[1] When beginning this collection, I thought that the focus on the Girl emerging in new fictions by women would stand in stark contrast to configurations of girlhood in earlier fiction: that new visions would interrogate assumptions about whose lives and perspectives are suitable for literary inquiry and would craft new plots and narrative renderings of females coming-of-age. To some extent, this notion has proven correct, in that new fictions of the Girl provide access to a constellation of themes and narrative patterns—including race and ethnicity, sexual orientation, class, female subjectivity, and nationalism—in ways far different than their earlier predecessors of centuries, or even decades, ago. However, despite the important ways in which the texts addressed in this work break open and into older narratives and plots of girlhood, I have found that contemporary literary investigations into the Girl continue to envision girlhood according to tropes and plots familiar since the dawn of novelistic fiction. While the "marriage or death plot"—the "heroine's text"[2] of eighteenth- and nineteenth-century British and American fiction—has expanded to encompass less homogeneous, compulsory heterosexual definitions of love, romantic fulfillment or the rejection of romance still propels many of today's fictional young women. Such themes as individuation from the mother, maternal loss or overpresence—staples of novels by the Brontës, Dickens, Eliot, Thackeray, and Woolf—continue to inform *Künstlerroman,* narratives of female coming-of-age. Physicality—the Girl's experience of her body, engagement in or denial of sex, her cultural "value" as young female body—remains crucial. Perhaps one locus of difference between contemporary fictions and those of earlier centuries or even decades is their focus on reaction and active subjectivity; in other words, while early women writers—such as Aphra Behn, Eliza Haywood, and Delarivier Manley, who, in Restoration and Augustan England, were among the first women to publish—might imagine violent responses to their young heroines' abuse or to her predicament in a sexist society, she is virtually never allowed to flourish after rebelling. In Victorian England, George Eliot's Maggie Tulliver and Emily Brontë's Catherine Earnshaw die, and modernist protagonists, such as Virginia Woolf's Mrs. Ramsay or Rachel Vinrace and Jean Rhys's Antoinette, either die because of their participation in the marriage plot or, like Woolf's Lily Briscoe and Willa Cather's Thea Kronberg, survive at the cost of denying their own sexuality. Contemporary protagonists, such as Toni Morrison's Pecola, Dorothy Allison's Bone, and Jane Hamilton's Ruth, endure physical and emotional abuse, and then either "escape" into madness or narrate their own stories with a matter-of-factness that indites the culture while reconfiguring the reader's notion of girlhood innocence, insisting upon the young heroine's value as a speaking subject.

This collection proposes that contemporary stories of girlhood constitute a new and generative lens for literary and cultural study. As they have in the past, girls remain fixtures in today's fiction, particularly in fiction by women; tracing the reverberations and dissonances between fictional visions of girlhood calls attention to new texts and contexts as it simultaneously provides us a new lens through which to re-vision older and perhaps more familiar plots and texts of girlhood. I have chosen the essays in this book for their intersections and the ideological debate they engender when read with and against one another. These essays speak to, complement, and contest one another in their multivalent interrogation of textual visions of growing up female at the end of the millennium. Part of the strength of this edited work is the way in which the essays negotiate shifting constellations of themes, motifs, and historical-cultural issues rather than falling into discrete treatments of any one of the many critical means of categorizing the Girl. Some of the thematic threads connecting the pieces include cultural minefields; the body as battlefield; maternal matrices; beauty and the bestial; looking glass reflections; and the complexities of coming-of-age.

These thematic threads often overlap in a single text. For example, in Jamaica Kincaid's *Annie John* we see how the changes in the protagonist's body create the demarcation between girlish freedom and, in Annie's mind, that whole "young lady business," which not only complicates her life but also drives a wedge between mother and daughter. Whereas in Louise Meriwether's *Daddy Was a Number Runner* or Dorothy Allison's *Bastard Out of Carolina,* the girl's childish body is vulnerable to physical invasion and abuse and is the battlefield on which adults wage their own emotional wars in a sexually permeated cultural context. In novels such as Toni Morrison's *The Bluest Eye,* we see the brutality of racism enacted on a vulnerable little girl whose mother has internalized the dominant American beauty myth from the movies, and whose father has been beaten down by racism. Pecola, raped and abused, goes mad in her desire for the blue eyes that she thinks will make people love her, always seeing herself through the skewed looking glass of white cultural prerogative. Overbearing and absentee mothers, themselves struggling with cultural imperatives, may do the best they can, as in Morrison's *Sula* or Lisa Vice's *reckless driver,* but their daughters bear profound emotional and psychological scars from which their mothers cannot shield them. And, in the looking glasses of literature, contemporary film, and the media that surround them, as well as in the conflict with their mothers, these modern fictional girls experience fierce competing battles for their bodies and souls.

The roots of this work are found in literature courses I have taught for the past twenty years; the class titles reflect my interest in the characterization of the female in fiction by women: "Women Writers," "Heroines in Love and Trouble," "Regional American Women's Fiction," "Fictions of Gender," "'Dead Angels': Mothers and Daughters in Fiction and Theory," "Contemporary Fiction by Women." From an initial interest in heroines in works spanning the eighteenth, nineteenth, and twentieth centuries—from Fanny Burney to Toni Morrison—my inquiry has led to a focus on the portrayal of the conflicting scripts of woman as mother and woman as creative artist, in which to become a mother means by extension to foreclose options of creative intellectual or artistic production. As I have become the age of the dead mothers who litter these texts whose plots focus on daughters, I have seriously questioned the unwitting misogyny of my complicity in teaching such novels. And, as a wife and mother for more than 30 years, I have increasingly questioned the implicit fictional assumption that not only must a woman choose between artistic creativity and procreation, but that lasting friendships between women and men are doomed and the space of creative subjectivity is always that of the beleaguered daughter.

For 24 years, while teaching in a women's college, I have raised a family that includes three children—two daughters 15 years apart in age, and a son just two years younger than his elder sister. An avid reader since my own childhood, I read to the children from the time they were born—fairy tales, the classics, whatever we could find at home or in the local library's children's collection that caught their eye. While working on this book, I have not only queried my daughters about what they read as young girls but wondered what I read as a girl. Which seven books did I choose each week from my neighborhood library during those interminable childhood summers before television? Memory is incomplete. I recall reading everything by Louisa May Alcott; multiple books about Sue Barton, nurse; the adventures of Narcissa Whitman and Helen Keller; Nancy Drew books; and novels by Pearl Buck—anything that extended my world of experience until finally I was checking out *Les Miserables* and *Robinson Crusoe,* without direction or goal, looking always for books into which I could escape, reading without direction whatever caught my eye.

Later, as an undergraduate English major, I read what was assigned. I cannot recall one book chosen just for leisure reading during those intensive years of study, community service, and work. Although I did not find myself in the literature I read, at the time I was not aware of the absence. I loved the language, the stories, the romantic quest—primarily the poetry—for I was assigned few novels. It was not until I was living in graduate student housing in Chicago, and contemplating teaching high school, that I began to fill in the gaps that I perceived in my own reading. It was in this way, in the early 1960s, that I read all of James Baldwin, Richard Wright, and Ralph Ellison in the coffee breaks and lunch hours of a secretarial job. Teaching high school at Hyde Park that first autumn after marriage, I sought out stories and poetry that might seduce my non-readers into wanting to read, showing them the connections between the assigned curriculum of Chaucer and Shakespeare's "Romeo and Juliet" and the then contemporary film and soundtrack of *West Side Story,* while extending my acquaintance with the writings of black male writers, still oblivious to the absence of books by women of color, and hardly aware of more than a handful of any women writers.

When I became a mother, I searched not only for "how to" books about raising children, but also books to read aloud to my baby girl. During the early years of reading to my children I discovered, rather than rediscovered, the Winnie the Pooh books, Beatrix Potter, C. S. Lewis's *The Lion, The Witch, and the Wardrobe* and then the entire Narnia series, and all those wonderful books written for British children—I was surprisingly untroubled by their subtle and blatant colonial messages. In spite of my own local activism in the 1960s' movements for social justice, I was oblivious to the complex and often constricting implications of race and gender in books for children.

When I returned to school in 1970 after remaining home with two children until they were five and three years old, I discovered I could take all English courses. The women's movement not only led me to form a women's consciousness raising group, but also made me acutely aware of women writers. Feminist books of outrage drew me in as I read polemical tracts, first-person accounts of sexism, and the rash of new fiction in which the female protagonist seemed always to go mad, leave her husband, or die. Anäis Nin's *Diaries,* Kate Millet's *Sexual Politics,* Erica Jong's *Fear of Flying,* Sylvia Plath's *The Bell Jar,* and Sheila Ballantine's *Norma Jean the Termite Queen* come to mind as I recall those days. While in a master's program, I eventually discovered the writings of Doris Lessing, Virginia Woolf, Alice Walker, Kathryn Porter, Tillie Olsen, Grace Paley, Toni Cade Bambara, Diane Johnson, and Anne Rice. I taught my first course on women writers in 1974, assuming I could include all the good fiction by women in a single course that began with *Evelina* and ended with *Ruby Fruit Jungle.* Later, in a doctoral program in literature, I searched out courses that focused on the writings of women, only then reading the grand novels by George Eliot and extending my knowledge of the Brontës beyond *Jane Eyre* and *Wuthering Heights* to *Villette* and *Shirley,* as well as looking to Restoration and eighteenth-century British women novelists such as Aphra Behn and Sarah Scott.

As part of the Modern Language Association's project "Teaching Women Writers from a Regional Perspective," I began reading unpublished and published diaries and letters and tried to make connections between my already internalized ideas about women from earlier times and the new voices I encountered in the archives. My acquaintance with fiction by women extended to works by Mary Wilkins Freeman, Sara Orne Jewett, Ramona Hunt Jackson, Rebecca Harding Davis, Kate Chopin, Dorothy Canfield Fisher, Zora Neale Hurston, Gwendolyn Brooks, and so many other "newly found" writers. Exposure to noncanonical writers made me reconsider the canonical writers of my early graduate study, and feminist criticism caused me to reflect on the unexamined assumptions with which I read literature.

In Jane Austen's novels, girls are cushioned by middle-class comfort, and their central project is to marry wisely. Attention for the female protagonist, unlike the male, is turned from matters of quest, vocation, or money to fashioning the self toward making a good marriage. Thus, Elizabeth Bennet needs to temper her pride and her prejudicial judgments of people. Taken for granted is intelligence and physical attractiveness—natural, rather than acquired at great cost. In a way, the Austen heroine's best legacy is genetic. She is healthy and spirited. In the Brontës' novels, genetic beauty gives way to plainness. Health, education, and a strong sense of self as well as passion lead to marriage. Jane Eyre, not unlike Elizabeth Bennett, must learn self-constraint, yet both these fictional characters reinforce the necessity of questioning public standards about women. The messages in these novels require girls to learn the social codes of obedience, reverence, appearance, modesty, thoughtfulness of others, while simultaneously subverting the most dastardly of those codes through developing an inner knowledge. These girls must participate in securing their own futures by marrying—not necessarily, and never ultimately, through paid labor. Where Elizabeth has no thought of working for pay, Jane has the ability to earn an income until she secures the even better situation of marriage. George Eliot's *Mill on the Floss* and *Middlemarch* demonstrate the ways in which girls are severely punished if they do not internalize the stultifying Victorian ideas about the place of women. Bright and desiring girls like Maggie Tulliver and Dorothea Brooke are not rewarded for being intelligent and vital. Emotional and spiritual development is what truly matters, and girls need wise protection. That Victorian umbrella of family and community protection nostalgically referenced by historians at the end of the twentieth century is not sufficient for Maggie, and we see evidence that even—or perhaps particularly—for a bright and deeply spiritual girl, the very suspicion of sexual impropriety can ruin her life.

In considering contemporary portrayals, not only against the novels written by women of the eighteenth and nineteenth centuries but more recently in comparison to the outpouring of American fiction by women 20 or so years ago, we note that while texts often open with the heroine as a girl, the focus is usually on the condition of young adult women, whereas today's writers seem increasingly to be portraying girls as the protagonists of their narratives. Many contemporary novels are set in an earlier time, often parallel to the time in which their authors were themselves girls. Such retrospective setting makes one wonder how much the backward glance distorts the account. A variation from the focus on a youthful narrative appears in two novels I read recently in which adult protagonists narrate their mother's lives, reconstructed through scrapbooks: *The Divine Secrets of the YaYa Sisterhood* by Rebecca Wells (a sequel to *Little Altars Everywhere*) and *The Cure for Death by Lightning* by Gail Anderson-Dargatz. Similar to the writings of second-generation immigrants who seek to render their parents' lives in literature, these two novels have a nostalgic flavor, of a time when girlish friendships and love and romance were still possible. In reading them, I realized that the experience of growing up in America in the 1940s and '50s is as strange for many younger readers as is the childhood set in another country or century. Unlike narratives such as Jamaica Kincaid's *Annie John* or Sandra Cisneros's *The House on Mango Street,* these books are narrated by daughters who seek to understand their mothers' youth after they themselves have grown up. These books begin with a state of separation from the mother and, through investigation of the mother's girlhood, the protagonist eventually comes to forgive and accept the mother as she is. In the recognition that one's mother is another human being—neither angel nor monster—these novels remind me of the insights expressed by students at the end of my first course on mothers and daughters as they tried to articulate what had been learned. One student, who had been embattled with her mother for years, remarked, "I learned that my mother is another human being."

From such a distance, even my own unremarkable fundamentalist childhood in the Pacific Northwest begins to seem like unplowed ground for fiction. And in saying that, I realize that today, virtually any girl can be the protagonist of fiction. It is in the telling that her story becomes memorable, rather than in her status as fairy princess, unknown royalty, middle-class romantic, marriageable daughter, outcast victim, or spunky rebel. As Jane Austen wrote of her protagonist in *Northanger Abbey*, her work about women and novels:

> No one who had ever seen Catherine Morland in her infancy, would have supposed her born to be an heroine. Her situation in life, the character of her father and mother, her own person and disposition, were all equally against her. Her father was a clergyman, without being neglected, or poor, and a very respectable man, though his name was Richard—and he had never been handsome. He had a considerable independence, besides two good livings—and he was not in the least addicted to locking up his daughters. Her mother was a woman of useful plain sense, with a good temper, and, what is more remarkable, with a good constitution. She had three sons before Catherine was born; and instead of dying in bringing the latter into the world, as anybody might expect, she still lived on—lived to have six children more—to see them growing up around her, and to enjoy excellent health herself. (3)

Austen gestures toward Catherine's "normalness" as an ironic and self-reflexive comment on the cultural categories of the novel and femininity as they developed and became intertwined during the late eighteenth and early nineteenth century. Contemporary women writers tend to begin with the assumption toward which Austen gestures: that there is no such thing as an "unremarkable" or "normal" girl, as it is in the telling of her tale, the excavating of the easily dismissed, that heroism is made. In Austen's text, Catherine Moreland discovers that the secret horror in the house is not a gothic monstrosity at all but a banal laundry list—a discovery that denies the tropic requirements of epic horror but reveals another, less visible, horror—that of the everyday female life of lists and domestic service. Much contemporary fiction by women continues Austen's legacy of demonstrating the momentous in the moment. The specificity and variance of the sorts of girls and the sorts of environments in which we encounter them result in a newly prismatic narrativization of the Girl, a medley of heroines whose variety is reflected in this book. Austen, however, uses Catherine Morland's "normalness" as an ironic gesture toward parody, while contemporary women writers focus on the unreliability of the very concept of the "unremarkable" or "normal" girl.

In my current course, " Contemporary Fiction by Women," as in this book, I do not have an overarching thematic focus, but combine ever-shifting lists of texts to chart and find meaningful connections between their echoes and silences on the infinitely varied and always remarkable story of the girl. I begin by reading selections from *Annie John* and *The House on Mango Street,* two popular books in freshman writing classrooms in American colleges and universities today. As I move beyond the canon that informed my own college and university studies to teach contemporary fiction from an ever expanding list of current writers, I am troubled by new questions, and I try to engage students, not in mere acceptance of one reading list or another, but in thoughtful reflection on their own reading assumptions and observations. Questions may include the following: How do these books differ from earlier fiction by women with which you are familiar? Who narrates these stories? At what age? What assumptions about girlhood in earlier texts do these recent works call into question? What is their portrayal of sexuality? Of innocence? Of education? Of female friendship? Of values among girls? Of mothers and daughters? What do these books, and others with which you are familiar, written in the latter part of our century celebrate? critique? What is missing in these recent books that readers have come to take for granted in earlier fiction about girls? What is new? Whose stories are available? Whose are still missing? And I ask myself whether in my desire to be inclusive I am inviting students to be voyeuristic tourists. In my desire to avoid stereotypes and to avoid reinscribing dominant cultural myths, am I merely inscribing alternative stereotypes?

Teaching at a women's college, trying to read new fiction by women, and raising two daughters with quite different reading tastes, I am always trying to extend my borders into places and people and ways of seeing the world that are unfamiliar to me. As a literature professor in English, I have taught fiction by women to women students for 24 years. Over the years, I have explored in my teaching the portrayal of mothers and daughters in literature and psychological theory, and I have noticed a deep split beween the surface stories and the covert messages about mothers in the literature written by the foremothers whose work I love. Just as that uneasiness about all those fictive portrayals of dead or ineffective mothers led me to write about the mother as the dead angel in the work of Virginia Woolf or the monster in the fiction of Doris Lessing, I have become increasingly aware that the daughters, the girls, in many of the contemporary novels by women, differ in many ways from the girls in earlier "more canonical" novels by women. These contemporary girl protagonists often are not protected from abuse, and, if abused, are not necessarily defined solely as victims. Protagonists are frequently immigrants, negotiating not only the boundaries of puberty, but also those of nation and language. Protagonists still hope for romance, but the novels often have open-ended conclusions. And as I have tried to make connections between the literature I teach, current psychological theory about female adolescents, and the social historical context within which I teach, I have noticed the ways in which fiction by women is changing. This project began as I tried to articulate these observations and to wonder how others read the fictional girl now being created by women.

In a literature that has previously privileged the white orphan or upper-middle-class child in England, the white immigrant child of extraordinary talent in America, or the tragic mulatta, these new girls often have two parents and at least physically intact families, are frequently poor, and are often children of color. Only recently have girls of color had their stories told in fiction that is assigned widely on English department reading lists. Only recently have college students been assigned texts by Maxine Hong Kingston, Toni Morrison, Jamaica Kincaid, and Sandra Cisneros. And once students read these girls' stories, they tend to ask for fiction from more perspectives; the empty places become visible as students ask for a story about a Puerto Rican girl or a Filipina or a mixed-race girl. An adopted girl wants to read fiction in which being orphaned by birth parents is not simply a trope to finding one's own identity free of the parental pressures that might have limited a Jane Eyre or Dorothea Brooke in an earlier fictional universe. The longing for an ever more inclusive bibliography of stories sends me constantly in search of new fiction or older fiction that is new to me. For the past three years, my students have published annotated bibliography projects to extend our awareness of contemporary fiction by women and to inform our library's acquisitions.

What about the literary qualities of these newer works? What about the language, the poetry, the tropes, the images? This book does not attempt to assess the formal quality of the texts it examines; rather, this collection as a whole interrogates the cultural stories we tell ourselves about girls and seeks to trace some of the ways in which contemporary women authors are subverting narrative genres in attempts to write with increasing truthfulness about the ways in which girls experience their varied lives. Each time I create a new syllabus, attempting to be inclusive of multiple perspectives, I am wary of the unconscious underlying assumptions that bring one book rather than another to the attention of students.

My most recent "Contemporary Fiction by Women" class includes works by Toni Morrison, Jamaica Kincaid, Fae Myenne Ng, Maxine Hong Kingston, Julie Shigekuni, Elmaz Abinader, Achy Obejas, Cristina Garcia, Sandra Cisneros, Doris Lessing, Dorothy Allison, Hisaye Yamamoto, Tillie Olsen, E. Annie Proux, Carol Shields, and Jeanette Winterson. I am impressed by what I see as a new focus on the Girl in many of these works, a change in narrative scripts. Envisioning the Girl differently from her predecessors in older canonical novels, which tend to be preoccupied with her as an object in the marriage market, these texts neither comply with the paternalistic plot that requires a daughter to reject her mother, nor assume that marriage is synonymous with adulthood, nor imply that to become a mother requires foreclosure of artistic achievement and self-fulfillment. Occasionally, this new Girl already is who she will become, her survival dependent, not on fitting into the culture, but on resisting its attempts to squeeze her into a generic mold, as proclaimed in the words of a character from Carolyn Chute's *The Beans of Egypt, Maine*: "I ain't no friggin wimp." In some novels, particularly those by immigrants to the United States, the Girl's maturation proceeds along lines parallel to her separation from her country of birth and her identification with the values and mores of the United States—a retracing of the colonial pattern in which womanhood is equated with assimilation. In others, she seeks her identity and survival, her changing body a battleground over which conflicting cultural values are fought.

If reading the earlier fiction enabled the female reader to identify with the self-fashioning project of the protagonist, as argued in Rachel Brownstein's *Becoming a Heroine: Reading about Women in Novels,* what is the experience of the reader of *Bastard Out of Carolina, The Book of Ruth,* or *reckless driver*? Does she substitute a new sense of self-fashioning from the survival tales of women writers whose fictional or autobiographical narratives are evidence of the power to shape one's own narrative, wresting one's own truth, subversively if necessary, from the dominant script—whatever that script encodes? Does reading the selection of multicultural texts reinscribe a cultural mandate for the girl in subtle ways not intended by author or teacher? Do first novels tend to retrace the steps of girlhood so that *Oranges Are Not the Only Fruit, A Bridge Between Us, Annie John, The House on Mango Street, The Book of Ruth,* and *Bastard Out of Carolina* are in some ways set in common emotional and epistemological territory—that place of childhood remembered from a different location or reimagined from the geographical or cultural place or age of the writer at the time she pens the fictional account, which never truly ever was as it is now told—and in the telling, how does it change?

In popular culture as well as in the literature we study in our college classrooms, the icons of the Girl are constantly being rewritten. The body of the young girl—whether athlete or potential Miss America—is the site of heated battles, not only among parents, teachers, and coaches, but also among those who would exploit her sexuality, lure her to internalize their fantasies and purchase their products. Told she can do anything and become anything, she is also infantilized and expected to keep to her second place in a patriarchal world of glass ceilings and second shifts. Told to develop her mind, she is simultaneously bombarded with messages that reinforce the ancient message that her body is the primary source of her power, that she is primarily decorative, that she should have a model's body, that she should be beautiful within a narrow range of cultural stereotypes. Portrayed as a social failure if she procreates as a teenager, she is simultaneously taught that to be a mother is a mark of maturity and the passage to adulthood in society. On the one hand the Girl in popular culture is an endangered species—in her own house as well as on the streets, vulnerable to rape, abuse, violence inflicted by others, and subject also to self-inflicted violence through diet pills, illegal substances, eating disorders, and self-mutilation. Yet on the other hand, girlish vulnerability is simultaneously being reinscribed as Girl Power by bands, zines, and films that acknowledge the culture's violence but portray girls as active perpetrators and self defenders rather than passive victims.

These new girls have multiple origins. On the one hand, the girl is more endangered than ever before yet she is simultaneously being told that she is freer than girls of previous generations to "just do it." In some cases, she enjoys the legacy of Title IX with its insistence on equal access, which has opened her possibilities to participate in sport, but with increased opportunities to play soccer or run cross-country and track is the concomitant recognition of mass-marketing firms that she is a consumer of dreams and goods. She also may be part of a generation of girls supported by parents and teachers who encourage her to fulfill her potential and who create at least an intellectual space for female sexuality and power while not being able to protect her from the dangers portrayed in movies such as *freeway* or Joyce Carol Oates's short story, "Where are you going? Where have you been?" Today, in multiple ways, from Riot Grrls to Spice Girls, from Nike ads to Feiffer comic strips and Xena, Warrior Princess, from girl gangs to

Seventeen, the Girl remains a central figure, not only in fiction and popular culture, but also in recent psychological, historical, and literary studies.

Since Freud, psychoanalytic representation of girls has relied on a male model to explain female development and the focus has been on early childhood as the crucial phase in human development, setting the stage for all that follows. More recent studies have focused on the developmental differences between males and females, and pointed to the importance of adolescence in female development. In the past decade, a number of psychological and historical studies have focused on girls, with perhaps the most well-known work that of Harvard psychologist Carol Gilligan. Even a cursory glance at some of the book-length studies of the past decade, indicates a new emphasis on the psychology and development of the girl. While it is outside the scope of this work adequately to attend to these books and others, I want briefly to touch on several of their salient conclusions.

Gilligan's work, beginning with *In a Different Voice* in 1982, argues that because girls and boys are socialized differently our models of adolescent development need to be differentiated by gender. Gilligan's insistence that confident, opinionated young girls become silenced between the ages of 11 and 16 is disturbing and has led to follow-up studies that move beyond her initial study to take into consideration race and class. The research results continue to be unsettling as they chart the ways in which contemporary culture silences girls in young adolescence. *The Girl Within* by Emily Hancock is a collection of women's life stories that concludes that, while women are at one time self-possessed, women easily lose sight of this autonomy because of a culturally accepted feminine facade they adopt in youth simply by growing up female in contemporary society. *Making Connections: The Relational Worlds of Adolescent Girls at Emma Willard School,* edited by Carol Gilligan with Nona P. Lyons and Trudy J. Hanmer, is a case study of girls from 1981 through 1984 that makes the case that the years between 11 and 16 are particularly important for girls and revolve around the "crisis of relationship." Noted sociologist and social critic, Ruth Sidel's study, *On Her Own: Growing Up in the Shadow of the American Dream,* contends that many of today's young women have absorbed aspects of the American Dream, but have not accepted or absorbed the tenets of contemporary feminism with the exception of their acceptance of the idea that a strong woman must succeed on her own. Both *The Beauty Myth: How Images of Beauty are Used Against Women* and *Promiscuities: The Secret Struggle for Womanhood* by Naomi Wolf examine the role of popular culture in shaping a girl's self-image. *The Beauty Myth* argues that society's emphasis on a woman's appearance makes women weaker than men socially, economically, and politically and is also a dangerous backlash against feminism. *Promiscuities* explores how the adolescent years of girlhood determine a sense of self-worth in contrast to images of the girl in popular culture and the mythology of feminine desire. *Meeting at the Crossroads: Women's Psychology and Girls' Development*, edited by Lyn Mikel Brown and Carol Gilligan, focuses its study on the importance of women guiding girls through adolescence as a means of political and cultural change. In *School Girls: Young Women, Self-Esteem, and the Confidence Gap*, Peggy Orenstein examines the narratives and situations of girls ages 9 to 15, links the discouragement of women students to the devaluing of students in general, and investigates the problematic social consequences that follow.

One of the most recent critical texts on the Girl, Joan Jacobs Brumberg's *The Body Project: An Intimate History of American Girls*, is particuarly relevant to this work in that she historicizes the contemporary figure of the Girl within a tradition of earlier representations. Brumberg argues that despite legal and social emancipation of Western women in the past century, the twentieth-century girl is not more free than her nineteenth-century predecessor. In fact, she argues, the modern girl, though not externally incarcerated in corsets, must nevertheless shape her body internally through a combination of dietary control and exercise. Although the area of the body most scrutinized changes over time, from breasts to waists, for example, or from a preoccupation with hair to skin, or from general leanness to a worry about one's thighs, what remains constant is an equation of the girl's body with her assumed worth. Bromberg's historical analysis makes for fascinating reading, but she offers little hope beyond suggesting that women of differing generations talk honestly about their own experiences and feelings. Her book is a reminder that contemporary girls, no less than and perhaps even more than girls of previous generations, are bombarded with fierce expectations that they should control and contrive their appearance if they are to be loved and valued.

Concomitant to the increased interest in psychological and social development of girls, literary critics have begun to investigate the figure and figurations of the Girl. This collection is preceded by three books whose projects, while substantively different than my own, reflect the current focus on the Girl. I will briefly summarize the findings of Sally Mitchell's *The New Girl: Girls' Culture in England, 1880-1915*, Rosemary Auchmuty's *A World of Girls*, and Barbara A. White's *Growing Up Female: Adolescent Girlhood in American Fiction* as these texts are most pertinent to the essays in this collection in their substantive theorizing of the figure of the Girl in the world of letters.

Sally Mitchell in *The New Girl: Girls' Culture in England, 1880-1915* argues that during this period, girls "increasingly occupied a separate culture," which she names "a provisional free space" discordant with adult expectations. Defining girlhood, not according to a particular chronological age, but as "a state of mind " (7), Mitchell sees the end of girlhood as the age at which she is considered a sexual being, the age of (heterosexual) consent, or the age of leaving school. She locates this new girl in the space between parental home and marital home, a space in which "the new girl moved into spheres where her mother had no advice to give; she did things her mother had not done and faced issues her mother did not face—if not in reality, at least in fancy" (9). This commercial girls' culture of "cheap and popular books and magazines" expanded girls' sense of possibilities in spite of their actual lives and allowed them to imagine lives quite different from those of their mothers (4). Mitchell credits L. T. Meade with making popular the "chief varieties of formula fiction" that dominated girls' reading for 50 years after her death (16). The formula school story creates "a community where the important rules are the children's own ethics and mores" and "emphasizes peer standards" (18). She concludes her study by noting the breakup of this girls' culture after World War I, arguing that the "free space" occupied by new girls diminished as they were sexualized earlier and girls turned into adolescents (152). Girls' literature became "increasingly youthful" as novels became "more adult" (180). She notes that with a new emphasis on joint recreational events for boys and girls and a steady decline in women's age at marriage, romance became central to both life and fiction, refocusing fictional attention from the self to the man.

Rosemary Auchmuty's study of girls' boarding-school stories, *A World of Girls,* points to the almost complete loss of separate spheres for men and women in the twentieth century and the "mixed blessings" of coeducation and greater sexual freedom of modern times for girls and women (3). She argues that the earlier enjoyment of women-only spaces, "once taken for granted" now arouses suspicion "since feminism has made people aware that women without men pose a threat to a society organized in the interests of male power" (3). She explains the popularity of the girls' school stories as appealing to women who "perceived the world depicted therein as a refuge and an alternative to the real world of patriarchal relations" (4). Auchmuty takes her title from an L. T. Meade book of 1886 and describes this world of girls as one in which "authority figures as well as colleagues and comrades are female, where the action is carried on by girls and women, and decisions are made by them. Girls and women rise to the challenges presented by ideals such as honor, loyalty and the team spirit. Women's emotional and social energies are directed toward other women, and women's friendships are seen as positive, not destructive or competitive, and sufficient unto themselves. School stories offer female readers positive role models to set against a reality which is often restrictive or hostile to them" (7). While Auchmuty acknowledges the contempt of literary critics for the school story, for being formulaic and unrealistic as well as dated and irrelevant, and promoting troublesome values, she asserts that the significance of the girls' story is not in its surface qualities but rather "in an implied message and an unstated set of assumptions about what *might* be possible for girls and women" (15). She traces the success of girls' school stories through the 1950s, notes their decline in the 1960s and 1970s, and their resurgence in the 1980s and 1990s, arguing that the decline of the girls' school story after World War II "removed a potential source of strength for girls," and that its current popularity "points to a continuing need for a separate literature for girls and women which presents positive role models . . . free from domination and control by men" (19).

Examining the portrayal of adolescent girlhood by women writers in approximately 275 novels with female adolescent protagonists, Barbara A. White in *Growing Up Female: Adolescent Girlhood in American Fiction*, reminds us that "the adolescent girl, yet to fulfill her function, is crucial to the replication of the social system. Whatever her present goal, whether it be 'social integration' or not, her society will insist on integrating *her*. . . . So long as women's main function is conceived to be marriage and childbearing, and so long as wifehood and motherhood carry lower status than male pursuits, the adolescent girl will be in conflict with society" (197). White asks whether future novelists will "continue to portray growing up female as a loss, as the entering of a tightly enclosed space that entails the death of the self?" (197).

The Girl explores the ways in which contemporary women novelists portray growing up female and the losses, gains, and vicissitudes of this process. While it seems common to read fiction within a context of nation or decade, within a particular racial or ethnic frame, a class frame, a geographic frame, as well as to group books as *Künstlerroman* or Coming Out stories, or survival tales, in this book I have intentionally tried to avoid such rigid categorization, leaving myself vulnerable to charges of omission or of invalid comparisons, of cultural myopia, of lack of breadth, lack of depth, ignorance. If I were to try to know all things, I would never publish this work. But even more importantly, I think it is necessary that we make connections between books, between authors whose reading and cultural and educational legacies differ greatly. Each of us approaches a book personally, through our own lenses of personal experience, accumulated reading, formal and informal education, and chosen critical theories. What else could we possibly do?

This book, then, began as a question: How do contemporary women construct girlhood in their fiction? The book is not a survey nor is it by any means exhaustive or fully representative; rather it is meant as a contribution to the conversation circling around the Girl. No particular theoretical lens dominates these essays, though they all have in common a careful look at particular texts. The texts examined in this collection frequently are discussed solely by theme, genre, or by their protagonist's or author's primary racial, sexual, or national identification; the following essays cross such boundaries and provide complicated readings of girlhood with simultaneous attention to varying calibrations of race, class, location, family, context, and sexual orientation.

PREVIEW OF THE CHAPTERS

In Chapter 1, "Where Is She Going, Where Are We Going, at Century's End?: The Girl as Site of Cultural Conflict in Joyce Carol Oates's 'The Model,'" Brenda Daly contrasts the 1966 story, "Where are you going, where have you been?" with "The Model" in which Oates transforms the rape plot into a feminist plot. Daly suggests that to analyze the Girl at century's end, we need a new developmental model in which daughters reintegrate aspects of the self that have been fragmented by the male gaze and overthrow the patriarchal injunction, "*away from the mother.*" Because the stranger-rapist in "Where are you going . . .?" is transformed into a father-rapist in "The Model," Daly argues that, in these stories, father-daughter incest functions as a paradigm of cultural imbalance between the masculine and feminine. She questions whether Sybil in the recent story, in contrast to the earlier Connie, knows both where she is going and where she has been, and asks in cultural terms what difference it makes that Oates has reconstructed the Girl.

In Chapter 2,"Self-Possession, Dolls, Beatlemania, Loss: Telling the Girl's Own Story," Gina Hausknecht explores the paradigm of the Girl's own story, which she calls "a counter-narrative" to cultural ideology and canonical authority about teen and preteen femininity through Toni Morrison's *The Bluest Eye,* Angela Carter's *The Bloody Chamber,* Kathy Acker's *Blood and Guts in High School,* and Jane Campion's short film, *A Girl's Own Story.*

In Chapter 3, "The Battleground of the Adolescent Girl's Body," Brenda Boudreau focuses on novels that "deliberately emphasize bodily experiences in an effort to subvert the cultural narrative that says girls are passive victims." Using Elizabeth Grosz's *Volatile Bodies* as a lens through which to illustrate the importance of understanding female subjectivity as embodied, Boudreau examines Louise Meriwether's *Daddy Was a Number Runner*, Sandra Berkley's *Coming Attractions*, and Dorothy Allison's *Bastard Out of Carolina*.

In Chapter 4, "When the Back Door Is Closed and the Front Yard Is Dangerous: The Space of Girlhood in Toni Morrison's Fiction," Deborah Cadman charts ways in which Morrison's girl characters negotiate knowledge in their movements through the highly charged spaces in which they live without maps or reliable guides. Asserting that their movement is circular and that characters reveal their sense of self through their use of spatial metaphors as well as their spatial movement, Cadman argues that such movement can destroy as well as enrich.

In Chapter 5, "Dizzying Possibilities, Plots, and Endings: Girlhood in Jill McCorkle's *Ferris Beach*," Elinor Ann Walker traces the ways in which McCorkle appropriates plots from biography, autobiography, and nineteenth- and turn-of-the-century British and American literary traditions to create frame narratives that vie for protagonist Kate Burns's "ending" or identity. Walker notes the ways in which McCorkle's appropriation of varied plots and textual allusions exemplifies some of the perils that confront girls on the brink of womanhood in a culture that bombards women with impossible female ideals.

In Chapter 6, "'I Ain't No FRIGGIN' LITTLE WIMP': The Girl 'I' Narrator in Contemporary Fiction," Renee R. Curry argues that contemporary girls, from the moment we meet them in fiction, already know who they are, where they live, and how they fit into their surroundings. Examining Carolyn Chute's *The Beans of Egypt, Maine*, Jamaica Kincaid's *Annie John*, and Dorothy Allison's *Bastard Out of Carolina*, Curry argues that the girls of this contemporary literature defy fragmentation and alienation, already occupying a self-aware "I" who speaks of the past, present, and future as if it were always already occurring. Curry notes that, in the face of rape, incest, death, or leaving her country, this new girl "ain't no friggin' wimp." Each girl simply grows into the person she was, living her "I" without innocent dreams.

In Chapter 7, "Coming-of-Age in the Snare of History: Jamaica Kincaid's *The Autobiography of My Mother*," Diane Simmons argues that in Kincaid's recent novel, the Girl no longer hopes for freedom to build an authentic self. Hopelessly trapped in a history of colonial oppression, such a girl's only outlet is revenge. Simmons sees in "this sad book" Kincaid's attempt to force her readers to "fully face the trap of history," with a recognition that only then may it be possible to find a way out.

In Chapter 8, "Subversive Storytelling: The Construction of Lesbian Girlhood through Fantasy and Fairy Tale in Jeanette Winterson's *Oranges Are*

Not the Only Fruit," Isabel C. Anievas Gamallo analyzes the ways in which Winterson uses storytelling as a way to relate to prevailing cultural ideologies and to achieve self-understanding and self-explanation in/and/or against them. Gamallo argues that Winterson renegotiates the position of the girl-heroine as a gendered subject in the male-biased realm of language, decenters the male hero position in the patriarchal story to celebrate female identity and sexuality, and demonstrates that the girl's access to the symbolic order is not necessarily as doomed by her subjection to "the Law of the Father" as Jacques Lacan has suggested.

In Chapter 9, "But That Was in Another Country: Girlhood and the Contemporary 'Coming to America' Narrative," Rosemary Marangoly George examines several contemporary novels written by women of color in the United States that have achieved substantial academic and mainstream success. She argues that novels such as Esmeralda Santiago's *When I was Puerto Rican,* Julia Alvarez's *How the Garcia Girls Lost Their Accents,* Jamaica Kincaid's *Annie John* and *Lucy,* and Bharati Mukherjee's *Jasmine,* rely on similar narratives—the coming-of-age of girls whose growth is calibrated by the stage during which they discard their associations with the places they lived before coming to America. George argues that ultimately, the radical politics of some of these texts is dimmed by the parallel established in moving from the Third World to the West and from girlhood to womanhood.

This collection is in no way definitive or inclusive. It does not gain focus through a single idea nor through a single theoretical perspective, but through diverse essays on diverse texts, all of which share a deep engagement with the Girl. The threads that hold it together are several, and you will notice connections between many of the works. I hope this collection helps to shape the ongoing conversation about the portrayal of girls' lives in books, not only in fiction, but also in the psychological theories that tend to shape many of the ways we see—not only girls in books but living girls. I hope that as we examine the multiple ways in which the Girl has become the site of competing ideologies we will not see her through biased or nostalgic or predatory eyes ourselves but will learn to listen to real girls, to expand our critical and theoretical lenses, and in teaching the works will learn to ask increasingly more provocative and open questions.

Notes

1. This book results from a special session I chaired at the 1996 MLA Conference in Washington, D.C. The number of submissions I received for the panel, as well as the energy of the discussion that followed the session, demonstrated a level of interest in the topic of The Girl that spurred me to proceed with this collection. As this book goes to press, other books on girls are being written, and the topic appears among calls for papers on the internet and in print as conference topics of specialized groups in literature, history, psychology, and education.
2. This term comes from Nancy K. Miller's study *The Heroine's Text: Readings in the French and English Novel,* 1722-1782.

ONE

Where Is She Going, Where Are We Going, at Century's End?

The Girl as Site of Cultural Conflict in Joyce Carol Oates's "The Model"

BRENDA DALY

"America today is a girl-destroying place" (44), according to Mary Pipher. If so, the question is, why? I examine this problem through the lens of Joyce Carol Oates's short fiction, analyzing how the girl of the 1990s differs from her prefeminist counterpart of the mid-1960s. Significant changes in the Girl are most obvious, as I shall illustrate, when she reappears under a different name in a later Oates short story. For example, when Connie, the female protagonist in the famous "Where are you going, where have you been?" (first published 1966)[1] reappears as Doreen in "Years of Wonder" (first published 1974), an important change is immediately evident: although both girls encounter the violence of the male gaze, only Doreen, a girl of the 1970s, survives. Initially, Connie and Doreen appear quite similar. Connie is at first attracted to Arnold Friend, but when she hears him croon, "My sweet little blue eyed girl" (31), she understands that he has not truly seen her, for her eyes are brown, *not* blue. Like Connie, Doreen is initially taken in by the male artist in a shopping mall, but when she sees his portrait of her, she recognizes that "the face in the sketch was a girl's face, but she was older" (350). In addition, both girls quarrel with their mothers and, following their encounters with the destructive male gaze, both yearn for reconciliation. However, only Doreen has the chance to make amends. In this way, through a daughter's reconciliation with her culturally devalued mother, "Years of Wonder" transforms a rape plot into a feminist plot.[2]

In the early 1990s, yet another change occurred in Oates's fiction: the Girl now frequently carries a weapon. For example, in "The Model" (1994)—another story that re-visions the famous "Where are you going?"—the girl carries a knife. As one reviewer puts it, the plot of "The Model" takes a "post-feminist twist: this time the girl brings a knife along for the ride" (Upchurch 34). Whether this change should be described as "post-feminist" is questionable; however, the reviewer is certainly correct about the knife: in contrast to Connie, who steps unarmed and defenseless into Arnold Friend's "golden car" at the close of "Where are you going?," Sybil Blake is carrying a steak knife when, at the end of "The Model," she accepts a ride in Mr. Starr's limousine. Is Sybil, whose story is set in the 1990s, going to the same place as Connie? Tragically, since the publication of "Where are you going," which appeared just as the second wave of the women's movement was gaining momentum, violence against women has increased dramatically, along with political attempts to gain control of women's bodies.[3] During the Reagan-Bush administrations of the 1980s, the struggle to gain control of women's bodies, especially the bodies of teenage girls, intensified: "In almost every state there are bills pending to further circumscribe teenage girls' control of their bodies" (Christian-Smith 208).

Oates herself has suggested that the 1990s is an era of increasing hostility toward women. For example, when asked why she had written *Black Water*—yet another story in which an older man takes a young woman for a ride that ends in death—she described the current era as "particularly inhospitable to women." She wrote *Black Water,* Oates explained, because she was "drawn back to the [Chappaquiddick] incident by Justice Thurgood Marshall's resignation from the Supreme Court and by accusations of rape against Senator Kennedy's nephew William K. Smith" (Hunnewell 29).[4] However, "The Model" differs from its famous predecessor from the '60s: first, the rapist in the 1990s "The Model" is no longer a stranger, he has been refigured as a father rapist; second, the girl's relationship with her mother has been complicated, in part by paternal violence, but also by the advent of the women's movement; and third, while Connie was absorbed by "trashy daydreams" (12), Sybil, a girl of the 1990s, is self-confident and goal oriented. In contrast to Connie, Sybil is a jogger who, as the result of "vigorous exercise," has acquired "a growing confidence in herself" (105). Finally, as stated above, the girl is also more likely to carry a weapon.[5] In short, as I shall demonstrate, Sybil, the white, middle-class[6] girl of the 1990s, whom Oates depicts as a site of current cultural conflicts, differs from Connie, a girl of the 1960s whose violent sexual initiation precedes the women's movement.

Yet, the fact that Oates is now arming girls with knives and guns does not mean, however, that she applauds violence. Indeed, it is difficult to understand why, given the increasing violence in the United States, critics accuse Oates of writing fiction that is "too violent." [7] As Oates herself has explained, "I write about the victims of violence . . . and yet my critics say I'm writing about violence. From my point of view, I've always been writing about its aftermath" (Hunnewell 29). In "The Model," for example, a seventeen-year-old girl is struggling, after having lost both her parents to violence at the age of two, to learn the truth about her past. In this story, as in many of Oates's stories, she is exploring the aftermath of violence, once again—as in "Where are you going?"—from the victim's perspective. Furthermore, neither Connie nor Sybil is a passive victim; both respond with considerable courage to the threat of male violence. As feminist critic Elaine Showalter says, "Oates does not see the Gothic as a revelation of female hysteria, but rather as the indictment of an American social disorder, the romanticization of the violent psychopath and serial killer" (139-40).[8] Showalter was referring to "Where are you going?" but "The Model" may also be interpreted as "an indictment of an American social disorder," and Oates certainly does not portray Sybil as a hysterical female despite the fact that, like Connie, she is completely isolated when she enters the car of a potentially violent man—in this case, her father.

Oates herself has stated that the addition of a father to "Where are you going?" would improve it. As she remarked in a review of *Smooth Talk,* a movie based on "Where are you going?," the director's addition of a "mysterious" father, with whom Connie has an "ambiguous relationship . . . is an excellent touch." She explains, "I had thought, subsequent to the story's publication, that I should have built up the father, suggesting, as subtly as I could, an attraction there paralleling the attraction Connie feels for her seducer Arnold Friend" ("When Characters" 1).[9] In "The Model" Oates achieves this artistic goal, not by suggesting a parallel between father and rapist, but by creating a composite figure: the father-rapist. What point is Oates trying to make with this change? In my view, by changing the identity of the rapist from an indeterminate male such as Arnold Friend, to a father-figure such as Mr. Starr, this story foregrounds the fact that patriarchal institutions, rather than a few psychopaths, perpetuate violence against women. Furthermore, because of its focus on the daughter's perception of paternal violence, "The Model" also points to a blind spot in the Freudian family romance: its failure to provide an analysis of the father's desire, along with its failure to acknowledge the patriarchal cultural context of the family romance.

Unfortunately, according to psychologist Ellyn Kaschak, even feminist psychologists such as Nancy Chodorow continue to employ an oedipal model of the family, a model that not only silences the mother, but leaves intact a theory that requires daughters *to see themselves through paternal eyes.* If we are to move beyond an oedipal psychology, Kaschak insists, we must take into account the perspectives of mothers and daughters, points of view missing or subsumed in Freud's conception of the Oedipus complex. To resist this silencing of the maternal voice,[10] we must listen to the mother while, at the same time, taking care to differentiate maternal voices from the voices of daughters. Furthermore, whereas the Freudian model of the family romance leads to blaming the mother, primarily by ignoring the patriarchal cultural context that empowers the father and devalues the mother, Kaschak's model allows us to examine the roles of both mothers and daughters while attending to gendered power relations that so often shape women's beliefs and actions. However, since my focus is on the girl's point of view, it is most important to note that the Freudian model, by ignoring the father's desire to possess the daughter, would lead to the conclusion—a seriously mistaken conclusion—that Sybil agrees to act as Mr. Starr's model because she has sexual fantasies about him.

As Kaschak argues, now that feminists have successfully challenged Freud's belief that hysterics lie, that they merely fantasized sexual abuse by their fathers,[11] we must formulate a new model of the family romance, a model that takes into account patriarchal power both within and beyond the family. She proposes a model, named after Antigone, in which daughters do not view themselves through paternal eyes, or through the eyes of an indeterminate male, but through their own eyes. A major developmental task for Antigone—that is, for the girl in a patriarchal culture—is to re-integrate aspects of the self fragmented by the male gaze. This fragmentation of the self occurs most often in adolescence, according to the research of Carol Gilligan and others; the tragic result is that girls begin to doubt their own thoughts and desires as they internalize the patriarchal view of their bodies and minds. In a patriarchal culture, as Judith Lewis Herman argues in *Father-Daughter Incest,* citing Phyllis Chesler's blunt assessment: "'Women are encouraged to commit incest as a way of life. . . . As opposed to marrying our fathers, we marry men like our fathers . . . men who are older than us, have more money than us, more power than us, are taller than us'" (57-8).[12] In other words, according to the Antigone model, whether or not Mr. Starr is Sybil's biological father, the relationship is incestuous because he is clearly older, wealthier, and more powerful than she.[13] It should be noted, however, that Sybil agrees to model for Starr, not because of a sexual attraction, but for an economic reason: she needs to earn money to pay for voice lessons and college.

At first Sybil refuses Starr's offer to pay her for modeling, but in parts two and three of the story, called "The Temptation" and "The Proposition," she is tempted by his proposition because it is "an exorbitant sum, nearly twice what Sybil made babysitting or working as a librarian's assistant . . . when she could get hired" (101). A mature seventeen-year-old, Sybil Blake recognizes that her aunt, a physical therapist who "by California standards" does not make much money, "could not be expected to support her forever" (102). Those who ignore such economic realities, choosing instead to interpret Sybil as engaging in romantic fantasies about Starr, are, quite simply, misreading the story. It is evident that Sybil is not sexually attracted to Starr when, for example, she finds it "repulsive" that Starr has sketched her to "look as if she were wearing a clinging, flowing gown; or maybe, nothing at all" (123). Rather, Sybil is puzzled about why Starr is attracted to her: perhaps because he disguises himself as an amateur artist she is at first "convinced it was not a sexual attraction but something purer, more spiritual, and yet—why? Why *her?*" (121). Why indeed. However, Sybil does find Starr *"interesting"* (103), partly because of his obvious wealth, partly because of his interest in her, but also because she recognizes that "there was something not *contemporary* about him" (104). She is curious about Starr: she doesn't know where he has come from or who he is and, until near the close of the story, she tries to find the answers to these questions. The important point, then, is that Oates does not depict Sybil's interest in Starr as sexual, but as a desire to know the truth—the truth about his identity, and her own.

Unfortunately, since her aunt hides the truth about the family's past, Sybil must rely on her own detective work—a secret exploration of the photographs and newspaper clippings hidden in her aunt's files and desk drawers—in order to reach the conclusion that Mr. Starr, amateur artist, is her biological father, George Conte. The timing of her father's return is just right: fifteen years have passed since the crime and, according to one newspaper account, Conte was sentenced to between twelve and nineteen years in prison. To suggest Starr's years in prison, his skin is described as "luridly pale, grainy, and rough" and his voice as "hoarse as if from disuse" (100). As if sensitive to sunlight and uninformed about current styles, "He wore glasses with lenses so darkly tinted as to suggest the kind of glasses worn by the blind; his clothes were plain, dark, conservative—a tweed jacket that fitted him loosely, a shirt buttoned tight to the neck, and no tie, highly polished black leather shoes in an outmoded style" (100). When Sybil first meets Starr, she immediately recognizes that he is old enough to be her father—"this strange person might have been in his forties, or well into his fifties" (100)—but only later does she see "a faint scar on his forehead above his left eye, the shape of a fish hook, or a question mark" (116), a detail consistent with a news report of a failed suicide attempt that had left Conte "critically wounded . . . with a shot to the head" (138).

In addition, and this detail may be the most disturbing of all, Sybil recalls that she has seen Starr before; obviously, and ominously, this supposed stranger has been watching her and has sought her out. Soon after their first encounter on the beach, "Sybil realized, as if a door, hitherto locked, had swung open of its own accord, that she'd seen Mr. Starr before . . . some where" (104). With some effort, she remembers that he had sought her out at school: "the school choir, of which she was a member, had been rehearsing Handel's 'Messiah' the previous month for their annual Christmas pageant, and Sybil had sung her solo part, a demanding part for a contralto voice, and the choir director had praised her in front of the others . . . and she'd seemed to see, dimly, a man, a stranger, seated at the very rear of the auditorium, his features indistinct but his gray hair striking, and wasn't this man miming applause, clapping silently?" (104) This memory makes Sybil wonder, "Why had he visited her high school, and sat in on a choir rehearsal? Had he known she would be there?—or was it simply coincidence?" (121). Later, when Sybil asks Starr if, in fact, he already knows that her first name is not "Blake" but "Sybil," he admits, "I must confess, I'd sneaked into a rehearsal too—no one questioned my presence. And I believe I heard the choir director call you—is it 'Sybil'?" (130). Like Arnold Friend, Mr. Starr seems to have mysterious prior knowledge of his victim. For example, it seems likely that prior knowledge of Sybil motivates Starr to observe her movements between December, when he visits her at choir practice, and January, in order to arrange the supposedly "chance" encounter on the beach.

Since Sybil is an intelligent and sharp-eyed observer, she begins to speculate, along with readers, about these very questions. These mysteries hint at danger, but at least initially there is nothing clandestine about Sybil's meetings with Starr, especially since she agrees to model only in public, and only in daylight. Nevertheless, with each modeling session, the danger increases. For example, the first time Starr offers Sybil a ride in his black limousine, she is ready to climb in when, "for some reason she could not have named—it might have been the smiling intensity with which Mr. Starr was looking at her, or the rigid posture of the whitegloved driver—she changed her mind" (119). Each time he repeats this offer, the hint of danger intensifies. In addition, Starr soon asks Sybil to move to a more secluded part of the beach. However, the most dangerous moment occurs when Starr asks Sybil to pose in a blouse and skirt, rather than her usual jogging outfit, in order to participate in an experiment. Starr explains her role in these words: "There are people, primarily women!—who are what I call 'conduits of emotion.' In their company, the half-dead can come alive" (124). With Starr's prompting, Sybil finally whispers, in the voice of a child, "Mommy," and Starr responds, "Ah, yes: 'Mommy.' To you, that would have been her name." (124). The implication is that Starr, who is concerned not with his daughter's memories but with his own, had expected to hear his model utter the name of his dead wife, Melanie Blake.

The question is, if Sybil is a mere "conduit of emotion" (125), whose memories, whose emotions, are these? As Starr's "model" is Sybil simply a projection screen for his memories and emotions? Starr hints at this possibility when he says, "Why, many times innocent children are given memories by adults; contaminated by memories not their own. . . . In which case the memory is spurious. Inauthentic" (123). To further complicate matters, a few evenings after this session, Sybil is reading a library book when she finds the following explanation of how repressed memories can be awakened: *"dormant memory-traces . . . can be activated under special conditions,"* including *"words, sights, sounds, and especially smells,"* but the same passage warns: *"Much of human memory, however, includes subsequent revision, selection, and fantasizing"* (133). This warning about the unreliability of memory makes "The Model" very much a story of the nineties, reflecting current debates over so-called implanted memory. This debate usually intensifies when a daughter accuses a father of incest, an accusation that has become commonplace since the advent of the women's movement. Such accusations, particularly when made by patients under the care of therapists, have engendered skepticism not only from the media,[14] but also from juries. This debate over the reliability of repressed memories also raises the question: whose testimony has greater authority, the father's or the daughter's?[15]

Readers of "The Model" confront a similar question: that is, how reliable are Sybil's memories and perceptions, particularly her inference that Starr is her father, George Conte? Some readers may question Sybil's credibility, but it is important to note that her conclusion—that Starr is her biological father—is not based on memory or fantasies—nor on some mixture of the two—but on textual evidence. Near the close of the story, Sybil finally learns from old news clippings that, contrary to her aunt's persistent claim—that both her parents died in a boating accident in Vermont when she was two—her father is still alive. According to the news clippings, George Conte succeeded in killing his wife and throwing her body into a lake, but he had failed in his attempt to commit suicide. Because Conte was a wealthy man who could afford a skilled lawyer, he had been convicted "of second-degree murder, and [given] a sentence of only between twelve to nineteen years" (140). Since the clippings also record the fact that Aunt Lora Dell had testified at the trial, surely she must know that Conte is still alive and might be released at about this time. Nevertheless, Aunt Lora, who is described as "incapable of being, or even seeming, docile, tractable, 'feminine,' hypocritical" (110), does not warn her niece that her violent father might, after his release from prison, track her to California. Its seems obvious that, in order to prevent just such an encounter, Aunt Lora Dell has tried to protect Sybil by changing her name from Conte to Blake. But surely Aunt Lora must have guessed that a change of name—especially when the "new" name is well known to George Conte—will not provide adequate protection for her niece.

Nevertheless, Aunt Lora maintains her lie of omission, even suggesting, based on her authority as a medical worker, that because Sybil did not attend her parents' funeral, she is now fantasizing that her father is alive: "'It's a theory,' she explains to Sybil, 'that if you don't see a person actually dead—if there isn't a public ceremony to define it—you may have difficulty accepting it. You may—' and here Aunt Lora paused, frowning '—be susceptible to fantasy'" (133). Despite her aunt's "theory," an assertive Sybil maintains her own perspective: "Fantasy! Sybil stared at her aunt, shocked. *But I've seen him, I know. I believe him and not you!*" (133), but she does not confront her aunt. In part four of the "The Model," entitled "Is the Omission of Truth a Lie, or Only an Omission?" Aunt Lora lies despite her niece's persistent questions and obvious desire to know and understand the truth. Aunt Lora's intentions are good—she wishes only to protect Sybil—but the decision to withhold the truth is a tragic mistake, not only because it makes her niece more vulnerable to danger, but because it de-authorizes the young woman's perceptions. Just as Freud undermined the perceptions of his "hysterical" female patients by redefining their memories as fantasies, Aunt Lora now undermines her niece's perceptions by suggesting that she is not actually seeing someone, but only fantasizing his existence. Here Aunt Lora Dell practices an adult habit so widespread that, according to Carol Gilligan, it frequently leads to a crisis in female adolescence: "a division between what girls know through experience and what is socially constructed as 'reality'" (Tolman 251).

However, rather than simply blaming Aunt Lora, it is important to acknowledge that, in a patriarchal society, the task of mothering is demanding, complex, and unjust. Patriarchal societies place mothers in a cruel double bind, holding them responsible for the well-being of children while, at the same time, denying them the power to alter the conditions of child care. Nevertheless, it is imperative that those who care for children carefully examine and re-examine the ways in which their practices might, unwittingly, perpetuate destructive patriarchal beliefs.[16] For example, Aunt Lora apparently believes, along with many parents, that innocence protects children from harm; however, as Tolman argues, "If both desire and danger are real forces in girls' lives, adults' impulse to focus on and protect girls from danger and to discount girls' desire may in fact endanger rather than empower girls" (251). "The Model" dramatizes Tolman's point, for by attempting to protect Sybil's "innocence" by denying the truth, Aunt Lora loses her niece's trust: upon finding the hidden news clippings, Sybil "understood that those who love us can, and will, lie to us; they may act out of a moral conviction that such lying is necessary, and this may in fact be true—but, still, they *lie*" (141). Equally pernicious is the fact that Aunt Lora unwittingly endorses a gendered code of morality—the belief that girls should be "good" and innocent, while boys can be "bad" and knowledgeable. Such a conception of morality is based, not upon the desires and needs of girls, but on adult denial and fears, especially the fear of female sexuality.

This habit of denying the desires of girls—whether sexual, intellectual, or spiritual—maintains a patriarchal moral code that, while failing to acknowledge the father's desire, holds the daughter responsible for her own sexual abuse.[17] In other words, girls are held responsible for what men do to them. Oates illustrates the dangers of such a patriarchal concept of "goodness" in "Where are you going?" when Connie's mother describes her as "bad" simply because she is pretty, while she views June, who is "plain and steady," as her good daughter. The major difference is that Connie, being prettier, is likely to become the object of male sexual desire. Aunt Lora, like Connie's mother, comes close to blaming her pretty sister, Melanie, for her own death when she tells Sybil, "I'd warned her it was dangerous" (114)—dangerous, that is, to marry George Conte. Neither Aunt Lora nor Connie's mother suggests ways of resisting the objectifying male gaze; rather, they assume that "good" girls should not acknowledge sexual desires, especially in themselves. Psychological research on adolescent girls has not challenged this assumption; even in the 1990s, Tolman finds, "The most striking feature of a review of the psychological research on adolescent girls' sexual desire is that there is virtually none" (250). As long as such adult denial persists, our institutions—our churches, schools, courts, or families—will enforce a concept of morality that denies women's sexuality while, at the same time, de-authorizing their perceptions of reality.

During the early 1970s, a more optimistic era, Oates predicted in the preface to "Where are you going, where have you been?" (1974) that this old binary morality was finally beginning to change. She believed that "a new morality is emerging . . . which may appear to be opposed to the old but which is in fact a higher form of the old—the democratization of the spirit, the experiencing of life as meaningful in itself, without divisions into 'good' or 'bad,' 'beautiful' or 'ugly,' 'moral' or 'immoral' "(9). Unfortunately, even in the 1990s, according to Deborah Tolman and Tracy E. Higgins, the sexuality of women, especially adolescent girls, is still "suspect in our culture" (205). As they explain, "The cultural and legal sanctions on teenage girls' sexuality convey a simple message: good girls are not sexual; girls who are sexual are either (1) bad girls, if they have been active, desiring sexual agents or (2) good girls, who have been passively victimized by boys' raging hormones" (206).

What we need, they point out, is an "affirmative account of women's sexual desire" (205). Lacking such an affirmation, goodness in girls continues to be construed as the absence of sexual desire. Feminist critic Elayne Rapping holds the media responsible because of its representation of women in a "simplistic," binary manner—portraying them as good girls or bad, as victims or survivors (267). However, recent feminist scholarship—for example, a study of girls' magazines by Kerry Carrington and Anna Bennett—points out that while "such magazines instruct the female sex how to fashion themselves into an object of the male gaze, as good wives, mothers, and daughters" (149), girls are not simply passive consumers of these images. "The Model" makes this same point, primarily by inviting readers to enter Sybil's very active and resisting consciousness.

Through Sybil's resisting consciousness, "The Model" also asks readers to consider the possibility that the patriarchal moral code—which makes daughters the property of fathers—is motivated by the aging male's jealousy. More than two centuries ago, as the story's allusions remind us, William Blake challenged this same moral code in "Songs of Experience." This coming-of-age poem depicts the father as jealous, not only of his wife's sexuality, but of his daughter's—just as in "The Model." It is the mother in

"Songs of Experience" who explains that her death is the result of her husband's jealousy: "Starry jealousy," EARTH says, "does keep my den/Cold and hoar, Weeping o'er" (Erdman 18). As we know, Sybil's mother's body has also lain "Cold and hoar" for many years—years when Sybil certainly needed her mother's care—because of her husband's jealousy. If Sybil's mother were alive, surely she would warn her daughter, as does Blake's EARTH, about this dangerous father: "Selfish father of men/Cruel jealous selfish fear/Can delight/Chain'd in night/The virgins of youth and morning bear" (Erdman 18-19). As EARTH recognizes, the jealous husband is also a jealous father who, "Chain'd in night," cannot "bear" the sight of "virgins of youth and morning." Such jealousy explains why, after killing his wife and throwing her body into the lake, George Conte had returned for his daughter. "He came for me too" (124), Sybil recalls. This memory prompts her to reflect, even before identifying Starr as her father, *"But Daddy isn't dead, you know he isn't. You know, and he knows, why he has returned"* (131). As suggested by Conte's hearse-like limousine, the father has returned, once again, to take possession of his daughter.

Unfortunately, both because Aunt Lora wants to protect Sybil's innocence, and because she shares, with many Americans, the belief that the past can be erased, she does not warn her niece about her father. Instead, Aunt Lora had moved Sybil from Vermont to California "'to erase the past, for the child's sake,' she said, 'and to start a new life'" (110). Because Aunt Lora assumes that she has erased the past, she refuses to give an honest answer when Sybil asks "How, again, exactly, had her parents died" (111). Again, when Sybil asks, "Is my father alive?" (132), Aunt Lora insists that her parents "'would have wanted you—your mother especially—to be *happy*.' Part of this legacy of happiness, Sybil gathered, had been for her to grow up as a perfectly normal American girl, in a sunny, shadowless place with no history, or, at any rate, no history that concerned her" (137). Yet the violent father still casts his shadow over Sybil's young life, a point emphasized by Starr's frequent association with shadows. For example, at the opening of the story, as Sybil stands looking at Starr's sketches, "his shadow" fell over the page where she saw herself "amid the joggers . . . a young girl with shoulder-length dark hair held off her face by a headband, in jeans and a sweatshirt, caught in mid-stride, legs swinging, arms caught in motion" (106). Toward the close of the story, while investigating her aunt's files, Sybil finds this same shadow in a family photo: "In the foreground, on the grass, was the shadow of a man's head and shoulders—'George Conte,' perhaps? The missing person" (136).

What Aunt Lora fails to understand, largely because she has not questioned the very American belief in a perpetually sunny present, is that the habit of denying the shadowy past, the so-called unconscious or repressed, only increases its power. As a result, at the end of "The Model," Sybil is alone and, like her counterpart of the 1960s, going for a ride. But where is she going? In "Where are you going, where have you been?" Oates answers this question through allusions to Dickinson's "Because I could not stop for death, he kindly stopped for me." Like the carriage in which Dickinson's gentleman arrives, Arnold Friend's golden car is a death carriage. Mr. Starr's chauffeur-driven limousine may seem very different from Friend's souped-up car, yet Sybil initially identifies it as a hearse: "'Look,' Sybil said, pointing, '—a hearse'" (118). Mr. Starr tries to correct her perception: "'I'm afraid, Blake, that isn't a hearse, you know—it's my car'" (118), but the old news clippings uphold Sybil's viewpoint. In addition, as Sybil learns, Starr is actually much stronger than he initially appears, a fact that becomes apparent when Sybil helps him up; "Sybil tugged at his hand (how big his hand was! how strong the fingers closing about hers!) and, as he heaved himself to his feet, grunting, she felt the startling weight of him—an adult man, and heavy" (128). Another time, after Starr exerts "kindly" pressure while offering Sybil a ride, she sees later that his strong hand has left "faint red marks on her wrist" (133). Starr also carries a cane that, while giving him the appearance of weakness, could be used by a strong man to fend off an attacker.

The fact that Sybil is carrying a weapon does not mean, then, that she can protect herself effectively. The story offers numerous hints that a steak knife may not be Sybil's best protection against a man like Starr. Despite the fact that Sybil is strong—"vigorous exercise had made her strong in recent years" (105)—the story suggests that her fate may be the same as Connie's. The major problem is that Sybil, like Connie, is alone. By contrast, Mr. Starr, like Arnold Friend, has a side-kick—in this case, his chauffeur—while Sybil has cut herself off from her aunt. But why, one wonders, doesn't Sybil have any girlfriends? Since *Foxfire, Confessions of a Girl Gang,* which was published just one year after "The Model," portrays girls as banding together to protect themselves from male violence, Oates's decision to isolate Sybil seems deliberate.[18] One might argue that Oates's choice is aesthetic—by focusing exclusively on familial relationships, the story achieves a more dramatic effect—but certain spatial ambiguities challenge this argument. Why, for example, does Oates locate a private (familial) story on a public beach? It is a strategy, in my view, for drawing reader attention to the permeable boundaries between private and public, familial and extrafamilial. Within this ambiguous space, readers are uncertain, just as Sybil is uncertain, of Starr's true identity: is he a stranger or a father, or both at once? I suggest, then, that Oates isolates Sybil from other girls her age, not primarily for aesthetic purposes, but rather to dramatize a crisis that occurs in the lives of many girls: their loss of supportive relationships, especially with other women and girls, while they struggle to achieve what our society, with its overemphasis on individual autonomy, defines as maturity.

In short, for many girls the crisis of adolescence is not one of achieving separation, but of maintaining relationships. In Sybil's case, she is alienated from her aunt, primarily because her aunt lies to her, but also because Sybil is attempting to resist the conventions of feminine goodness that her aunt has failed to examine; at the same time, perhaps in the quest for autonomy, or self-sufficiency—Sybil jogs alone, for example, rather than participating in a team sport—she has cut herself off from other girls. Carol Gilligan states the problem this way: "For girls to remain responsive to themselves, they must resist the conventions of feminine goodness; to remain responsive to others, they must resist the values placed on self-sufficiency and independence in North American culture" (Preface to *Making Connections* 10). In short, girls face a developmental task that would be daunting to many adults—the task of recognizing and resisting damaging cultural definitions of female goodness and mature selfhood. It seems obvious that girls cannot be expected to transform damaging patriarchal codes without adult and peer support; however, according to researchers, girls will stay in relationships only with those who listen to them in nonjudgmental ways. Unfortunately, as the authors of *Between Voice and Silence* discovered, it is uncommon to find "those who truly know how to listen when girls speak about thoughts and feelings that fall outside the social bounds and cultural expectations of appropriate or acceptable behavior" (Taylor et al. 120). As illustrated in "The Model," Aunt Lora fails to listen and respond in a nonjudgmental way to her niece's questions. Moreover, by cutting herself off from family and friends—"They had no one but each other" (111)—Aunt Lora models the kind of self-sufficiency that ultimately isolates and endangers Sybil.

From a feminist perspective, however, Sybil's father must be held equally accountable for the care of his child, a task at which he fails completely, and not out of good intentions. While Aunt Lora does her best to care for Sybil, Starr is trying—as he had years earlier—to kill her. When Sybil finds the old news clippings, she understands that her murderous father had "misrepresented himself" (141), pretending to be an artist whose professional goal is "'redeeming the world'" (109). However, not only has Conte lied about his identity, according to the testimony of witnesses at the trial, Conte had also planned to kill his daughter. After killing his wife, the "jealous" Conte had "tried to take his two-year-old daughter, Sybil, with him, back to the boat—saying that her mother was waiting for her" (140). In order to resist her mother's fate, Sybil arms herself with a steak knife and enters Starr's limousine. Readers are left to speculate: Will Sybil be reunited with her mother, or will she use her steak knife to stab her father? And will she use her weapon only in self-defense or will she launch a surprise attack? If she chooses the second course of action, a court of law would surely define her as a killer, like her father before her. From a legal point of view, then, she becomes more of a Conte, her father's daughter, than a Blake. Indeed, when Sybil finally learns the truth about her violent father, she thinks: *"Now you see, don't you, why your name had to be changed. Not 'Conte,' the murderer, but 'Blake,' the victim, is your parent"* (139). Tragically, if Sybil attacks her father in order to escape a legacy of maternal victimization and silence, she must act within the constraints of a violent binary logic—"to be or not to be"—that is, to be either her mother's daughter or her father's, to be either good or evil, victim or victimizer.

The fact is, of course, that Sybil is entitled to both her family names: both Blake and Conte. By resisting the either/or logic of Western culture in order to "solve" Sybil's dilemma, readers may discover such creative "both/and" interpretations in Sybil's full name. For example, the name "Conte," which translates from the French as "story," may initially suggest that the father maintains rightful possession of his family story, but this surname also rightfully belongs to Sybil—who has her own story to tell. As Sybil's story, "The Model" may be understood, not only as a story of paternal violence, but as an analysis of the consequences of telling or not telling certain stories. For instance, Aunt Lora chose *not* to tell Sybil the truth about her family's past, but her niece's full name—Sybil Blake Conte—tells readers what Aunt Lora tries to deny, not only about Sybil's past, but about her possible future. The name Blake, which Aunt Lora associates with her victimized sister is also, as some readers know, the name of a male poet, perhaps the first to name "patriarchy" and identify many of its dangerous effects on the young.[19] Is it possible, then, that Sybil will develop a voice? By naming her protagonist, Sybil, Oates also suggests the girl's kinship with the legendary sibyls who had the power to interpret disaster. Taken together, then, the girl's three names—Sybil Blake Conte—identify her possible future as a storyteller (Conte), poet (Blake), and prophet (a sibyl) with the power to interpret, and perhaps thereby avoid, disaster. Such a powerful legacy authorizes Sybil to fulfill her own desire, to claim her own voice, rather than serving as model and "emotional conduit" for the male artist, whether stranger or father.

When Starr hires Sybil as his model, he certainly is not acting benevolently; rather, he exploits her body and her voice to feed his own desires. By making Sybil into a "conduit of emotion," he hopes to re-establish contact with aspects of himself that he has repressed or "killed" to maintain his masculine (oedipal) subjectivity. As Starr's artistic conduit, Sybil does recall the repressed, maternal unconscious: "Mommy's face," and Mommy's voice on the phone, "Yes, yes? Oh hello" (126). So strong is Starr's response to this memory that it knocks him to the ground. In short, having killed (and repressed) the mother in himself, the male artist is forced to exploit the body and consciousness of a young woman in order to reclaim his own vitality. In this vampire-like manner, "the half-dead can come alive" (124), as Starr himself acknowledges, by feeding on the emotional vitality of a young girl. Starr describes himself as "one who redeems by restoring the world's innocence" (108), but he actually defiles Sybil's innocence in order to maintain his belief that the "profane" earth can be redeemed only by the "sacred" creation of the male artist. Such a view of the art—in which "sacred" male artistry redeems the "profane" (female) earth—perpetuates the very gender hierarchies that lead to violence against women. For this reason, as suggested in "The Model," the legacy of most male artists, including Blake himself—who was both a poet and a visual artist—is complex. As feminist critic Mary Lynn Johnson explains, although Blake participated in the Romantic movement that "reclaimed for the 'human' certain aspects of consciousness that had traditionally been identified with nature, with extra-rational, and the feminine" (58), he "invariably personifies the creative genius as male, his creation as female" (59).

Oates challenges this tradition, not only by giving Sybil the name "Blake," but also by portraying her as an intelligent critic of Mr. Starr's artistry. Furthermore, although the story suggests that Sybil may be in danger when she agrees to become Starr's emotional conduit—and this is a paradox—the role also empowers her, primarily because in order to recall the "political" unconscious she must overthrow the patriarchal injunction, "*Away from the mother.*"[20] This injunction, as Oates has pointed out in an analysis of "King Lear," is dangerous not only for daughters, but for society as a whole. She explains, "The patriarch's unspoken imperative, *Away from the unconscious, away from the mother,* is dangerous precisely because it is unspoken, unarticulated, kept below the threshold of consciousness itself" ("Is This the Promised End?" 75). The result of such widely shared repression, Oates argues, is a collective paranoia that, perhaps especially at century's end, engenders apocalyptic visions. The time has come, then, to ask whether the struggles of girls—especially their struggles to know and assert their truths—might be emblematic of a larger social crisis. As Gilligan asks, "Does a girl's sensibility, her fascination with the human social world, and her knowledge about relationships cue her at present to the specter of disconnection on a societal and global scale?" (Preface to *Making Connections* 11). If so, isn't it time that we—that is, all adults, not only parents—begin listening carefully to girls?

Notes

1. The story, which has since appeared in numerous anthologies, was first published in 1966 in *Epoch*; it was also included in *The Best American Short Stories 1967*; *Prize Stories: The O. Henry Awards 1968*; and *The Wheel of Love* (1972) . For an analysis of "Where are you going, where have you been?," as well as the movie *Smooth Talk*, see my "'An Unfilmable Conclusion': Joyce Carol Oates at the Movies."
2. In *Lavish Self-Divisions: The Novels of Joyce Carol Oates*, I argue that this same feminist plot—in which the girl reconciles with her culturally devalued mother—became a recurrent feature of most of Oates's novels of the 1980s.
3. "The number of rapes reported to the UCR [Uniform Crime Report] has risen steadily over most of the past twenty years: From 1972 to 1991, there was a 128 percent increase in the number of reported rapes. During the same time period, the forcible rape rate per 100,000 inhabits increased 8 percent." (Buchwald, Emile, Pamela R. Fletcher, and Martha Roth, eds., "Are We Really Living in a Rape Culture?")
4. As most readers will recognize, *Black Water* is based on events that took place at Chappaquiddick in July 1969. In its account of the tragedy, *Newsweek* pictured a troubled Senator Kennedy on its cover, and its title emphasized Kennedy's "'Grief, Fear, Doubt, Panic'—And Guilt," while the article itself concluded by speculating about Kennedy's political future. As Richard Bausch says of *Black Water*, "The Senator, though never named, is recognizable not only as a certain politician from a big political family with a lot of money, but also as a certain modern type, the man with power and charisma on the prowl for susceptible women" (1). "Her Thoughts While Drowning: Review of *Black Water*." Oates deliberately and dramatically alters the media focus on Kennedy in order to give the victimized woman a voice.
5. In *Foxfire, Confessions of a Girl Gang*, the female protagonist uses a knife, while in *What I Live For*, she uses a gun. Except in *Black Water*, a novella set in the 1960s, the female protagonists in Oates's trilogy of the 1990s—which includes *I Lock*

My Door Upon Myself and *The Rise of Life on Earth*—also tend to be more aggressive. In *The Rise of Life on Earth,* for example, the female protagonist, who is severely victimized as a child, becomes a serial killer.

6. I do not have space in this essay to account for differences of class, race, or sexual orientation. For a concise review of theories of adolescent development which takes into account such differences, see Janice M. Irvine's "Cultural Differences and Adolescent Sexualities" in *Sexual Cultures and the Construction of Adolescent Identities,* 3-50.
7. For Oates's brilliant reply to the charge that her writing is "too violent," see her essay "Why Is Your Writing So Violent?" *New York Times Book Review.* 29 March 1989: 15-35.
8. Oates comments on the kinship between the grotesque and the gothic in her "Afterword: Reflections on the Grotesque" for the collection *Haunted: Tales of The Grotesque* (303-07).
9. Since both Arnold Friend and Mr. Starr employ verbal manipulation, rather than overt acts of violence, I understand why Oates uses the term, seducer; however, since the threat of violence lurks behind the words of both men, I prefer to use "rapist."
10. I develop this point more fully in the introduction to *Narrating Mothers,* co-edited with Maureen T. Reddy. In *The Mother/Daughter Plot,* Marianne Hirsch also argues that mothers are silenced by oedipal models of the family.
11. See, for example, Florence Rush's *The Best Kept Secret: Sexual Abuse of Children,* Judith Lewis Herman's *Father-Daughter Incest,* and Alice Miller's *Thou Shalt Not Be Aware* . In my view, whether or not the daughter has sexual fantasies about her father, the fact remains that the father, being an adult and more powerful, is responsible for any actualized incestuous relationship. Furthermore, such sexual fantasies about a father or a father-figure should not automatically define the girl as a "hysteric" whose perceptions should be discounted.
12. Chesler's comment is frequently cited; for example, see *Daughters and Fathers* edited by Lynda E. Boose and Betty S. Flowers.
13. In *Black Water,* for example, the father-lover is not the girl's biological father, but a man old enough to be her father who is identified only as "The Senator."
14. During the 1990s, the media frequently covered cases in which incest victims later dropped their charges because their memories had been proven unreliable. For example, on "Sixty Minutes" (17 April 1994), Morley Safer reported on a number of legal suits that were dropped by patients who later acknowledged that they were not remembering the experience, but responding to suggestions by their therapists. One month later, NBC (10 May 1994) reported that Gary Romana, a father accused by his daughter of incest, was suing the two therapists who had assisted his daughter in remembering

paternal sexual abuse. During the same month, *The New York Times Review of Books* (15 May 1994) published a front-page review called, "The Monster In the Mists," with the subtitle: "Are long-buried memories of child abuse reliable? Three new books tackle a difficult issue" (1). Only one of the books, Lenore Terr's *Unchained Memories: True Stories of Traumatic Memories, Lost and Found*, argues, though not to the complete satisfaction of the reviewer, that repressed memories of childhood trauma may turn out to be valid.

15. For example, as reported by NBC (10 May 1994), even though Holly Romana's father was found guilty of incest, a different jury recently awarded him damages when he sued his daughter's therapists for malpractice, charging them with "implanting" memories of paternal sexual abuse in his daughter's mind. Despite the fact that Holly's therapists as well as her mother and sisters believed her, jurors felt that, because of the methods the psychiatrist had used, they could not determine, beyond a reasonable doubt, whether Holly was remembering experiences of childhood sexual abuse or fantasizing them. This method of discrediting the daughter's story has a familiar ring: almost 100 years ago, Freud reversed his own theory—his belief that hysteria was usually caused by sexual abuse—when he concluded that his female patients had fantasized, rather than actually experienced, paternal sexual abuse.
16. For example, as Lyn Mikel Brown and Carol Gilligan found in a study of adolescent girls at Laurel School, many "good women," not only mothers but also teachers, undermine girls' experiences "by implying that 'nice girls' are always calm, controlled, quiet, that they never cause a ruckus, are never noisy, bossy, or aggressive, are not anxious and do not cause trouble" (*Meeting at the Crossroads: Women's Psychology and Girls' Development* [61]).
17. As feminist scholars have argued for some time—see, for example, Chesler, Gilbert, Herman, Miller, Rush, as well as Boose and Flowers—because the daughter is viewed as the father's property, the taboo against father-daughter incest is much weaker than the taboo against mother-son incest. By contrast, the taboo against mother-son incest is so intense that, when repressed and unresolved, it leads to the construction of a violent masculine (oedipal) subjectivity so evident in Mr. Starr.
18. As in "The Model," the greatest threat in *Foxfire* comes from "fatherly" men: a man with "a fatherly, an avuncular look to him" (233); a man who takes "the hook in his smug little purse of a mouth" (234) with the comment, "I have a daughter myself" (235); a man who is "a good Catholic husband and father" (236); and another man "with a fatherly-bullying smile" (239) who almost kills one of the girls.

19. "Blake may actually have been the first writer to use the word *patriarchal* pejoratively" (58), according to Mary Lynn Johnson, "Feminist Approaches to Teaching Songs."
20. Oates used this phrase in "'Is This the Promised End': The Tragedy of *King Lear*," first published in *The Journal of Aesthetics and Art Criticism*, Fall 1974, the same year she published "Years of Wonder."

TWO

Self-Possession, Dolls, Beatlemania, Loss

Telling the Girl's Own Story

GINA HAUSKNECHT

> It's not very pleasant for women to find out about how they are represented in the world.
>
> —Angela Carter, 1988 interview

> Being born into and part of a male world, she had no speech of her own. All she could do was read male texts which weren't hers.
>
> —Kathy Acker, *Don Quixote*

Jane Campion's short film *A Girl's Own Story* opens with three girls silently thumbing through a medical text; they pause at a drawing of a naked man and we read along with them the caption, "This sight may shock young girls." In the next image, they strum tennis racquet "guitars," performing a rousing rendition of the Beatles' "I Should Have Known Better." Soon we watch two of the girls, Pam and Stella, kiss each other wearing Beatles masks; a row of Barbie dolls, small impassive semi-smiles perched on their lips, rims the foreground of the image. Twenty minutes later the film concludes with abstract, disconnected images of the three girls, isolated, folded into themselves, singing a slow, sad song (lyrics by Campion), the refrain of which is "I'm feeling the cold. . . . I want to melt away."

Girls' stories are about accommodation, acquiescence, and fitting in: Jo March's great destiny is marriage; Nancy Drew is a bossy country club matron in miniature; Laura Ingalls learns to control her temper; the assorted Judy Blume protagonists come to accept their situations and realize they aren't as different as they believed. On the other hand, what I will call the Girl's own story is precisely about not fitting in, about failing, willfully or unwittingly, to fulfill normative cultural expectations. Staples of the Girls' story are triumph over the various adversities associated with adolescence; acquisition of self-knowledge; assertion of control over character defects (often having to do with not being socially graceful, popular, or feminine enough); and getting the boy. All of these involve socialization by the cultural imperatives of femininity; the knowledge granted the Girl at the end of her story is of a narrowly defined feminine self. The Girl's own story, by contrast, relates how it feels to encounter such imperatives and definitions. The latter reveals the former as a bewildering script that a Girl cannot enact without the surrender of her own self-image and self-imaginings. Campion's short film is paradigmatic of a transgressive response to the Girls' story in contemporary fiction by women.

What I am calling the Girl's own story is a counternarrative that responds to corporately produced cultural ideology and canonical authority about teen and pre-teen femininity. In this essay I will explore the paradigm of the Girl's own story through an analysis of Campion's film and then turn briefly to three works of fiction—Toni Morrison's *The Bluest Eye,* Angela Carter's *The Bloody Chamber,* and Kathy Acker's *Blood and Guts in High School*—which, while very different generically and stylistically, demonstrate the Girl's own story at work in contemporary British and American fiction. Taken together, the four texts form a useful unit for the study both of narrative and of representations of girls in literature, a unit that may be understood in terms of narratives of loss and narratives of resistance: Campion and Morrison tell stories about the gradual loss of self-possession; Carter and Acker challenge and resist the terms on which stories about young women are told. Father-daughter relationships, incest, absent or delinquent mothers, isolation, the perilous edge of insanity, inchoate sexuality, encounters with a master narrative, and the experience of popular culture are recurrent motifs throughout this set of texts. Each consciously reworks the materials of the Girls' story, revealing the ideological machinery of that story, and each offers a distinctive critique of it.

The Girl's own story responds to the authority of the book that offers a highly prescriptive account of female youth. In their postmodern retellings of the Girls' story, authors like Morrison, Carter, and Acker, and, from a younger generation, Jeanette Winterson, Amy Herrick, and Carole Anshaw, among others, manipulate both the narrative structure and social structure of fictional girlhood, radically interfering with storytelling technique and convention in order to interrogate assumptions and instructions about being a girl. Central to *The Bluest Eye, The Bloody Chamber,* and *Blood and Guts in High School* is a struggle with a book: Morrison's Pecola Breedlove is done in by the child's primer of white middle-class life from which she is excluded, Carter rewrites familiar European fairy-tale tropes, and Acker overwrites a number of canonical authors, including Nathaniel Hawthorne and Jean Genet. In various ways, these works explore permutations of violence, popular culture, and heterodox sexualities, responding with skepticism to a culture that, deeply ambivalent about teen female sexuality, both eroticizes and denies erotic agency to girls. To be female in these works is to grapple with the task of understanding oneself in terms of a cultural iconography that refuses to provide recognizable points of identification. Girlhood, these texts suggest, is a frequently incoherent fiction. They depict girls constructing themselves out of pictures they are shown, the captions of which often read, "unsafe for girls."

This essay emerged in large part from my use of *A Girl's Own Story* in a college course on fiction by women. *A Girl's Own Story* works particularly well in a literature classroom for several reasons: it is rich in compelling imagery, it traffics in familiar elements (Barbie dolls and the Beatles), and, not insignificantly, it is short enough to invite detailed study, especially for students who may not be conversant in the methodologies of film analysis. Teaching this film in the context of contemporary fiction by women, I found that it served as a touchstone for one of the main issues around which my course circulated: how women's representations of female experience reflect, at the formal level, resistance to and interrogation of inherited narrative paradigms. Literary theorist Rita Felski, writing about contemporary feminist novels of self-discovery, stresses that "it is in narrative that the governing ideological conceptions of male and female roles are fleshed out, the configurations of plot mapping out the potential contours of women's lives" (124). The means of telling stories of girlhood are in the service of reigning ideologies about femininity that strenuously resist granting young people in general and young females in particular the authority to name their vision of the world. Hence, almost necessarily, to tell the Girl's *own* story is to disrupt familiar ways of telling.

Female adolescence in *A Girl's Own Story* is a series of risks and losses, connections attempted and severed. The camera details the troubled relationships the protagonist, Pam, has with each member of her family and narrates the dissolution of her friendships with her schoolmates Gloria and Stella. Pam's mother is neurotic and withdrawn, resentful of her husband's philandering but uncommunicative until an explosive, violently sexual final scene. Pam's older sister is angry and abusive, threatening Pam at knifepoint for having borrowed the pair of white go-go boots in which we see Pam dancing at the beginning of the film, in the only moments in which we see her energetic and happy. Pam's relationship with her father is shrouded in ambiguity: she sides with him against her mother in a dinner-table argument; later we see Pam dressed up and excited on her father's arm as they begin a birthday "date" that turns disastrous for Pam when her father has his girlfriend join them; a dreamlike sequence shows a young Pam being lured into a car by a man who may be her father; finally, a male hand, clad in the dark suit sleeve we associate with Pam's father, caresses Pam in the film's final montage. Over the course of the film, Pam loses both of her friends. Gloria, impregnated by her brother, is sent away to a Catholic home for unwed girls. Stella drifts away, moving towards a clique of girls at school and becoming Pam's tormentor.

Narratively economical, the film tells this story in twenty-seven minutes through recurrent images of heaters and coldness, the Beatles, Barbie dolls, and forms of play, and by means of a shifting deployment of music both in the foreground and background. The film is permeated with sex. The Girl's own story is, among other things, a narrative of adolescent female sexuality, developing around the edges of experiences and relationships which are ostensibly not sexual. All of the sexual activity happens within the domestic sphere: between Pam and Stella in Pam's bedroom; between Gloria and her brother in the living room of their home; and in some sense between Pam and her father, perhaps only in Pam's imagination, perhaps in memory. Dark interiors and repetitive shots of waning heaters make the film feel claustrophobic and cold; the characters seem driven together into postures of intimacy simply to keep warm or to have something to do. In the film's closing scene, each of the three girls is huddled into herself, spatially separated from the others, and apparently unaware of the others' presence. Just before this last, abstract set of images Pam has watched a fight between her parents culminate in sex in the hallway of their house and Pam's voice tells us, "I was shocked to see Dad kiss Mom like that. How could he do it?" It is unclear what she is asking. Attraction, fear, and passivity combine in Pam's attitude toward her father as they do in the film's other depictions of sexual play and possibility. By the end of the film Pam and her friends Stella and Gloria have turned from exuberantly inhabiting the roles of their teen idols to the alienated chill of womanhood. Their imaginative sexual play has given way to invasive, sadomasochistic forms of adult sexual behavior. Pam has effectively become her lonely, neurotic mother.

The camera treats the girls and their bodies with a shifting regard to their status as objects of our gaze. While their bodies are fragmented in the first two scenes, it is a fragmentation that focuses on their agency. In the first scene we see a hand tracing a drawing of a naked male body, seeking to understand its contours. The second scene opens in extreme close-up on Pam's face and before we are able to absorb that she is playing lead Beatle we see her mouth and eyes, open and active. At the film's end, not only are the girls still and silent but the camera moves away from them, closing in on a male hand touching Pam, and then widening out to show us her profound isolation as she sits crumpled into herself. In contrast to scenes in which Pam, pretending in various ways, presents a self-styled persona to our view, as the hand caresses Pam in the final scene, followed closely by the camera, we see her body as someone else's plaything.

The film is filled with forms of play: the three girls play at being the Beatles in concert; Pam and Stella, alone in Pam's room, play at being Beatles in bed; Gloria and her brother Graeme play a game they call "cats," which lets them tumble around together and that finally gives way to actual sex; finally, Pam on her birthday plays at being her father's date. In all of these games, the girls act out experiences they can never have (sex with George Harrison, life as a cat) and people they will never be (the acknowledged girlfriend of one's father). All of the scenes that aren't of play are of conflict; the play provides the only instances we see of connection, the only moments when Pam receives nonthreatening attention. The play is all role-playing; there are dolls in Pam's bedroom, a pantheon of Barbies, but they are untouched. The games we watch are unmediated by dolls; the make-believe is precariously close to the real, a division that Pam herself questions and that falls quickly away in Gloria and Graeme's game of cats. Nor is the division absolute: "the onset of puberty creates the essential dialectic of adolescence—new possibilities and new dangers. The sensual, diffuse longings of childhood now become more focused. Fantasies that press themselves upon the imagination are at once more exciting and more frightening than earlier wishes: with the maturation of the body, moreover, these fantasies are now capable of fulfillment" (Dalsimer 6). Throughout the film we see Pam excited and frightened; by the end of the film the excitement has drained away, leaving her prone and still.

The scenes of Pam's play chart her struggle to comprehend and incorporate the possibilities and dangers of adolescence. The Barbie dolls serve as an emblem of Pam's liminal state, poised between ignorance (if not innocence) and awareness (if not wisdom). We see the Barbie dolls twice. When Stella and Pam, after arranging themselves carefully on the bed and discussing various points of play etiquette, finally begin to kiss, Pam lying on top of Stella, the camera leaves them in the background and pans a long line of Barbie dolls. Later, the dolls form a bridge between the scene that ends with Gloria and Graeme about to have sex and the nighttime scene in which Pam is threatened by her sister with a knife. The dolls are juxtaposed against moments of sex and violence in which the innocence of girlhood, such as it is, gives way to a tentative emergence of adult knowledge, such as it is. The Barbie dolls, static, never the object of Pam's attention, abandoned perhaps, remind us of Pam's strenuously maintained balance between girlhood and adolescence. The dolls' molded busts and vacuous smiles, heads at that odd tilt from the torsos, become a grotesquerie against scenes of Pam's young, doubting, fearful body. Their fleeting presence in this film signals both Pam's movement away from childhood play and the forces that shape and sexualize that play.

With their endless, interchangeable outfits, their ostensibly adult status, and a prescribed play activity that mostly involves dressing, undressing, and redressing the dolls, Barbies are powerful indicators of ways in which girls practice gender.[1] When she goes out with her father for her special birthday dinner, Pam is dressed up, "dolled up," in clothes and accessories that are ill-fitting and awkward on her youthful frame. Here she masquerades as a grown woman as much as in the earlier scene she has masqueraded as a Beatle; playing at being her father's girlfriend—only, mortifyingly, to be replaced by his actual girlfriend—Pam "practices for later" (as Stella has said of their kissing). But the role is a demanding one and Pam has not yet mastered its complexities. In the early scene the camera cuts away from Pam mid–Beatles' song. By contrast, in the birthday sequence, we see her role-playing break down. Pam suddenly beats out a spontaneous, silly tap-dance while her father looks on in amused impatience. The tap-dance expresses a gleeful reluctance to let go of childishness; the dance and the Beatles' song are the two moments in the film where Pam is most physically active and among the few places where she appears happy. It also destroys the illusion of maturity Pam has been working on. Adult femininity, to the extent that it involves wearing rather than inhabiting identity—putting on the costumes that register the feminine (and the matching shoes)—requires extensive practice in order to construct a convincing performance.

The rehearsal of femininity is filled with role conflict for Pam. We see her playing parts but at the same time doubting them; Pam resists her own scripts. In an early scene, Pam and Stella walk around Pam's bedroom kissing pictures of the Beatles decorating the walls. They then tumble onto the bed, pull Beatle masks over their faces, and, lying together in an embrace, begin to kiss. In various ways Pam hesitates over this activity. She and Stella squabble briefly about the masks: Pam wants them both to wear masks but Stella asserts, "If I wear one too it'll just be like two boys kissing, not a girl kissing a boy." Pam gets angry when Stella talks about wanting to have sex with George Harrison, Pam's favorite Beatle. Stella is clearly more knowledgeable about what they're doing. When Pam asks, "Do you think this is all right?" Stella responds, "Sure, why not? We're only practicing for later, aren't we? It's not like Gloria and her brother." Pam doesn't understand this reference: "What?" Stella replies, "Just something she said." Pam, sounding as if she doesn't want to hear the answer, asks, "About what?" "About what he and she did," Stella replies. The camera shows us Pam in close-up looking pensive, then turning to look at Stella; the music box begins to play as the screen goes black and the scene ends.

Pam is both eager and ambivalent. It is Stella who connects what they're doing with "real" sex: Stella who speaks longingly, dreamily, of sex with a real Beatle, Stella who makes the connection between Gloria's incestuous play with her brother, and Stella who understands their game in terms of "practice." In a brief scene later in the film in which we see Stella abandoning Pam at the school swimming pool, Stella's new clique is admiring an older looking girl's bathing-suit and, perhaps, her developing body. The girls humiliate Pam for not having figured out or accepted that Gloria is not, in fact, at boarding school. When the girls, Stella among them, sweep away from Pam, the only girl who remains behind in Pam's company is the youngest looking one. Pam remains girlish even while she plays at adolescence, desperately attempting to stave off knowledge that will mature her. At the end of the film a fight between Pam's parents turns into a sexual encounter from which Pam flees. Her sister grabs hold of her, attempting to stop her: "What's the matter with you? They're only having sex. Grow up, you little baby." Pam breaks away and is seen in close-up crawling up the stairs, away from her parents' interlocked bodies. On all fours, her face illuminated, trying to escape the implications of the display going on below, her infantile posture expresses her determination not to grow up.

The passing allusion that Stella has made about Gloria and her brother is explained two scenes later: Gloria and her brother Graeme, on the living room floor, pretend to be cats. Graeme talks Gloria into undressing but when she stops at the underwear he gives up the game in disgust while Gloria tries to purr him back into action. "I hate cats," he says, sitting above her on the sofa, arms folded tightly across his body, "nothing ever happens." Gloria, attempting to cajole him back into play protests, her face luminous in the dim room. "Yes it does," she replies, rubbing against him and purring. Graeme is unresponsive, withholding. The room is suffused in dusk, the patterned rug on which Gloria kneels the only ornamented surface. Their clothes, by now shed, are stark school uniforms. "What do you want to do then?" Gloria finally asks. "I don't know," he first answers, but we are sure he does know what he wants to do and then, after a pause, he suggests, "Have sex?" Gloria considers his request: "What do *I* do?" "Just lie there, I suppose." During a long pause we listen to the sound of the music box playing, menacingly slowly; finally Gloria stretches out on her back: "C'mon."

The scene is ultimately at least as disturbing for its depiction of Gloria's passivity and surrender as for its portrayal of incest. Gloria wants imaginative play; she takes great delight in it, a delight clearly sensual as she joyously wriggles and stretches in imitation of a cat. Yet to re-engage Graeme's attention she will lie prone in a sex act in which neither supposes she can actively participate. Earlier in the scene, when Graeme has tried to get her to remove her clothes, she is reluctant but finally acquiesces: "turn the heater on then," she commands and Graeme, perhaps surprised at his success, scrambles to comply. When we see her next, Graeme is paying her a brief visit at a Catholic home for pregnant girls; she begs him to stay: "Don't go—I hate it here—it's so cold—there's no heaters." As a consequence of the game of cats, Gloria, who has wanted heat and connection, is left colder and more alone.

Juxtaposed with the explicit story of Gloria's incestuous relationship with her brother is a more ambiguous narrative of Pam's sexualized relationship with her father. Both of the scenes between Gloria and her brother are followed immediately by a scene suggestive of intimacy between Pam and her father. The cats scene fades to black as the music box plays, the camera opens onto the row of Barbie doll faces as the tune ends, and we are back in Pam's room. After her sister menaces her with a knife for having worn her go-go boots, we enter what we assume to be Pam's dream. The scene is the film's least narrative. Images of a girl's feet jumping rope and the feet of an ice-skater are cut into a sequence in which a girl walks at night by herself in a slicker and white go-go boots. When we first glimpse her face we see a younger version of Pam. She is lured towards a car by an unidentified man whose clothes are like her father's. As the car door opens she starts to run away; in turning towards the camera to move away from the car, we see she is Pam. Then a kitten is proffered; when the camera cuts back to her face, it is the little girl who smiles happily and reaches a hand towards the kitten.

She climbs into the car, her face temporarily obscured by her motion; when we see it again it is Pam's, frightened. The kitten is now laden with sexual suggestion, given the scene's position after the siblings' game of cats. The oscillation back and forth between little-girl-Pam and teen-Pam again suggests Pam's ambivalence about her transition out of childhood; the fear and eagerness with which she regards the car may reflect tensions in the assumption of sexual identity. It is unclear how much of the dream sequence is memory and how much fantasy.

The incest between Gloria and her brother, however disturbing, is tellable. Like the other make-believe we watch, the sex that seems taboo emerges out of play that seems natural. It's easy to follow the trajectory by which first two friends and later two siblings wind up in bed together. By contrast, the suggestion of incest between Pam and her father remains that: something suggested, a possible interpretation of what we are seeing. The "story" of this scene, to the extent that there is a story, is hard to follow. The incest—or Pam's erotic attraction to her father—is palpably not shown. A reviewer asked, "Is the apparent molestation of a child by an unseen stranger in a car one more incident in a pathological sexual history or a metaphor for the general loss of innocence the film painfully chronicles?" (Quart 62). The film allows us, perhaps compels us, to ask such questions but refuses to answer them. There is never any confirmation or assertion; incest remains in the realm of the unnarratable.[2] Pam's feelings about her father are coded through a shadowy dream sequence that disallows us from sorting out fantasy, fear, projection, and memory. It is not that film cannot tell or show incest. Rather, this film, intent on capturing the experience of girlhood in its moments of unfolding—not retrospectively or from an adult, observational position—cannot show what has happened or is happening between Pam and her father, because it is something Pam cannot tell herself.[3]

The dream sequence is only the most dramatic of the ways in which the narrative of this film is visually disjointed. Form mirrors content: the film, with its abrupt and impressionistic segues, tells a story of disjunctive experience. At the same time, even as the visual narrative relies on montage and juxtaposition, as opposed to continuous and linked scenes, and on highly suggestive and symbolic images, as opposed to a clearly representational, "realist" aesthetic, the music of the film operates to integrate and interpret the visual elements. Film theorist Mary Ann Doane reminds us of the ways in which the "ideology of the audible" brings its own truth to bear on the "ideology of the visual": "The ineffable, intangible quality of sound—its lack of the concreteness which is conducive to an ideology of empiricism—requires that it be placed on the side of the emotional or the intuitive" (49).

Narratively, we move from the early image of the girls staring into the camera and shouting out a Beatles' song to an abstract, atmospheric, dirgelike tune in the film's closing scene. The final song has a narrative voice—the refrain is "I'm feeling the cold"—yet we don't always see the source. Some images are of the girls standing against a shapeless, colorless background singing, not looking at the camera or one another; other images show them hunched, separately, over their bodies, silent as the song plays on the soundtrack: "feel the cold, feel the cold is here to stay." In contrast, the Beatles song is lip-synched by the girls as they play at being the Beatles: "I should have known better with a girl like you. . . ." By the end of the film, the "I" has moved outside the girls' bodies; their voices have become disembodied. The story, which is told in visual fragments, is directly coded through the musical progression, from vocalization to alienation.

The music, guiding us through the film's quick succession of symbolic images, comments on the action. Other than the opening and closing songs there is little music. Many scenes are played against silence; a few others incorporate background sound. One motif, the sound of a music box, runs throughout. It is introduced in the first moments of the film, the only sound we hear as the girls look at the medical book. One girl runs her finger along the outlines of the male body, tracing around the erect penis, and coming to rest at the caption at the bottom of the page. The music box continues to play across the title of the film and then gives way to the sound of girls screaming in Beatles ecstasy over a loud rendition of "I Should Have Known Better." We hear the music box at the end of Pam's and Stella's Beatles play scene and again through the climax of Gloria and Graeme's play scene, under their final discussion, rising in volume as Gloria spreads herself out in preparation for sex that is wrenchingly childish yet will mark the end of Gloria's childhood. The slow tinkle of the music box becomes both menacing and sad, creepy and poignant, underscoring the surrender of a tenuously held innocence.

Just as the sound of the music box evokes the realm of childhood at its most fragile, the sound of the Beatles evokes adolescence at its most fervent. Beatlemania, with its collective and deeply performative female energy, is both a musical and visual theme, and it saturates the film. The familiar newsreel images of girl mobs screaming at Beatles' gigs suggest a safe, if noisy, channeling of heterosexual impulses; we implicitly understand that the girls are "in love with" the Fab Four. Yet Sue Wise, in her 1984 essay "Sexing Elvis," argues that the male rock critics who have iconized the performer's "uncontrolled and rampant male sexuality" serve their own psychosexual interests and ignore other sources of his appeal

(392). She counters with a personal memoir of fandom, in which her identification with Elvis provided comfort and safety during the profoundly lonely teenage years before her lesbian self-recognition. In Campion's film the Beatles are not simply objects of desire. Pam and Stella have aroused themselves by fingering and kissing pictures of the various Beatles on Pam's bedroom wall before turning to each other; when they do make out, Stella wears a Beatles mask. Pam and Stella's sex play involves being with their favorite Beatles and being them at the same time. It involves suspension and stretching of their own identities; it denies the fundamental lack that in psychoanalytic terms defines them as female. The other make-believe in the film, the game of cats, also turns into sex. Indeed, the film may suggest that sex is the adult version of make-believe, the opportunity to be at once yourself and not yourself, fleetingly to cast off or transcend your social script. Fandom, too, is a release into private self-construction; it may be deeply social, as the screaming girl mobs suggest, but it is also an alternative story the fan tells herself about herself. The Barbie dolls looking on like prim, normative sexpots at Pam and Stella's play remind us that what is "wrong" with the girls' game is not that it is sexual but that it is sexual in ways that defy the gender conditioning of the toys and tools of girlhood.

Both visual and musical motifs, then, move us from the vibrancy of an exploratory girlhood to an isolated, chilly female adolescence. At the beginning of the film, the three girls are reading a book that should be off limits to them (the camera moves from the warning, "This sight may shock young girls" to their impassive, unshocked faces). In two respects this initial image resembles the film's ending: the girls are absolutely still, and we focus in close-up on a slowly moving hand, with the difference that this hand is one of theirs. Immediately after showing us the cautionary caption, the film's title appears onscreen, as if in response to the book's authority. We shift from silence to the girls' own Beatles act, boisterous and loud. Pam is in the middle and foregrounded, the center of the action, wearing white go-go boots. In the course of the film she is punished by her older sister for wearing those boots that aren't her own. By the end of the film, authority can no longer be resisted, and we see Pam by herself, wearing very little, claiming nothing of her own. In the closing scene Pam is silent and hunched over; we watch her, still and nonresponsive, as an adult male hand explores her body. The transgressive act of reading a dangerous book is the last successful piece of defiance we witness. Campion's short film presents a trajectory of girlhood in which active, busy play surrenders to threats, fears, and the suppression of desires rendered unworkable by conventional expectations.

All of the texts discussed here revolve at a figurative or literal level around reading practices. The Girl's own story dramatizes the dissonance for girls of reading the prescriptive cultural narratives of female adolescence. From such narratives girls learn to acquiesce to their adult status as passive objects of male erotic attention; meanwhile, their own bodies relate a different story. To resolve the dissonance without cutting herself off from the norm, the Girl erases the story written by her own will and desire. That norm is at the center of fiction for and about girls, frequently represented as the world of high-school social competition and its macrocosm, an upwardly mobile, white, consumerist middle class.

The paradigm of the Girl's own story is useful, especially for students, in requiring attention to how social identity is constituted by the tyranny of norms. It is not the drama of sorting things out and finding one's place but the record of facing confused and confusing demands. In *The Bluest Eye,* as in Campion's film, we watch girls absorb a master narrative and accept its ability to tell their story. Both novel and film depict coming-of-age as a process of loss rather than an acquisition of identity. Morrison's novel dramatizes a girl's reading of a seductively normative book, a book that reifies whiteness and upward mobility. Morrison tells us in a 1993 afterword that the novel responds to "the damaging internalization of assumptions of immutable inferiority originating in an outside gaze" (210). In *A Girl's Own Story,* we observe Pam negotiating role conflict as she teeters on the brink of adolescence. In *The Bluest Eye,* the conflict is not negotiable: while girlhood can and will be relinquished for adulthood, brown eyes cannot be traded for blue.

Like Pam, Claudia MacTeer and Pecola Breedlove in Morrison's *The Bluest Eye* look for themselves in the images of pop culture iconography. When Claudia, one of the novel's narrators, doesn't find herself in those images, she reacts with a rage that reflects self-knowledge. Like Campion's Pam, Pecola's identification with those cultural images she finds most attractive and compelling finally fails her. *The Bluest Eye,* like *A Girl's Own Story,* narrates a passage from relative innocence to a devastatingly alienating experience that is thick with cultural representations of girlhood. Pecola's mother, Pauline, grew up obsessed with white movie stars; in adulthood, she neglects her own family in favor of the white family for whom she works. The young, black Pecola looks for herself, futilely, in popular culture images of girls; she is entranced with Shirley Temple, and even Mary Jane candy wrappers fill her with wistful desire. Pecola's longing for blue eyes and blond hair, like that of Pauline's employer's daughter, is her legacy from her mother. The imperatives of a culture driven by consumerism and divided by race and class subvert and replace maternity. Claudia, on the other hand, whose mother is a strong, protecting presence in the novel, responds with ferocious violence to a white doll. We understand by the end of the book that if Claudia is spared the immolating self-hatred that consumes Pecola, her salvation lies in her ability to destroy the doll that invites self-loathing identification with the white world.

As in Campion's film, the doll is an important icon in *The Bluest Eye*. Critic Michael Awkward, in a discussion of the liminality that results from Claudia's conflict between black and white standards, comments on the doll's function: "adults' gifts of white dolls to Claudia are not pleasure-inducing toys, but, rather, signs (in a semiotic sense) that she must learn to interpret correctly" (60). Claudia survives precisely because she does learn to interpret the signs produced by a hostile culture: "we had defended ourselves since memory against everything and everybody, considered all speech a code to be broken by us, and all gestures subject to careful analysis" (191). She learns to observe and analyze adults' behavior, ultimately able to pass judgment on them—and on herself. Pecola never learns to interpret the world around her or her own longings. She reads uncritically, absorbed by cultural inscriptions of whiteness, and, finally, in her madness, absorbing herself into them.

As in *A Girl's Own Story*, we see Pecola on a directionless quest to learn about love, sex, and relationships between men and women. Adults are no help; the only adult women who talk frankly with Pecola are the prostitutes who live upstairs, whose company is forbidden. Their own knowledge base a patchwork of observation and surmise, "the children are forced to rely on each other for information, since adults make themselves so inaccessible" (Rosenberg 439). "How do you get somebody to love you?" Pecola asks Claudia and Frieda but gets no reply (32). Later, remembering hearing her parents having sex—her father making mysterious sounds, her mother making none—Pecola wonders, "Maybe that was love. Choking sounds and silence" (57). Eventually Pecola learns a profound and isolating silence: in the novel's final glimpse into her consciousness she carries on a conversation with an imaginary friend. Evoking sterility and abandonment at the end of the story, as Campion's film does with its closing images of coldness and withdrawal, *The Bluest Eye* ends with barrenness and separation: Claudia and Frieda, despite their concern for Pecola, have drifted away, dismayed that nothing has grown from the seeds they planted on Pecola's behalf. Claudia and her sister Frieda are perplexed by the adult reaction to Pecola's pregnancy by her drunken father: "They were disgusted, amused, shocked, outraged, or even excited by the story. But we listened for the one who would say, 'Poor little girl,' or, 'Poor baby,' but there was only head-wagging where those words should have been" (190). Even as Pecola's story is about parents who are not where they should be and are where they shouldn't be, it is also a story in which coming-of-age is marked by the absence of meaningful language. Because Claudia is capable of critical observation, she has tools of resistance that Pecola does not; to the extent that Claudia survives this minefield of silence, it is because she can recognize what is missing in the adult response to Pecola.

The story about how the girls are shaped by normative white standards is itself, in the telling, shaped by a normative white narrative. *The Bluest Eye* is structured around interpolated phrases from a children's primer. Critic Linda Dittmar's study of the structural elements of the novel calls our attention to the fact that "narrative form, like thematic content, is never politically neutral" (140). Each of the elements of the Dick and Jane story is reflected back, ironically, in the story of Pecola's anything but picture-perfect life. By the end of the novel the friendless Pecola, raped and impregnated by her father, succumbs entirely to her fantasies and the Dick and Jane story becomes a barely legible jumble: "Pecola's grasp on sanity, gradually loosened and finally destroyed, is enacted in the narrative structure, where Pecola's disintegrating sanity is reflected in the dislocation between the norms of the reading primer and the child's perception of the real world" (Birch 156). The novel concludes as Campion's short film does: girlhood comes to a frayed end; the protagonist's sexuality appropriated, her attempts to forge an identity defeated.

Like *A Girl's Own Story*, *The Bluest Eye* begins with a book and ends with an ironic revisiting of the consequences of reading that book. In a certain sense, the entire story of *The Bluest Eye* is told on the first two pages, represented typographically. Text from a "Dick and Jane" book describing a happy family—complete with house, pets, clothes for the children, a friend, a laughing mother, and a smiling father—appears three times. The first time it is presented in standard print, obeying all typographical conventions; the second time, punctuation, capitalization, and spaces between the lines have vanished, obliterating formal sentences although the eye can still distinguish units of thought; finally, spaces between letters have disappeared and the text becomes illegible.

Just as the opening of *A Girl's Own Story* resonates in the final scene, pointing towards Pam's defeat by the prohibitions of adolescence, this primer sequence suggests the way the novel will end: Pecola's hopes for a safe childhood are diminished and finally her sanity itself destroyed. The typographic technique is aggressive in its interference with the conventions of the print book, underscoring the violent impact of normalizing discourses of whiteness on the girls: "numbing the imagination with their simplifications of grammar and life, both the form and the substance of the 'Dick and Jane' passages violate the integrity of the life Morrison depicts" (Dittmar 141). The Dick and Jane story, repeated a few sentences at a time as section headings, corresponds loosely and ironically to Pecola's story. In one of the novel's most important scenes, Pecola's mother throws Pecola out of the house where she works, turning to comfort the daughter of that household; the next section begins: "SEEMOTHERMOTHERISVERYNICE" (110). Pecola's increasing losses drive her deeper into an alienated fantasy until in the novel's final pages, headed "LOOKLOOKHERECOMESAFRIEND," Pecola manages, in her madness, to manufacture a loyal playfellow (193). In fulfilling the imperatives of the primer ("PLAYJANEPLAY"), Pecola cuts herself off not only from contact with the world outside her mind but also from all possibility of self-recognition (193).

While Campion and Morrison's stories of emergent adolescence are precisely about failures to come fully and safely of age—about the impossibility of girls' doing so—Carter and Acker's stories revise the archetypes from which the coming-of-age story is constructed. While Pam and Pecola are defeated by the books in whose stories they become absorbed, *The Bloody Chamber* and *Blood and Guts in High School* absorb canonical sources into their tales of girlhood. Both Carter and Acker rely on our familiarity with a set of texts that shape Anglo-American moral, aesthetic, and literary values. Carter and Acker rewrite these stories in their own images, ransacking the texts and topoi that constitute our cultural mythology and demythologizing them, sometimes violently. Acker snatches stories and characters from across the spectrum of Western literature and culture, peopling her novels with women named Don Quixote, Toulouse Lautrec, and Paul Gaugin.[4] Carter rewrites the folktales that form the basis of our canon of children's literature, placing female agency and interiority at the center of the marriage plot and altering the endings to include rescuing mothers and girls deciding their own fates.

The Bloody Chamber and *Blood and Guts in High School* provide narratives of resistance that counterpose the narratives of loss in *A Girl's Own Story* and *The Bluest Eye*. Carter and Acker, as the epigraphs to this essay suggest, are highly conscious of the omission of women from the circuit of public language, and therefore they select as their medium the very stories from which women are most obviously excluded. Acker's books are "adult" not only in their pornographic content but in their reliance on an audience fairly widely read in European and American novels and drama. Carter, on the other hand, takes as her point of departure children's literature, fairy tales whose familiar plots and characters constitute a kind of mythology primer. Feminist literary theorist Rachel Blau DuPlessis's discussion of revisionary mythopoesis illuminates the challenge Carter assumes: "When a woman writer chooses myth as her subject she is faced with material that is indifferent or, more often, actively hostile to historical considerations of gender, claiming as it does universal, humanistic, natural, or even archetypal status" (106). Like H. D.'s re-casting of classical mythology, the stories in *The Bloody Chamber* reveal that their source material is fundamentally ideological, rooted in a given perspective, and indebted to particular arrangements of authority.

Carter depends on our having been steeped in Grimm and Perrault's tales and their later adaptations. Because we know from these sources exactly how perilous the dark forest of female adolescence is and precisely how necessary a prince for salvation, the resourcefulness and determination—the selfdetermination—of Carter's girls reveals to us our own immersion in the values of these myths. The endings come as a surprise because we are so thoroughly conditioned by the narrative expectations of fairy tales with their aura of universality. While an ongoing discussion debates the nature of Carter's feminist revision, with some readers contending that the tales in *The Bloody Chamber* remain saturated in patriarchal authority, the stories do at least defamiliarize and thereby allow us critical access to these narrative expectations.[5]

The Bloody Chamber is a kind of serial novel, its short stories functioning together to form an answer volume to the books with which American and British children are raised. In revising a handful of fairy and folktales, *The Bloody Chamber* vamps, parodies, and riffs on the themes foundational to children's literature. Rather than simply rewriting "Beauty and the Beast," or "Little Red Riding Hood," Carter meditates—and compels us to meditate—on these stories' motifs, structures, and sexual politics. The book contains two beast stories and closes with three wolf stories, not offering one variant but hinting at the possibility of infinite revision. Because "The Tiger's Bride," with its reversal of the "Beauty and the Beast" formula, follows "The Courtship of Mr. Lyon," which maintains it, the book moves us gradually towards an expanded field of narrative possibility: "As much about the act of storytelling as it is the subversive undoing of old stories and sexual politics, *The Bloody Chamber* ultimately recodes literary history to sanction the feminist writer who comes to embrace her own desire" (Linkin 307). The "anti-moral" of the story of *The Bloody Chamber* is that the ability to imagine alternative endings is profoundly liberatory.

For Campion's Pam and Morrison's Pecola, self-discovery involves loss. Carter's heroines travel a similar and recognizable path but not to the conclusion we expect; each story drives through familiar territory toward an unfamiliar ending. At the end of "The Bloody Chamber," a version of "Bluebeard," the adolescent wife is saved at the last minute by her mother. In "The Tiger's Bride," instead of the beast turning into a man ("The Courtship of Mr. Lyon" follows this conventional ending), the beauty turns into an animal. In two variants on "Little Red Riding Hood" the girl saves herself at her grandmother's expense. The girls in *The Bloody Chamber* have keen senses of self-preservation, they have strong sexual impulses, they have wills, and they laugh. Their laughter resounds through the muffled atmosphere of the fairy-tale world, through the dank, elaborate castles and deep, intriguing forests. The protagonist of "The Tiger's Bride" laughs at the Beast's first proposal: "no young lady laughs like that! my old nurse used to remonstrate" (58). When the wolf in "The Company of Wolves" intones his famous threat, "All the better to eat you with," "the girl burst out laughing" (118). The laughter saves her, not from death, but from a cultural insistence on her vulnerability, her passivity, and her sexual submissiveness. Both of these stories conclude with sexual union with the beasts initiated by the girls.

Most of the *Bloody Chamber* stories forcefully reject the static, stultifying definition of goodness—manifested as extreme physical beauty—around which Grimm and Perrault's tales revolve. Critic Sylvia Bryant argues that "this social scenario of reward based on essential goodness presents an essential problem, particularly for the 'girls' seeking their own stories and experiences other than those which literature and history has proffered to them" (440). Rather than being rewarded for appropriately feminine behavior, Carter's girls, in most cases, have to reject some element of the feminine to survive and triumph. Carter takes apart "that 'moral' which positions the female character, and hence the subject-seeking female reader, at the definitional mercy of the dominant culture's inscribing pen" (Bryant 440). The pragmatic girl in "The Company of Wolves" examines and then rejects her initial reaction to the wolf's threatening virility: "since her fear did her no good, she ceased to be afraid" (117). Her subsequent misbehavior—bestiality, cohabitation with her grandmother's murderer—not only saves her own life but is a manifestation of a powerful, transformative love.

While Campion and Morrison's stories are anatomies of loss and Carter's are legends of loss transformed, in Acker's work it is harder to talk of loss, betrayal, rescue, recovery, or survival. Survival (arguably the end point of all narrative in one way or another) is a fuzzy category in Acker's novels; acquiescence and resistance are bound together in roiling narrative frenzy. The master narrative to which Acker responds is the canonical novel, from Cervantes to Hawthorne; her response divests it of the realism and linearity constitutive of the genre. In Acker's novels the pretense of a stable, organized, nonquixotic reality dissolves under the barrage of experience. There is no progression toward love or death; nearly every episode of her novels is saturated in both. For Janey, the protagonist of *Blood and Guts in High School*, the attempt to escape a psychologically and emotionally devastating affair (with her father) leads to increasingly intense physical suffering, insanity, and finally death. Janey's main sexual partners are men with virtually unlimited power over her: first her father and then the Persian slave trader who has imprisoned her. The novel serves as a brutal repartee to the girls' story about accommodation, conformity, and deference to authority. In its formal dimensions as well, with its pastiche of narrative, dramatic script, interior monologue, book report, and hand-drawn illustrations and diagrams, *Blood and Guts in High School* does violence to the generic shapes and methods of the novel. Like *The Bluest Eye*, it responds to a canonical book, probing that book's values and following its outlines closely, only, finally, to render the original unintelligible.

Blood and Guts in High School is deliberately hard to read in two different but intentionally parallel ways. With its frequent digressions away from narrative, its drawings, ideograms, Persian language lesson, and free-form rants, the story is hard to follow. With its relentless sexual violence toward Janey, a young girl who has been used sexually and then abandoned by her father, it is horrifying to follow. Most disturbing are the various ways in which Janey, victimized first by her father, then by the slave trader who teaches her to be a whore, and along the way by a surfeit of other men, comes to participate in her victimization. The novel suggests self-destruction and profound physical, mental, and emotional pain are inherent in sexual relations. After the first of multiple abortions, Janey tells us "abortions are the symbol, the outer image, of sexual relations in this world" (34). Critic Sylvia Söderlind's comments on abortion in *Don Quixote* apply equally to *Blood and Guts in High School*: "the abortion, with all its attendant pain, is a consequence of the love/hate relationship between a female reader and the male texts that have represented her to herself. The abortion is the impregnation by and consequent expulsion of the canonical (or more accurately, seminal) texts of the male tradition" (252). The recurrent abortion motif in Acker's work is indicative of an underlying argument: female sexuality will always be self-destructive because the male texts out of which women construct that sexuality are filled with loathing.

Acker's reaction to this double bind is a novel that does all it can to dismantle the canon that produces the double bind. *Blood and Guts in High School* is a rebellious book. One of its chief methods of resistance is relentless borrowing from a male canon: the novel makes passing references to world literature (including Shakespeare, Catullus, and Dostoyevsky) and focuses long sections on rewritings of Hawthorne and Genet. This complicated exploitation of literary history is at the center of much of Acker's work; her *Great Expectations* and *Don Quixote* allude to novels that we understand to be peculiarly canonical. Acker's deployment of the Western literary tradition is so extensive that it is frequently referred to by critics not as allusion but as a deliberate form of plagiarism, what the critic Gabrielle Dane refers to as "a parodic plagiarism" (247). It is one of the most challenging aspects of Acker's work, in its own way as shocking and disquieting as the graphic depictions of sex and violence. While imprisoned, Janey writes a book report on *The Scarlet Letter* to occupy herself; the book report gives way to a jagged retelling of Hawthorne's tale, in which a character named Hester tries to figure out her relationships to Chillingworth, Dimwit, the repressive society around her, and her own desires: "'I go crazy when I want to fuck a guy,' Hester thinks to herself. 'How will any man ever love me? How can I be happy if a man doesn't fuck and love me? But look at Pearl. She's happy and she doesn't fuck'" (93).[6] But allusion in Acker's work does not serve the function it serves elsewhere of forging ties across time and space. While allusion conventionally creates and reflect literary community, Acker's borrowings dismantle our sense, which seems artificial under Acker's gaze, of a body of literature with corporeal integrity and wholeness. Janey's story can only be written at the expense of the stories organized around female docility and shame. Her short and violent life can only be related by doing violence to the narratives that precede and organize hers. In Acker's terms, to tell the Girl's own story is not only to critique but to act out against a repressive and silencing culture.

Blood and Guts in High School, with its long, strange version of Hester Prynne's story doesn't revise Hawthorne as Carter revises the folktales of the Grimm Brothers. Instead, it overwrites and overrides *The Scarlet Letter* and it is, indeed, itself overwritten in its verbal prolixity, switching abruptly from linear narrative to chaotic jumbles of words and phrases. Woven into the narration of the life and death of Janey are poetry, translations, streams of consciousness and unconsciousness, emphatic repetitions, handwritten lists of Persian phrases, and passages that can only be described as written shouting. The *Scarlet Letter* passages parody, not only Hawthorne's story, but his rendition of character and language: "She's going to fuck Dimwit, she's going to have Dimwit for ever and for ever, the moon and the stars in the sky, pluck them out with your hand, put them in your pocket and keep them, a dream of a limitless world, of the sun and the moon and the stars. As far as I can go. Love love love. Want want want" (98). Acker's Hester, like Janey, is formidably verbal. While both are constantly frustrated in their desires, their narration of that frustration is the source of a potent creativity. Acker's Don Quixote is described as having "no speech of her own" (39); while incarcerated Janey writes, "There's going to be a world where the imagination is created by joy not suffering. . .(a woman's going to come along and make this world for me even though I'm not alive anymore)" (100). Her wish is at once powerful and despairing. To name the hope of a better world is to begin to forge that world, yet the hope of a savior, in the form of a woman artist, remains in the secondary, enclosed space of the parentheses.

The novel asserts the power of the enraged imagination even in its most wrenching depictions of Janey's vulnerability. One of many examples of literal overwriting in *Blood and Guts in High School* is the repetition of a passage describing an evening Janey and her father-boyfriend, Johnny, spend together shortly before Janey is due to leave, reluctantly, for America. She is in despair about losing her father to his new girlfriend, Sally. The passage ends, "Johnny left her, telling her he'd be home later" (21). We expect, given previous episodes, that Johnny will not be home, that he will, in fact, spend the night with Sally. The novel proceeds for a paragraph and then the passage repeats itself. This happens six times; six times the threat of Johnny not returning to Janey is deferred. The repetition illustrates Janey's longing to hold on to the relationship while her father pulls away; it literalizes her desperate wish to have the evening over again, or more evenings like it. If the repetition does indeed enact Janey's desire, then we see that desire being powerful enough to interfere with the shape of narrative itself. Similarly, Acker's Hester intervenes in the very act of literature. If Acker only alluded to *The Scarlet Letter*—if Janey's book report simply nudged us toward a gentle parallelism between the two novels' preoccupations with cultural attitudes toward female sexuality—the result would be participation in and even reverence toward the tradition. But Acker's use of Hawthorne is violent, and the link it forges between her novel and *The Scarlet Letter* grotesque. Like the highly irreverent treatment of President Carter (he has sadistic sex with Janey), the use of Hawthorne attacks the sanctity of a cultural icon. Allusion in Acker has the effect of graffiti; the observer can still discern the original, but the image of the penciled-in mustache remains in the mind's eye. While Angela Carter's response to the Girls' story is reform, the energies of *Blood and Guts in High School* are annihilating.

Acker's novels show, in critic Martina Sciolino's phrase, that "'coming to be' is full of gaps, folds, and disappearances" (438). Only fairly recently has a range of fiction and cinema emerged that tackles underlying cultural and narrative assumptions about the outlines and outcome of the Girls' coming of age story. In her study of American fiction of female adolescence, literary historian Barbara White points out that the feminist Bildungsroman that emerged out of the women's movement of the '70s focused on adult women awakening into recognition of sexuality and self-determination, rather than girls coming-of-age: "a patriarchal society is less inimical to an independent woman past childbearing age and less hesitant to assimilate her or at least leave her alone to pursue a personal quest" (196). Reflecting on her success with *The Piano* (1993), the first film for which she wrote the screenplay without collaboration, Campion told a reporter, "*The Piano,* like *A Girl's Own Story,* is my territory—things I know about, that nobody else could easily get access to" (Cantwell 51). The Girl's own story is the telling that explores private territory, the folds and gaps in which the materials of one's own story are hidden; it is the story that belies the narrative of conformity in which success means being accepted by one's peers and learning to rein in one's oddity. It is the Girl's own in that it resists the injunction towards conformity embedded in the didacticism of consumer culture.

The Girl's own story—necessarily disjunctive and unfamiliar, as lived experience is—skirts the margins of a highly conventional cultural text, using that text and its artifacts, but to its own ends. In each of the works discussed here, girls use narratives in which they don't find themselves to generate stories in which they do figure. The pleasure of this self-authored text may be fleeting, as in Pam's Beatle-vamping, or it may both rescue the girl and enable her to rescue the boy, as in Carter's "The Tiger's Bride" and "The Company of Wolves." The Girl's own story shows us girls entering into conversation with the books they read, a dialectic that may be destructive to the girl, as in *The Bluest Eye,* or to the book, as in *Blood and Guts in High School;* it shows us girls whose relationship to the cultural images presented for their consumption defy the boundaries implicitly presented with those images.

Notes

1. This is not to say that children's play with Barbies actually revolves around the dolls' outfits, despite Mattel's emphasis on wardrobe and grooming.
2. When I taught *A Girl's Own Story* there was no question in any of my students' minds that the film depicted an incestuous relationship of some sort between Pam and her father.

3. Another Campion short film, *Passionless Moments,* is remarkable for capturing the silent, unthinking perception that constantly filters through the mind in repose. Acute and banal at the same time, its dramatization of the observational detritus that never makes it to the level of thought or articulation offers a compelling study of point of view.
4. This particular technique of feminist appropriation is also used by Jeanette Winterson in her 1994 novel *Art and Lies.* Among its protagonists are a doctor named Handel and a distraught young girl named Picasso.
5. For a critique of the politics of *The Bloody Chamber,* see Robert Clark, Patricia Duncker, and Susanne Kappeler; for defenses, see Nanette Alterers and Elaine Jordan.
6. Even in less deliberately provocative forms allusion raises issues about the writer's relationship to her or his predecessors. Ellen G. Friedman sees Acker as interrogating the masterworks' "sources in paternal authority and male desire" (244); Arthur F. Redding holds that despite its subversiveness, the use of powerful literary forefathers is masochistic (287). Certainly both views are accurate; neither, I think, fully measures the violence Acker does to her source material.

THREE

The Battleground of the Adolescent Girl's Body

BRENDA BOUDREAU

In her 1985 study *Growing Up Female: Adolescent Girlhood in American Fiction,* Barbara White suggests that despite the feminist consciousness informing many recent novels of adolescence, the picture of growing up female remains overwhelmingly negative. A survey of common problems confronted by girls in literature in the latter half of the twentieth century, such as AIDS, teenage pregnancy, sexually transmitted diseases, eating disorders, and depression, would seem to support White's claim. White, however, underestimates the subversive potential of many of these narratives. These novels do not simply reflect the lived realities of the adolescent girl; instead, these novels deliberately emphasize bodily experiences in an effort to subvert the cultural narrative that says girls are passive victims, reframing the terms by which the body has been traditionally represented.[1]

Girls clearly do not experience their bodies for the first time in adolescence, but at this stage their self-identities become closely linked to the physical body, particularly as the body takes on more visibly sexed characteristics. At the same time, the body becomes an obstacle to autonomy and self-agency as the girl tries to reconcile her body to the demands of a socially proscribed gendered identity, leading, paradoxically, to feelings of disembodiment. Contemporary novels of adolescence certainly deal with these difficulties, but by foregrounding the adolescent girl's body, these novels effect a re-embodiment, one in which the body is not simply a negative obstacle to be overcome. These novels recognize the body as a site of contestation, a "battleground," as autobiographical critic Sidonie Smith suggests, "upon which the struggle for cultural meaning is waged" ("Identity's Body" 184).[2]

Recent feminist theoretical efforts to recognize the subject as a corporeal being offer a particularly useful framework to understand the body as a site of struggle for the adolescent girl. As feminist theorist Elizabeth Grosz writes in *Volatile Bodies,* the link between corporeality and subjectivity is problematic for women who "have been objectified and alienated as social subjects partly through the denigration and containment of the female body" (xiv). The female body continues to be coded in patriarchal discourse as weak, incompetent, and unstable, but these representations are also open to (re)presentation, creating more positive images of the female body.

Because the link between subjectivity and the corporeal body is not a simple, direct one, it is far more productive to focus on body image, which is, as Grosz points out, the subjective representation to the self of the physical body: "The body image is a map or representation of the degree of narcissistic investment of the subject in its own body and body parts . . . measuring not only the psychical but also the physiological changes the body undergoes in its day-to-day actions and performances" (83). The body image is not self-contained but is dynamic and fluid, taking in perceptions of others' bodies, as well as external objects, including clothing. The subjective representation of the body, then, is necessarily historically and culturally contingent: "The body image is as much a function of the subject's psychology and sociohistorical context as of anatomy" (79). This focus on body image allows for a consideration of the physical body without falling into totalized, essentialized thinking; focusing on an "embodied subjectivity" (22) insists that the body must be considered in its sexual, racial, ethnic, and class particularities.

The body image is particularly tenuous for the adolescent girl, who is often confused and frightened by the radical physical changes taking place in her body, as well as by the cultural response to her body. It is in adolescence that "the subject feels the greatest discord between the body image and the lived body, between its psychical idealized self-image and its bodily changes" (75). Because of its tenuousness, the body image is particularly amenable to external influences during adolescence, making it susceptible to political and ideological inscription. Grosz's insistence that the body image is relational, that it is "the result of shared sociocultural conceptions of bodies in general and shared familial and interpersonal fantasy about particular bodies" (84), offers a useful way to read alternative narrative possibilities in contemporary novels of development. The focus within many of these novels is not exclusively on the adolescent girl's body but on female bodies, including mothers, friends, and siblings, linking the girl to a community of women in (potentially) empowering ways.

Several recent novels of development illustrate the importance of understanding female subjectivity as embodied, emphasizing that a positive body image (or lack thereof) directly affects how girls engage with the social struggle for autonomy and self-agency. In Louise Meriwether's *Daddy Was a Number Runner* (1970), Sandra Berkley's *Coming Attractions* (1988), and Dorothy Allison's *Bastard Out of Carolina* (1992), the girl's body reflects various cultural attitudes and values about the body, as well as being constituted by them; her body becomes a literal battlefield, the target for, and a means of, humiliation and control, particularly by men.[3] In all three novels the struggle begins when the girl is prepubescent, emphasizing that a girl's sexually specific body makes her vulnerable long before she takes on a position as a sexual subject. As these novels also suggest, however, the girl's body can be a potential site of contestation when she claims control over her own self-representation, allowing her to escape cultural objectification and containment.

While Sandra Berkley's *Coming Attractions* critiques patriarchal culture's representations of the female body, this novel offers a contrast to Meriwether's and Allison's novels because it does not actually empower its adolescent protagonist to fight back against cultural oppression. Instead, it is a cautionary narrative about what can happen when an adolescent girl's body image is so externally mediated that she never becomes a subject, never develops a self-identity that will allow her to exercise agency. In fact, Berkley emphasizes her main protagonist's containment within a femininity script by writing several sections of the novel as a film script, replete with shot directions.

The novel traces the development of Cassandra Keen, a girl whose anatomical body *is* her identity. Grosz suggests that it is only in adolescence that sexuality "acquires social recognition and value" (75), but as this novel makes clear, the line separating a girl from a woman is sometimes an arbitrary one; indeed, the girl's body is often sexualized before she understands what "sex" is and long before her body takes on secondary sexual characteristics (breasts, widening hips, pubic hair). Cassie is only five years old when her stepfather, "Daddy Dick," becomes sexually aroused by Cassie's imitation of Mae West. He begins bouncing Cassie up and down on his lap, laughing and tickling her. Cassie finds Daddy Dick's roaming fingers amusing until he touches her genitals under the elastic of her underwear, "where her special place is!" (20). The vocabulary Cassie uses to explain her body suggests that she is already internalizing a cultural objectification of female genitalia. Cassie is upset by Dick's behavior, but when she tries to tell her mother, Hedy, that Daddy Dick has touched her "there," Hedy refuses to listen, accusing Cassie of having a wild imagination and insisting that she apologize to Dick (21). This denial protects Hedy's marriage, but it also negates Cassie's control over her own body.

Ironically, Hedy herself has endangered her daughter by making Cassie a spectacle of adult sexuality in the way she dresses her and in the way she encourages Cassie to imitate adult movie stars in front of a video camera or to entertain guests. Cassie is never actually raped by her stepfather, but Daddy Dick continues to come into her bedroom at night, "accidentally" touching her as he covers her with blankets. The very fact that Cassie feels she must keep silent suggests that she is learning behavior that will make her more vulnerable to this male threat as her body physically matures. By the time she is ten, Dick is constantly trying to sexualize Cassie's image, telling her to pull her skirts up higher for the camera. The adolescent Cassie doesn't question Dick's behavior, partly because her own mother seems perversely fascinated with Cassie's physical changes, particularly Cassie's development of breasts: "Worst of all, they bring a creepy look to Hedy's face, and jokes about baby boobies. Hedy often gets that look now—a secret grin-wink when Cassie's body is mentioned" (56).

Grosz suggests that adolescents often experience their bodies as an "undesired biological imposition" (75) because their physical bodies are temporally out of step with their body images. Cassie's body image has, however, been constructed by a visibly sexed adult sexuality that never accords with her physical body, and this discordance does not allow Cassie to develop any "real" sense of identity. Adult sexuality is a role Cassie imagines she can "try on" through the accouterments of adulthood (makeup, clothing, bodily movements) and by miming film stars: "CUT TO Cassie in room furtively trying on one of Hedy's pink satin bras. . . . QUICK CUT TO LONG SHOT OF her swooning onto the covered-wagon bed and lying there, smiling. PAN her body as she breathes heavily, making her little chest heave in an out, up and down, as if her breasts are *enormous* . . ." (56). Cassie is imitating what she has seen in films and in the adults around her, but it is this kind of behavior that makes her vulnerable to the physical and psychological abuse she is subjected to at the hands of virtually every male with whom she comes in contact. The only thing that keeps Cassie "fighting" in the novel is her mother's warning about protecting her virginity so that she can use it as a bartering tool, a commodification that also distances Cassie from her body.

Unlike the central protagonists in the subsequent two novels discussed, Cassie is left stranded at the end of the novel, her dreams of romantic love destroyed, and forced to marry a man considerably older than she is because her mother has abandoned her. She is also left without any alternative role models, so the novel suggests she is locked into a "script" over which she had no control, one that she is ready to pass on to her own daughter.

Developing a positive sense of self can be particularly difficult for girls subject to racial and class oppression, as Louise Meriwether's *Daddy Was a Number Runner* emphasizes. Set in Harlem in 1934, the novel focuses on Francie Coffin growing up during the Depression, surrounded by gangsters, prostitutes, and gang violence. Francie has the advantage of loving family members who try to protect her from the worst influences of this environment, although there is a pessimistic, almost deterministic, sense in the novel that the main characters cannot really escape the dehumanizing effects of poverty and racial oppression. Thus, although Francie's father insists that she and her friends keep off the street where the prostitutes congregate, he himself is engaged in illegal activity, running the numbers in the neighborhood. A woman seems to have only three role possibilities in this neighborhood—virgin, mother, or whore—and which one she will be seems to have less to do with her own agency than with circumstances beyond her control. The body can become, however, a locus of cultural protest, suggesting that women must take ownership of their own bodies if they are going to be able to escape oppression.

Like Cassie, Francie's physically immature body is sexualized in various ways; she is forced to see herself through an objectifying lens, which leaves her feeling incompetent and unattractive. Even before puberty, Francie's body becomes the means for the males around her to assert their power and control by calling attention to her "flawed" body, which in Francie's case is too thin: "'Hey skinny mama,' one of them yelled. 'When you put a little pork chops on those spare ribs I'm gonna make love to you.' The other boys folded up laughing and I scooted past, ignoring them" (15). Francie is only vaguely aware of what their comments might be alluding to, but she internalizes their insults: "So I was skinny and black and bad looking with my short hair and long neck and all that naked space in between. I looked like a plucked chicken" (15). As it becomes clear throughout the novel, this self-distancing is dangerous for Francie, since she sees her "self" and her body as mutually exclusive.

Francie is further distanced from her body through her naiveté; the novel suggests that while sexual ignorance is culturally endorsed for many young girls, it can lead to bodily shame and confusion. Francie's first menstrual period is frightening and alienating, feelings for which her mother has little patience: "Shut up that screaming Francie. You ain't dying. You're just starting your period" (73). Suddenly her mother sees Francie's entire body as being sexualized, and she says she is going to need to buy Francie a bra. More importantly, Francie's body becomes linked to its reproductive capacities, and her mother's only explanation is, "'It means . . .' she hesitated. Her eyes dropped and her voice became crisp. 'It means don't let no boys mess around with you? Understand?'" (74). Francie, however, isn't quite sure of the connection. Francie wants to understand what is happening to her body, but unfortunately her mother voices a common maternal response to her daughter's puberty; culturally menses becomes associated with danger and vulnerability, since it literally means that a girl is now physically capable of bearing children. Francie's mother is well-intentioned, but her refusal to really explain what is happening to Francie's body does not prepare Francie to deal adequately with these changes.

Francie's mother fears pregnancy, but the danger to Francie's body is perhaps even more serious than her mother realizes. Francie may be able to walk away from the insults by the boys on the street, but she is unable to escape the various men who try to take physical advantage of young women in the neighborhood. Indeed, one of the most depressing observations made in this novel is that circumstances can force a woman to distance herself from her own body, so much so that she does not even question her own willingness to allow her body to be "used." In fact, poverty almost seems to force Francie to offer up her body in a kind of pseudo-prostitution; her body becomes a tool she can use to make money or get more food. Throughout the novel Francie is followed around by an older white man who usually corners her in the movie theater, and gives her dimes for "feels" (16). The man shows up even on the roof of Francie's apartment building, offering to give her a dime if she will touch his penis. Despite her disgust, Francie seems vaguely fascinated with men and male sexuality. This instance is clearly not the first time a scenario of this kind has occurred since Francie barely reacts to the man's exposure and does not even report the incident to anyone. Her lack of fear also points to her naiveté; she only wishes her best friend Sukie were around because "she'd know what to do to make us some safe money" (27).

These men represent annoyances rather than real threats, and Francie and Sukie are confident that they can somehow manipulate male sexual desire to make money, unrealistically believing that they are not in any danger. At one point Francie and Sukie go to a park and are stopped by an old white man, dirty and unshaven, who offers them both a nickel if they will let him "feel [them] a little" (43). They refuse, but he offers the nickel just for allowing him to look. Without hesitation, the two girls both take the nickel, and oblige his request: "Sukie lifted up her skirt and pulled down her bloomers and I did the same, watching the man's face all the time" (43). When he starts to come closer, they run away, laughing and shrieking. "I was glad Sukie never let any of these bums touch us. It was bad enough having the butcher and Max the Baker always sneaking a feel, but at least they were clean" (43). Here again there is a strange sense of disempowerment because Sukie is completely in control of how far Francie will go to get her share of the money.

In many ways there is a thin line between Francie and her friends and the prostitutes with whom they are so fascinated; the prostitutes actively solicit customers and have physical encounters with them, but both groups of women are resigned to their place within this environment. Sukie's sister, China Doll, feels that being a prostitute at least gives her an edge over women like her mother who are working for pennies a day: "She said ofays were gonna get you one way or the other so you might as well make them pay for it and try to give them a dose of the clap in the bargain" (109). Francie recognizes China Doll's power as illusory, however, when she notices the bruises and scratches left by Alfred, China Doll's pimp.

Virtually all male characters represent a threat to the female body, and there is initially a feeling of hopelessness in the novel, a sense that women cannot refuse male attention, no matter how unwelcome it might be. Francie sees it as matter of course that she will have to use her body to get an extra soup bone or rolls from the neighborhood butcher and baker. When Francie goes to Mr. Morristein, the butcher's, for example, she is usually cornered by him if no other customers are in the store: "I stood there patiently while his hands fumbled over my body" (41). The disturbing part about these scenes is Francie's utter indifference and resignation to the molestation.

Francie's indifference, however, is part of her defense against these attacks, allowing her to feel in control; only when she finds herself responding to the attention does she feel defiled, and experiences her own sexual responses as problematic. Francie's sexual awakening occurs, significantly, in the movie theater, one of the few places she can escape into her fantasies. The fat, bald, white man she has seen on the roof follows her into the theater and sits down next to her. Francie's response illustrates her ignorance: "I had to giggle. He sure was crazy about Westerns. Almost every time I came to the show by myself he would sit next to me, hand me a dime, and start feeling me under my skirt. We never said a word to each other, he would just hand me the money and start feeling" (82). He is clearly watching Francie to see where she goes, but it never crosses Francie's mind to be frightened by the strange coincidence of continually meeting this man. We sense Francie's allowance of a kind of pseudo-prostitution; she is so engrossed in watching the film that she seems almost oblivious to the man's presence, other than being careful that his hands do not get very far inside her underwear.

This scene portrays another way that the adolescent girl's body is socially contained within a femininity script in which she experiences her own sexual desire as "bad." Francie gets caught up in the movie she is watching and forgets about the man next to her until she realizes he has gotten his fingers all the way inside: "I was throbbing down there like a drum. I squirmed. My legs opened wider, and his fingers moved higher. . . . My God. I was on fire" (84). Francie quickly escapes, but she is left confused and ashamed by her wet underwear and her own feelings. Francie's response is representative of how social attitudes toward female sexuality can leave girls confused and dangerously ignorant, since female sexuality has been left unspoken and unacknowledged.

The picture in this novel of growing up in America as a young, poor black woman is bleak; however, a glimmer of hope at the end of the novel suggests Francie will try to refuse sexual objectification by asserting control of her own body. Her observations of the oppression of women around her empower Francie to rebel. A turning point in the novel happens shortly after her thirteenth birthday when Francie, fed up with Max the Baker's groping, knees him in the groin and runs away. When she realizes that she has seen Sukie having sex with Alfred, China Doll's pimp, Francie suddenly realizes that the "games" she and Sukie have been playing with their bodies can have far-reaching consequences if Sukie will follow in her sister's footsteps. Neither girl is entirely sure how to escape, however, and the novel ends with them sitting on the stairs crying, as Francie thinks, "Either you was a whore like China Doll or you worked in a laundry or did day's work or ran poker games or had a baby every year" (187). Part of Francie's coming-of-age, then, has been to accept her body as the inevitable site of her struggle with her environment. Given the focus on Francie's body throughout the novel, Meriwether makes it clear that Francie can refuse victimization by asserting the autonomy of her body.

Bastard Out of Carolina presents an even more horrific picture of the adolescent body becoming a battleground, but this novel is, paradoxically, more uplifting than *Coming Attractions* and *Daddy Was a Number Runner* because the adolescent protagonist remains determined not to let herself be destroyed completely by the oppressiveness of her environment; although the struggle is played out on her physical body, she becomes an active participant by trying to control her own self-representation.

The narrative is told in the first person by Ruth Ann Boatwright, nicknamed Bone as an infant. Bone grows up poor and white in Greenville, South Carolina, in 1955; she is haunted by issues of identity throughout the novel, beginning with the fact that she is "certified a bastard by the state of South Carolina" when her fifteen-year-old mother Anney, unconscious at the time of birth, is unable to identify a father (3). Anney is appalled and goes to the courthouse every year to try to get a new birth certificate that would legitimate Bone's birth. Anney's mother cannot understand her daughter's obsession, however: "The child is proof enough. An't no stamp on her nobody can see" (3).

Ironically, visual verification of her identity is what Bone seems to want most as a small child, particularly since she looks so different from most of her Boatwright relatives. Bone eventually hears stories from her grandmother and aunt about her father, but he remains a topic her mother refuses to discuss. This missing link in her history leaves Bone feeling that she doesn't quite fit in, particularly since she cannot be certain that what she hears is the truth. She desperately wants to believe the stories she hears, even if it might mean she has Cherokee or even "colored" blood (54). Despite her difference in looks, being a Boatwright is an identity that Bone holds onto tenaciously.

Bone is torn throughout the novel between needing to identify herself with her family and being deeply ashamed of her "white trash" background. Even as a child, Bone never has any sense of optimism that she might be able to break away from her background because the only identity she can claim is her Boatwright heritage. Sometimes the "battle" for identity, then, becomes an internal one.

It is not unusual in novels of female development for girls to experience their bodies masochistically, imagining that they somehow do not deserve love and respect, simply because they have been born female. As feminist literary critic Patricia Waugh notes in *Feminine Fictions*, "The radical dissatisfaction that women feel with their cultural position is turned back in rage against their own bodies because they masochistically perceive this site of 'femininity' to be itself, in its imperfections, the source of their frustration and depression" (175). Throughout the novel, Bone observes that there are two codes of acceptable behavior, one for women and one for men. It becomes clear that it is the Boatwright women who bear most of the burden of their family's survival, yet the women idolize the men in the family, excusing their drunken and irresponsible behavior, making Bone resentful. Bone also learns, very early on, that her class increases the vulnerability of her female position. She feels certain that her cultural heritage is inescapable and that, as a woman, she is destined to be used by the men around her: "This body, like my aunts' bodies, was born to be worked to death, used up, and thrown away" (206). The females around Bone represent limited models of who she can become, resigning her to a future of oppression.

For Bone, the battle being fought on and through her body is really a battle for her mother's love and affection. Anney is an attractive, strong woman trying to raise two children by working in a truck-stop diner, but she subscribes to conventional ideas about a woman's role. After she meets Glen Waddell, she subordinates everything to his needs and wants. Anney knows Glen is like an insecure little boy, but she also seems to sincerely love him, despite his mean temper. Bone is an atypical adolescent protagonist in that she is very aware of her mother's sexuality and almost seems to understand it. Bone senses that understanding sexuality will explain everything in her life: "Mama and Daddy Glen always hugging and rubbing on each other, but it was powerful too. Sex" (63). Bone also sees her mother's strength and beauty slowly drained within this marriage, a destruction Bone blames on her mother's inexplicable love for Glen. Her mother's sexual desire becomes, then, a *lack* of control of her body in Bone's eyes and one that threatens to break up her family.

Bone has internalized the belief that women are somehow weaker than men, and throughout her childhood, it is ingrained in Bone that boys are inherently better than girls. This belief is driven home when her mother becomes pregnant with Glen's child. Glen is absolutely convinced that Anney will bear a boy. Bone's uncle Beau, however, is disgusted by Glen's pride before the baby is even born and says, "'A man should never put his ambition in a woman's belly. . . .Serve him right if she gave him another girl'" (45). Bone hears this sentiment expressed at the hospital as she waits in the car with Glen while her mother delivers the baby: "'She thinks if it's a girl, I won't love it. But it will be our baby, and if it's a girl, we can make another soon enough. I'll have my son. Anney and I will have our boy. I know it'" (46).

Bone's inferior position as a female is asserted in this scene in a disturbing sexual molestation by her stepfather. Bone and her younger sister Reese have been asleep in the backseat, and Glen pulls Bone forward into the front, clearly wanting company. He then pulls Bone onto his lap and pushes her skirt aside, rubbing his hand between her legs and rocking her against his pelvis. Bone is afraid but silent, despite the fact that Glen is hurting her: "I'd seen my cousins naked . . . but this was a mystery, scary and hard. . . . He was hurting me, hurting me!" (47). This scene becomes important in the novel because it is associated for both Glen and Bone with the time that Anney loses the son she bears and finds out that she can have no more children.

Bone's rather unstable sense of identity is further fragmented when the control of her body is forcibly taken from her as Glen becomes increasingly abusive sexually and physically. Bone is suddenly caught in the middle between her mother and Glen because Glen feels threatened by Anney's love for Bone. Bone's body becomes the tool Glen uses to drive a wedge between Anney and her daughter. When financial conditions in the house begin to worsen, Glen takes out his anger and feelings of incompetence on Bone, beating and sexually molesting her. Bone can turn to no one for protection, believing that she is somehow responsible for Daddy Glen's abuse.

Bone convinces herself that if she were more attractive, Daddy Glen would be less likely to be so angry with her all the time. Ironically, Bone wishes for a more visibly mature body: "I didn't want to be tall. I wanted to be beautiful. When I was alone, I would look down at my obstinate body, no legs, no hips, only the slightest swell where Dedee and Temple had big round breasts" (206). Like so many girls in novels of development, Bone is obsessed with her own image, always wanting to see herself as other people do: "I took to watching myself in mirrors to see what other people saw, to puzzle out just what showed them who I really was" (206). Her representation of herself as ugly, however, is completely distorted as a result of Glen's abuse and her mother's willingness to look the other way.

Bone is so emotionally scarred by Daddy Glen, in fact, that when she begins to discover her own sexual feelings, she continually masturbates to scenes of violence and death, even taking masochistic pleasure in fantasizing about Daddy Glen beating her while other people look on: "Those who watched admired me and hated him. I pictured it that way and put my hands between my legs. It was scary, but it was thrilling too. Those who watched me, loved me. It was as if I was being beaten for them. I was wonderful in their eyes" (112). The result is that Bone begins to internalize Glen's perception of her as somehow "evil." She is left feeling shame that these images excite her sexually, further reinforcing her sense that she deserves Daddy Glen's anger and disgust: "I hid my bruises as if they were evidence of crimes I had committed. I knew I was a sick disgusting person. I couldn't stop my stepfather from beating me, but I was the one who masturbated. I did that, and how could I explain to anyone that I hated being beaten but still masturbated to the story I told myself about it?" (113). Ironically, however, Bone is empowered through the control she takes of her own fantasies, one of the few places Daddy Glen cannot have any control. As Allison explains in an interview, Bone's storytelling becomes "'a technique whereby she retains a sense of power in a situation where she has none'" (Megan 72).

Bone's body becomes a literal battleground in the novel as Daddy Glen begins to physically change her body with his beatings. So, for example, he leaves a rumpled ridge of bone on the top of her head, and her collarbone fuses with a lump for the second time after one of his beatings (113). When she is questioned in the hospital by an angry intern, however, Bone is suddenly afraid, particularly when he questions her mother accusingly about Bone's broken coccyx. Here in the hospital, there is visual evidence of her abuse that Bone is unable to hide when the x-rays come back. Rather than being comforted by the young intern who tells her he can help if she will tell him the truth, Bone feels betrayed by her body in yet another way because this kind of evidence threatens her mother's safety and stability. When the doctor is rude and overtly angry with her mother, Bone's body is used as a wedge to separate her from her mother in a completely different way.

While Anney makes some attempt to protect her daughter from Glen, she is partly responsible for the abuse inflicted on her simply by her refusal to open her eyes to what she sees. As authors of *The Adolescent in the American Novel Since 1960,* Mary Jean DeMarr and Jane S. Bakerman, write that adolescent girls have a fear "that resistance to parents' wishes could mean disapprobation, the loss of love and approval" (40). Most adolescent girls' self-images are dependent on feeling loved. Bone senses that what her mother wants is to avoid conflict by pretending it doesn't exist, and throughout the novel, Bone puts her mother's needs above her own. She responds to the pain she sees her mother experiencing by refusing to reveal Glen's abuse to anyone, including her mother. Ironically, it is Bone's fierce, blind love for her mother that gives her the strength not to break under the physical and psychological abuse inflicted upon her. However, this is a little girl who really doesn't understand what is happening to her.

The final "battle" in the novel happens through Bone's body when Glen severely beats and rapes her. At this point Anney has left Glen yet again, and he has come to coax Bone to convince Anney to return to him. At first, he seems to be sexually responding to Bone's body, making comments about her getting bigger, the fact that she will be ready to start dating boys soon. He punches her, and his fist becomes a caress: "His hand touched the side of my face, my ear, my neck, slid down my front, the slight swells of my breasts" (283). The scene is incredibly violent, and it is Anney who comes in and finds Bone lying on the floor with Glen still on top of her. Bone's feelings for her mother finally turn to rage as she lies bloody and broken in the backseat of the car as her mother holds Glen while he cries.

Of course, this conclusion is far from positive, but in the end Bone has asserted control of her own body by fighting back against Glen. Actively engaging in this ongoing "battle" leaves Bone stronger and able to blame her mother's own weakness for her final desertion rather than herself. Allison empowers Bone, then, to face the future: "'I constructed [the novel] in such a way that Bone gets angry at thirteen, and I think it'll save her. . . . She begins to hold people responsible" (73).

Neither Meriwether nor Allison suggests that the battle for self-autonomy has been won at the end of *Daddy Was a Number Runner* or *Bastard Out of Carolina,* but both of these novels portray adolescent protagonists who recognize their bodies as sites of contestation, and actively engage in the struggle. In *Subjectivity, Identity, and the Body,* Sidonie Smith observes that writing can be a means of subversion: "Writing her experiential history of the body, the autobiographical subject engages in a process of critical self-consciousness through which she comes to an awareness of the relationship of her specific body to the cultural "body" and to the body politic. That change in consciousness prompts cultural critique" (131).

Daddy Was a Number Runner and *Bastard Out of Carolina* are not autobiographies; however I think the impulse to write the body is the same as that of autobiography, particularly since these novels are written in the first person.[4] Both Francie and Bone recognize at the end of the novel that other female characters in the novel are subject to the same oppression they are; this link allows both girls to claim their anger and to realize that they can script an alternative future for themselves.

Daddy Was a Number Runner and *Bastard Out of Carolina* illustrate the importance for the critic to keep the girl's body at the forefront of her/his critique if we are to trace the ways a girl can be manipulated and constrained by a patriarchal culture, leaving her questioning her own self-worth. Asserting control of her body, however, can be the starting point for changing the traditional narrative of female development, one that refuses the impossibility of self-agency with which *Coming Attractions* concludes. Extending Grosz's understanding of an embodied subjectivity suggests that the adolescent girl can *re-embody* her subjectivity, taking control of who and what she will become.

Notes

1. Of course, not every recent novel of development subverts traditional narrative descriptions of growing up female, but given the plot summaries in bibliographies such as Jane S. Bakerman and Mary Jean DeMarr's *Adolescent*

Female Portraits in the American Novel 1961-1981, I can safely say that most of the novels written in the last 40 years are trying to implicitly, if not explicitly, critique patriarchal representations of the female body.

2. This "battleground" metaphor has been used by other feminist theorists. See, for example, Susan Bordo's essay "Material Girl" in *Unbearable Weight: Feminism, Western Culture and the Body*.
3. Virtually every novel of development that focuses on adolescence presents girls struggling to establish a secure sense of identity. The three novels I have chosen to deal with here, however, present the body as a literal battleground; gaining control over their bodies becomes the only way the central characters will escape destruction.
4. Allison has said in many interviews that *Bastard* is autobiographical, although it is not necessarily all true: "I make fiction, construct it, intend it to have an impact, an effect, to quite literally change the world that lied to my mother, to my sisters, and me. The fiction I make comes out of my life and my beliefs, but it is not autobiography . . ." ("Context," *Skin: Talking About Sex, Class and Literature*, 55).

FOUR

When the Back Door Is Closed and the Front Yard Is Dangerous

The Space of Girlhood in Toni Morrison's Fiction

DEBORAH CADMAN

Toni Morrison represents girlhood in her fiction not as a linear unfolding of time and a movement through initiation rites that are associated with Bildung traditions,[1] but as a confrontation with powerful and contradictory forces that are suggested by her figures of the closed back door and the dangerous front yard. In one sense, Morrison's figures are metonyms for property, for the owned or rented houses where her fictional girls encounter forces beyond their control in an intimate and physical way that make them knowledgeable even at very young ages. In another sense, her figures of the closed back door and the dangerous front yard depict a kind of space that her fictional girls occupy, one that is simultaneously enclosed and open to the physical dangers and the metaphysical terrors present in the milieu of each of her novels. If we imagine Morrison's fictional girls moving within the fictional space they occupy, then we can see the necessity of their circling within and around the spatial boundaries of the closed back door and the dangerous front yard.

Morrison draws on these spatial metaphors most explicitly to figure the girlhood of Denver Suggs in *Beloved*, which begins shortly after her birth in 1855 and ends after she steps into the front yard of her grandmother's house in 1873. The back door of this house at 124 Bluestone Road in Cincinnati, Ohio, which is boarded-up and enclosed within an exterior storeroom, serves as a physical sign of the end of enslaved life and a storehouse for the memory of slavery, both individual and collective.[2] The front "yard" of the house extends into the black community of Cincinnati and into a road traveled by slave catchers in pursuit of the most valuable property in mid-nineteenth-century America—fugitive slaves. The spatial boundaries of Denver's girlhood, then, hold the possibility of communal life as well as the dangers and the terrors that are locked behind the closed back door and poised to invade the front yard.

In modified forms, these spatial metaphors appear in novels that historically follow *Beloved* because the powerful and contradictory forces that Denver confronts—disinterested violence, the economics and the laws that sanction it, the life and the culture of the "village," and the memory of a familial and cultural past—are inscribed in the girlhood spaces of Morrison's more contemporary narratives. The house in East St. Louis where nine-year-old Dorcas Manfred of *Jazz* lives with her parents and makes her clothespin dolls that she so carefully dresses in bits of red, white, and blue cloth is "torched" by white rioters who enter her yard one morning in 1917, the fire burning up her girlhood home and everything in it, including her mother who returned to the house that morning after seeing the body of her murdered husband (57). By 1917, seven-year-old Sula Peace of *Sula* is already "wedged" into the labyrinthine structure of her grandmother's house that reflects the terrible instability of her girlhood as it throbs with disorder and is "constantly awry with things, people, voices and the slamming of doors" (51-52). Dorcas and Sula, Morrison's "new" fictional girls of the era of World War I and the Harlem Renaissance, embrace the dangers and the terrors of their milieus in ways that Denver cannot.

The most contemporary girls in Morrison's novels, Pecola Breedlove in *The Bluest Eye* and Hagar Dead in *Song of Solomon,* live in spaces that reflect their marginal position in America near the beginning of U.S. involvement in World War II. In 1941, eleven-year-old Pecola lives with her parents and her older brother in "an abandoned store on the southeast corner of Broadway and Thirty-fifth Street in Lorain, Ohio" (33). In 1942, seventeen-year-old Hagar lives with her mother and her grandmother in a "narrow single-story house whose basement seemed to be rising from rather than settling into the ground" on the outskirts of a Michigan town (27). Hagar's "natural" girlhood home that grows from the ground like a plant and opens only to the woods in the yard contrasts sharply with the abandoned store where Pecola lives, but both girls confront and "swallow" the same powerful forces that make them embrace what is most antithetical to their sense of themselves.

All of Morrison's fictional girls "swallow" the forces that they encounter between the closed back door and the dangerous front yard. At twenty-eight days old, Denver swallows her mother's milk along with the blood of her sister whom her mother has just murdered in order to prevent her from being taken back into slavery. At nine years old, Dorcas swallows a live ember from the burning front porch of her childhood home in East St. Louis. Before Sula turns nine, she repeatedly tastes sugar in her imaginative daydreaming that offers her a way out of the unstable conditions that are inscribed in the architecture of her girlhood home. At eleven, Pecola swallows three quarts of milk that she drinks from a Shirley Temple cup at the MacTeer house after her father tries to burn down the abandoned store. At seventeen, Hagar surprises and hurts both her grandmother and her mother by revealing that she has had "hungry" days, until the women realize that Hagar's hunger has nothing to do with the food and the love that they always provide for her. What each girl "swallows" determines the locus of her circling within and around the spatial boundaries of the closed back door and the dangerous front yard. The circling of Morrison's girls is both a literal movement through fictional space and an imaginative movement around specific moments, memories, or questions.

From the literal and imaginative circling that Denver Suggs makes around specific moments of her life in *Beloved,* readers can reconstruct the story of her girlhood. The incidents around which Denver circles include her birth in a canoe on the slave side of the Ohio River (in Kentucky) in 1855, the question that ended her one year of formal schooling at age seven and made her go deaf for two years, the losses of her two brothers and her grandmother just before the Civil War ended (when she was ten), her play in a circle of boxwood bushes, and her inability to step into the yard of her house at 124 Bluestone Road between 1863 and 1873. Denver's imaginative circling occurs within the spatial boundaries of her girlhood home, which reflects the borders of her knowledge and the degree of her terror about what she knows and does not know. Denver knows that her grandmother remade the space at 124 Bluestone Road so that she would not have to repeat in her free life a ritual of slave life, that she took control of her space by boarding-up the back door and building a storeroom around it, and that she assumed her rightful place as matriarch, protector, guard, woman, and self—the one whose presence was there at the front door. Denver knows that her grandmother "had done everything right" and that white people "came in her yard anyway" (207, 209). The terror of this trespass, which Denver aptly calls the "thing" that made it all right for her mother to murder Beloved, becomes for Denver the constant threat of annihilation. Since Denver can neither rid herself of this terror nor fully identify the "thing" responsible for it, she cannot cross the literal boundary of her yard from the time she is eight years old until she is eighteen.

To step into the yard is to step off the edge of the world and fall into the terror that threatens her life. As Denver tells us, she is always "afraid the thing that happened that made it all right for my mother to kill my sister could happen again." Although she does not know "what it is" or "who it is," she understands that this force "comes from outside" her house and her yard and that "it can come on in the yard if it wants to" (205). Denver's words suggest an invasion of the body's space by an outside force and recall the violations of Sethe's body and psyche by the slave master called Schoolteacher and his nephews, which critic Pamela E. Barnett sees so clearly as part of Morrison's figuring of the rape of black women and men by whites in the novel, a figuring that redefines rape in terms of race rather than gender.[3] Although Denver's references to a past and a possible future invasion are oblique, her image of a terrifying moving thing that exists beyond the village and can enter at will to satisfy its desires conveys the sense of the crimes suffered by Sethe as well as the agency that could compel her to kill Denver too.

Denver's terror is so extreme that it seems ever present, but Morrison locates the moment in her girlhood when she becomes unable to cross the yard. The moment occurs after an independent, seven-year-old Denver succeeds in getting almost a full year of schooling at the house of Mrs. Lady Jones and becomes known for her intelligence. At that point, Nelson Lord, the boy who was as smart as she was, shocks Denver into knowledge of her own past and her connection to her mother's past by asking if she went to jail with her mother for the murder of Beloved. The trauma of Denver's identification with her mother's imprisonment not only makes her go deaf for two years, but also alters the boundaries of her world in several other ways.

First, Denver cuts herself off from the black community of Cincinnati, which is an extension of her "yard." Morrison links the yard with the formal and informal schooling available to Denver in the community, just as West Indian writers of Bildung often make the yard synonymous with the village and the informal education available there (LeSeur, *Age of Darkness* 22). In Morrison's novel, part of what Denver loses by cutting herself off from her village is access to any knowledge she might gain about the political and cultural events that shaped her girlhood including the workings of the Underground Railroad in Cincinnati. Although Denver might not have felt any safer knowing that it was the Fugitive Slave Act of 1850 that sanctioned the trespass in her yard or that from the end of the Civil War through the "present" of the novel the Ku Klux Klan "swam the Ohio at will" like a dragon "desperately thirsty for black blood," such knowledge would have helped her to identify the thing (66). Contact with the village would also have separated what Denver conflates in her own mind: the terror of the question asked by her schoolmate and the terror of the "thing" that comes into her yard that merge into a world "out there" that can hurt her.

Second, since Denver's trauma makes her go deaf from age seven to age nine, she becomes a keen observer and a visionary who sees through the barriers between the living and the dead more clearly than other characters in the novel. This otherworldly seeing suggests her imaginative vision or her move toward embracing some form of art, which scholar Sondra O'Neale, writing more generally about fiction by black women authors, sees as "one of the few choices left to women characters once they are fully aware of the onus of being Black and female" (35). When seven-year-old Denver becomes aware of her association with Sethe's infanticide, she learns what "the onus of being Black and female" is in America in the year of the Emancipation Proclamation.

Third, because Denver's knowledge is terrifying, she seeks a refuge, a place "closed off from the hurt of the hurt world" (28). Even though the house at 124 Bluestone Road is haunted by Beloved's spirit and isolated from the black community, it is a refuge for Denver because it embodies her grandmother's lessons about the difference between the ideology of slavery and the need for black girls and women to love and trust their bodies. Baby Suggs told Denver that slaves "were not supposed to have pleasure deep down" because that powerful reality contradicted everything slave masters said. She also told Denver that she "should always listen to [her] body and to love it" (209). It is this lesson that Denver enacts in her private refuge, a ring of boxwood bushes arching together to create a room seven feet high with walls that are "fifty inches of murmuring leaves," where she dances in perfumed splendor and lets her imagination create "its own hunger and its own food" (28-29). In a sanctuary closed off from the appetites of slave owners and klansmen, Denver nurtures herself, embracing her body and mind within an embrace of trees. Denver's joyful dances not only serve as a counterpoint to her mother's brutal rape and beating but also show that Denver knows what Sethe only begins to imagine at the end of the novel: that she is her own "'best thing'" (273). Self-love also makes Denver ask her mother to tell and retell the story of her birth, particularly the parts about Amy Denver, the poor white girl who helped Sethe reach the Ohio River and deliver Denver into the world.

Although the circling that Denver makes in the direction that Geta LeSeur calls "back to the place of origin" seems affirming, it is dangerous (*Age of Darkness* 19). At two points in the novel, Denver literally steps into the story of her birth. The first instance occurs when a light snow drives an adolescent Denver out of her emerald closet and toward her house where she sees Sethe and a white dress kneeling in the keeping room, the empty white sleeve in a "tender embrace" around her mother's waist. From her dance of self-love, Denver enters a moment where past and present literally meet and where her keen observation and otherworldly vision come together. At this point in the novel, Morrison figures the circular path around the house as rememory, an opening in a time-space continuum where Denver enters her prehistory and makes a connection with her mother. Denver's first step into her story prefigures the physical intrusion of the past into the present of the novel, which occurs when the murdered child Beloved returns as a young woman. After Beloved appears, she brings the psyches of both mother and daughter into the past by her incessant questions about it, by her continual prompting of Sethe to "tell" her stories that Sethe herself does not know she remembers, and by the quality of insatiable hunger in her listening. In these ways, Beloved controls the storytelling of Sethe and Denver even though she narrates nothing.[4]

With Beloved as her hungry listener, Denver enters her mother's story a second time to narrate what can only be in the mind of Sethe—including the sexual violation by the nephew who stole her breast milk. Denver imagines her mother as a "nineteen-year-old slave girl—a year older than herself—walking through the dark woods to get to her children who are far away." Denver feels her mother's fatigue, her fear, her sense of being "lost" and alone, and her concern for the baby "inside her." Denver also imaginatively sees what is spatially "behind" Sethe: "dogs, perhaps; guns probably; and certainly mossy teeth" (77-78). Because Denver experiences the story of Sethe's escape from Sweet Home "through Beloved," she is able to narrate what she has never been told. This supernatural link between Denver and her mother shows that the living daughter is in danger of getting her psyche as locked in the past as are the minds of Sethe and Beloved. In fact, Denver stays in her house watching her mother and sister play an endless game of blame and explain until she realizes that she and her mother are in danger of starvation. Even then Denver cannot step into the front yard without hearing the laughter and the words of her grandmother from the realm of the dead telling her to remember that there is no defense against the thing and to "go on out the yard. Go on" (244).

In order to become part of the village that her grandmother helped to create through her public preaching about self-love, Denver must be able to move through dangerous space. Her step into terror is also a return to the communal life that she experienced during the first 28 days of her life, one full lunar cycle, with its echoes of African traditions surrounding the birth of a child that African cultural critic John S. Mbiti describes. After those 28 days, Denver learns that the arresting contradictions of her girlhood on the free side of the Ohio River make murdering a beloved child necessary and link the act of slicing one daughter's throat with nursing another. More explicitly than the curved smile under Beloved's chin, the "mossy teeth" of Schoolteacher's nephew, and the lash-carved tree on Sethe's back, the moment of Denver's nursing makes visible the intimate, physical links between past and present as well as the terrible truth of Sethe's need to keep her own past from becoming Denver's future. Yet Morrison makes it clear that Denver swallows the unspeakable trauma and terror of the thing without knowing fully what it is. Unable to identify the thing as the uncontrollable and legally sanctioned actions of slave masters and slave catchers as well as the Ku Klux Klan and their sympathizers, Denver cannot move beyond the closed back door and the dangerous front yard of her grandmother's house on her own.

A "new" girl of the era of World War I and the Harlem Renaissance, Dorcas Manfred of *Jazz* embraces the force and the contradictory meanings of fire in her fictional milieu to such a degree that she begins at age nine to seek out the kind of physical dangers and metaphysical terrors that confine Denver to her girlhood home for ten years. Although Dorcas cannot avoid the violence of white rioters any more than Denver can protect herself from the acts of slave masters and klansmen, Morrison's new fictional girl confronts the power of fire directly. Dorcas is sleeping across the street at her girlfriend's house when rioters set her own house ablaze, but she wakes to the sounds of shouting and the sight of people running. Since her first thought is her box of clothespin dolls on the dresser, she runs to get them, and yells "to her mother that the box of dolls, the box of dolls was up there on the dresser can we get them? Mama?" (38). This is the moment when Dorcas swallows one of the "ignited and smoking" wood chips from her porch, the burning ember entering "her stretched dumb mouth" and traveling "down her throat" (60-61).[5] The most minute and seemingly most insignificant part of the trope of burning in the novel, the wood chip that Dorcas swallows suggests the pain of her losses, the self that she makes with a fragment of burning space, the "glow" of both her sexuality and her daring, and the extent of her power.

A "bright wood chip" lodged in the throat of a nine-year-old girl is minute compared to the larger contextual framework of Morrison's novel: the conflagration of World War I, the burning of racial violence in northern American cities in the hot summer of 1917, and the fires set by klansmen to destroy cabins and cane fields in southern communities during the late nineteenth century. Yet the smallest detail of Morrison's figuring creates a number of metaphorical links in *Jazz*: between Dorcas and her first lover, fifty-three-year-old Joe Trace, between rioting in East St. Louis and the marching of silent black men down Fifth Avenue in Harlem to the beat of drums, between the seductive sound of jazz and the complex anger within it, between the body and power. The wood chip connects the painful loss of the mother Dorcas knew with the loss of the mother Joe Trace never knew: a woman called Wild who burned to death during what Joe himself calls "the dispossession" of the black community of Vienna, Virginia, in 1893: "Red fire doing fast what white sheets took too long to finish: canceling every deed; vacating each and every field; emptying us out of our places" (126). Their shared loss and crossgenerational connection is what the narrator, reflecting Joe's sensibility, calls "that inside nothing," which Dorcas "knew better than people his own age" and perhaps even better than Joe himself because she remembered the burning slap of her mother's hand on her face while he recalled physical signs of his mother's presence—four or more redwings in a group and the rustling of hibiscus leaves—but never felt the touch of her hand (37-38).

Although red fire empties Dorcas out of her girlhood space in 1917, it also moves her with her Aunt Alice Manfred to Harlem where the burning ember becomes a source of knowledge and power as well as a sign of her losses. Morrison represents Dorcas's arrival in Harlem as her entrance into a space of gathering forces and expressive drums, a communal response by black men to racial violence in northern American cities. As Dorcas watches "a tide of cold black faces" move slowly down Fifth Avenue in what she rightly imagines as "a kind of funeral parade for her mother and her father," the burning ember in her throat sinks "further and further down until it lodge[s] comfortably somewhere below her navel" (54, 60-61). Morrison links the comfort of the burning within Dorcas to the sound of the drums that speak for the silent marching men and assures Dorcas that the "glow" inside her "would be waiting for and with her whenever she wanted to be touched by it. And whenever she wanted to let it loose to leap into fire again, whatever happened would be quick. Like the dolls" (61). This small but powerful internal reality includes a kind of trust and love of her own body that resembles what Denver learns from her grandmother, but it is also a fiery dragon that eats the legs and dissolves the eyes of clothespin dolls with its hot breath and makes a quick end to the little girl art of Dorcas.

Swallowing the contradictory meanings of fire makes Dorcas more knowledgeable than either Joe Trace or Alice Manfred. Joe perceives the burning within Dorcas only as the pain of her losses that connects the two of them across generations: he is born in 1873, the year Denver steps into the yard, and Dorcas is born in 1908, a date that puts her at one remove from a generation who left the violence and poverty of the South for the promise of new life in cities of the North. Living in Harlem during the 1920s, Alice Manfred is aware of the powerful sexuality of the city that is expressed, for example, in the sounds of jazz and in the way young women wear their coats slipping off their shoulders like bathrobes, but she fails to see this power burning within her niece, who she thinks can be protected from such a dangerous force by being made to wear unattractive clothes and by learning to avoid eye contact with boys and men. Dorcas, however, knows in her body what her aunt Alice only thinks she hears in the music of Harlem: "a complicated anger, . . . something hostile that disguised itself as flourish and roaring seduction" (59). The self that Dorcas makes with a fragment of burning space knows that her body is "all she has" (67) and that for her the "life below the sash" is all the life there is (58). She knows the power of paradise and what women will do even for a taste of its power: "go right back after two days, two! or make a girl travel four hundred miles to a camptown, or fold" in paralysis the arm of her after school caregiver, Neola, "the better to hold the pieces of her heart in her hand" after she is jilted at the altar (63).

Since Dorcas has learned what endings as well as beginnings are, she also has a comprehensive vision of her life that includes a certain ironic detachment that makes her "bold" (61). As her friend from high school, Felice, explains: "'Everything was like a picture show to her, and she was the one on the railroad track, or the one trapped in the sheik's tent when it caught on fire'" (202). The force of fire within Dorcas is reflected in her daring and in the power she tries to wield over others. From the time Dorcas is nine, she has been trying to re-create and to re-enter dangerous space where adults "play for keeps," primarily by pushing boys and men into it (191). Felice points out that Dorcas always wanted boys "to do something scary," to "[s]teal things," or to "go back in the store and slap the face of a white salesgirl who wouldn't wait on her" (202). By the time she is eighteen, Dorcas relishes adult parties where "[e]veryone is handsome, shining just thinking about other people's blood. As though the red wash flying from veins not theirs is facial makeup patented for its *glow*" (191 emphasis added). During the last three months of 1925 when Dorcas shares paradise with Joe and becomes, for him, the first, the whole, and the only apple, she is not satisfied to enjoy her power in private. Instead, she pushes him to take her to public places—the nightclub called Mexico, rent parties, Coney Island—where he puts himself at risk. After Dorcas abandons Joe for a younger man called Acton with whom she can wield her power in public space, she pushes him too. Dancing with him, she reveals how she rubs her "thumbnail over his nape so the girls will know I know they want him" (191). At the same time, Dorcas is fully aware that Joe is coming for her "to complete" something that started with the voice of drums (60).

A number of Morrison's circular metaphors show that Dorcas and Joe "complete" each other in some way and that the two of them help to define the milieu of *Jazz*: the pimples on her cheeks that look like little "hooves," the "track" around the city that pulls Joe "like a needle through the groove of a Bluebird record" (120), the apple, the smoky jazz that fills the air, the cone of the victrola, the curved openings of the horns and the clarinets. As Joe becomes her end, so Dorcas takes him back to his beginnings. If Dorcas is complicit in her death, as Henry Louis Gates, Jr. claims in his early review of the novel, it is not simply because she refuses to be driven to Harlem Hospital, but because she has known this moment of "completion," envisioned it, and waited for it since she was nine. The parallels that Morrison establishes between the burning of her girlhood home and her bleeding to death after Joe shoots her in the shoulder at an adult party on the first day of January 1926 are explicit: the blaze and the blood, the failure of the fire truck and the ambulance to arrive, the imagined presence of the clothespin dolls, the screams of the neighbors, and the words Dorcas thinks she is screaming to Felice: "They need me to say his name so they can go after him. Take away his sample case with Rochelle and Bernadine and Faye [her clothespin dolls] inside. I know his name but Mama won't tell" (193). Joe's black sample case becomes Dorcas's final metaphor for her girlhood home. Perhaps that is why her last words are a message to Joe that gives him back what he thinks he has lost from her: "'There's only one apple.' Sounded like 'apple.' 'Just one. Tell Joe'" (213).

Another "new" girl of the era of World War I and the Harlem Renaissance, Morrison's Sula Peace embraces the physical dangers and the metaphysical terrors of her fictional milieu with the same degree of knowing and daring that Dorcas Manfred does, but Sula does not court fire. She crosses boundaries instead. Although violence seems more remote in *Sula*, it is inscribed in the space of the neighborhood known as "the Bottom" and in the households of the Peace and the Wright families. The neighborhood originates from what the narrator calls "A joke. A nigger joke" and what

Houston Baker calls "the tricky economics of slavery" that deprive the community of a "means of production" and make "betrayal" and "broken promise[s]" part of the milieu of the novel (237-38). The joke and the trick are set in motion by "a good white farmer" who promises his slave "freedom and a piece of bottom land" in exchange for completing some difficult tasks, but who gives him unyielding hilltop land, which the farmer represents as the rich and fertile "bottom of heaven—best land there is" (5). No one in the village escapes the violence perpetuated by "capitalism's joke" including the Peace and the Wright families: Sula's grandmother, Eva Peace, sacrifices "a leg for the sake of insurance premiums," which give her enough money and power to build her labyrinthine house 50 feet from the one-room cabin where her husband left her and her three young children to starve in 1895; Helene Wright, the mother of Sula's friend Nel, constructs her orderly household to erase her origin in the exchanges at the "Sundown House of prostitution in New Orleans" (Baker 241, 240). These new spatial arrangements in the Bottom create different but violent constraints for Sula and Nel. Sula is "wedged" into her grandmother's house as tightly as the "rocking chair top" of Eva's makeshift wheelchair is "fitted into" the "large child's wagon" that she maneuvers around her third-floor bedroom (31); and Nel, sitting on the steps of her back porch, is "surrounded by the high silence" of her mother's house and touched by "the neatness pointing at her back" like a finger or a knife (51). Their friendship begins in their efforts to cross restrictive boundaries and ends in the varying degrees of danger and terror that each girl is willing to embrace.

The way that Morrison brings Sula and Nel together in the novel suggests the crossing of spatial boundaries. Although the girls see each other at Garfield Primary for five years and even imagine each other as the friend who shares "the delirium of their noon dreams," they actually meet in 1920 when they are ten (51). The timing of their meeting coincides with Nel's crossing of boundaries—she returns from a trip to New Orleans that gives her access to her familial past and a rebellious spirit of selfhood that prompts her to invite Sula to her house against her mother's wishes. Sula is first introduced in the context of Helene's oppressively neat house, which she loves, and Eva's "woolly house" is described first in terms of Nel's appreciative perceptions of it (29). Both girls set out to cross the boundaries of identity that forbid them "all freedom and triumph" because they are "neither white nor male" (52). The boldness of their ambition links them to Dorcas Manfred of *Jazz* and takes them into dangerous space beyond the yard in 1922 when they are twelve.

At first, both Sula and Nel cross physical and metaphysical boundaries to confront the dangers and the terrors beyond the doors and the yards of their girlhood homes. With Nel at her side, Sula reclaims the shortcut home from school that has been usurped by four white teenage boys who have threatened Nel and forced the girls into a more circuitous route. Pulling Eva's paring knife from her pocket, Sula lets the boys contemplate what she could do to them after she so calmly slices off the top of her own finger. This triumph is followed by Sula and Nel's discovery of the powerful internal reality of their sexuality, which prompts them to look for "mischief" in the Bottom, and Sula's inadvertent crossing of a boundary away from her mother when she overhears Hannah say that she does not "like" her daughter (56-57). These events lead the girls into dangerously free territory down by the river and under trees where the two of them dig holes in the ground with creamy white sticks until the separate holes become one, the sticks break, and they fill up "the grave" with all the debris they can find (59).[6] The girls enact their new identities not only in their ritual earth play but also in their responses to a very young boy called Chicken Little who wanders into their drama and their wild, "unspeakable restlessness and agitation" (59). Nel taunts the boy, but Sula helps him climb a beech tree high enough to see the river and the diminished figure of Nel below. Once on the ground again, Sula spins him around until he slips from her hands and disappears under the water. She quite literally makes the earth move and the sky fall for the child named after the little chicken who terrifies the barnyard animals with his prophecy of doom until his authority is undermined by the farmer in the fairy tale.[7] In this scene, Sula usurps the power of Chicken Little and the farmer, the profession of the man who initiates the joke that determines the conditions of life in the Bottom, and assumes the godlike control that Eva wields within her household.

Nel, the interested witness to Sula's embrace of dangerous power, pushes her into more terrifying space by pointing out a second witness whom both girls believe to be the mad veteran of World War I, Shadrack. Alone, Sula crosses the footbridge that leads to the house of Shad on the other side of the river and enters his surprisingly neat and unthreatening dwelling that reflects the order of Nel's girlhood home. The comfort that Sula feels at his house, both before he arrives and after he speaks a word that answers her unspoken question, suggests a supernatural link between the characters somewhat like the connection that Beloved's hungry listening makes between Denver and Sethe in *Beloved.* Sula and Shad are linked in their confrontation with terror and in their knowledge. The veteran who has seen the face and the head of a fellow soldier fly off during a battle in World War I learns what Sula knows as a little girl growing up in the Bottom—that her own head could fall off as easily as the heads of her paper dolls: she "used to walk around holding [her neck] very stiff because [she] thought a strong wind or a heavy push would snap" it (136). Though the truth of her perception is not confirmed until she returns to Medallion after a ten-year absence, Sula confronts in the "throbbing disorder"(52) of her girlhood home what Baker calls the "terrifyingly unstable conditions of existence" that Shadrack experiences in the First World War (Baker 239).

The spatial distance between Sula and Nel when they are on opposite sides of the river figures their different responses to danger and terror that contribute to the ending of their close girlhood friendship. Sula embraces those conditions in a way that is unavailable to any other character in the novel including Nel, Shad, and the village as a whole. Although Shad has confronted the terrifying instability of life, he creates National Suicide Day—the one day each year when people in the neighborhood are free to kill themselves or each other—in order to control rather than to accept those conditions. The one word that he speaks to Sula—"always"—is meant to be his false promise that her head will stay attached to her neck, a reassurance that she wisely misinterprets as the promise of a "sleep of water always" (149). When Sula returns to the Bottom after spending ten years of her life in various cities, the village as a whole begins to fear the young woman who is not afraid to cross any established boundary and who is linked to every misfortune or excess in the neighborhood. Thus Sula becomes the "thing," an enemy or a witch who has invaded the Bottom in order to cause the evil occurrences there.

Sula's awareness of her status as the "thing" in the village and the reasons for such a communal judgment against her are reflected in her circular metaphors of the spider's web, the cobra below it, and the free fall through the space between them. The members of the community are "the spiders whose only thought [is] the next rung of the web, who [dangle] in dark places suspended by their own spittle, more terrified of the free fall than the snake's breath below" (120). The word spittle evokes both Sula's disgust for the way the village clings to conventions, including a moral order that makes them good and her evil, and their disgust at her willful breaking of boundaries: consigning Eva to a nursing home and establishing herself in the house, taking and abandoning numerous sexual partners including Nel's husband Jude and perhaps white men as well, and refusing marriage and motherhood. In Sula's view, the eyes of the spiders are "so intent on the wayward stranger who trips into their net" that they are "blind" to both the forces of the natural world beyond the social fabric that they have constructed and their link with the cobra below (120). Spiders are snakes too even though they do not know it. Stuck in their webs in the dry corners of a structure that someone else built and could tear down, the spiders live without knowing their creative potential or the full sense of being alive that the dangerous free fall represents to Sula.

The venom in Sula's metaphor comes from her conviction that Nel betrays her and their girlhood ambition by choosing to be one of the spiders instead of reaching for the clarity of vision that Morrison gives to Sula alone. Sula's vision of Nel as a maker of webbed netting in dusty corners is confirmed by Nel's own figuring of her grief for the loss of Sula and Jude as a little gray "ball of fur and string and hair always floating in the light near her" (109). Sula's vision of the village itself as a web dangling in dark places that the spiders neither make nor control fits the fictional history of the Bottom that begins with the farmer's joke and ends with the uprooting of "nightshade and blackberry patches" in order to make space for the Medallion City Golf Course (3). The blindness that Sula ascribes to the spiders is reflected in Nel's refusal to see until 25 years after Sula's death, that it is her friend, not her husband, whom she misses. The blindness of the town is reflected in their inability to see the actual "thing" as an economic system that restricts meaningful work on the New River Road in 1927 and on the tunnel "to connect Medallion to Porter's Landing" in 1937 to white men (81). When the village sees the betrayals and the broken promises in the unfinished tunnel on National Suicide Day—January 3, 1941—they miss the terrifyingly unstable conditions of the earth on that glittering warm day, and many of them drown in their attempt to kill a symbol of the system.

Morrison associates the clarity of Sula's vision with her girlhood ambition to make a new identity for herself within the dangerous and unstable fictional world of the era of World War I and the Harlem Renaissance. The pleasure that Sula takes from her milieu is evident in Morrison's figure for her early imaginative play: "galloping through her own mind on a gray-and-white horse tasting sugar and smelling roses" (52). Sula's simultaneous pleasure in the taste of sugar and the speed of the galloping horse is repeated in her metaphor of the spiders who must "taste their tongues" as they fully "surrender" to the free fall if they wish to be alive (120). In her emphasis on *tasting* sugar or fear rather than *swallowing* it, Sula suggests her own ironic detachment from the milieu that she sees so clearly. This detachment along with her "gift for metaphor" makes Sula a "dangerous" artist who has no vehicle for expression (121). Instead, she has a way of seeing some of the people around her materialize into objects of art before her eyes. At thirteen, Sula is rapt by the dance of agony that her mother, the beautiful Hannah Peace with "skin powdered in lilac dust," performs as she burns to death in the *yard* (Morrison "Memory" 386). As a young woman,

Sula imagines the layers of gold and black loam that must be hidden under the beautiful face of her lover, A. Jacks, who leaves before she has a chance to tear off his skin to find what is underneath it. After a little boy in the village breaks his leg falling off his front porch, Sula stops to examine the way the bone pierces his flesh. Although Sula's vision is clear, it is infected with the disinterested violence that insinuates itself in the space of her girlhood and pervades the economic system that makes betrayals and broken promises defining features of the milieu of *Sula*.

The most contemporary of Morrison's fictional girls confront forces within their milieus that are kept as "quiet" in certain quarters as some of the global atrocities of World War II. Both Pecola Breedlove of *The Bluest Eye* and Hagar Dead of *Song of Solomon* encounter in the spaces of their girlhood homes the force of an economic and social system that consigns them to the margins of existence in both a physical and a metaphysical sense during the years prior to U.S. involvement in World War II. In these novels, Morrison figures the margins of existence as household properties: the abandoned store at the corner of an intersection in Lorain, Ohio, where eleven-year-old Pecola Breedlove lives with her family in 1941; and the "narrow, single-story house" on the outskirts of a Michigan town where seventeen-year-old Hagar Dead lives with her mother and grandmother in 1942. Property itself, including the things that Pecola Breedlove and Hagar Dead own or do not own, becomes a dominant trope in Morrison's portrayal of girlhood in the mid-twentieth century.

In *The Bluest Eye,* Morrison represents the rented storefront property that is Pecola's girlhood home as a place of failed capital enterprises and a physical space that denotes economic, social, and personal worthlessness. The house is a "box of peeling gray" where the family "[festers] together in the debris of a realtor's whim" (38, 34). The word "debris" figures the position of the Breedloves at the bottom of a hierarchy of economics and status into which both of Pecola's parents are born: her father, Charles (Cholly) Breedlove, is abandoned by his mother at birth and left "on a junk heap" to die; and her mother, Pauline (Polly) Breedlove, is made to feel separate and unworthy by her large family who refuses to confer a nickname on her (160). Through the "whim" of a realtor, the legacies of family pain and the ideology of slavery are re-inscribed in the space of Pecola's girlhood home, where she shrinks from the violent rages of her parents and tries to make her body disappear from the "anonymous misery" of the "storefront" (34, 39).

The dangerous and terrifying conditions of Pecola's household are also present in the community beyond her "yard." Several scenes show the painful and humiliating ways in which Pecola is rejected by people outside the storefront: the white shopkeeper, Mr. Yacobowski, whose eyes reflect his distaste for the young black girl and whose hands will not touch hers when she pays him for Mary Jane candies; the black boys who taunt Pecola about the color of her skin and the sleeping habits of her father; the "high-yellow dream child" named Maureen Peal who befriends Pecola long enough to confirm that the taunts of the boys about her father sleeping naked are true (62); the son of the "sugar-brown" woman named Geraldine who coaxes Pecola into his beautiful house in order to taunt her and throw a blue-eyed black cat in her face (82); and Geraldine herself who whispers a curse to Pecola through the black fur of her dead cat: "'You nasty little black bitch. Get out of my house'" (92). In this milieu, the only parts of the world that Pecola owns are "the crack" in the sidewalk over which she stumbles and "the clumps of dandelions" who offer their alternatively white and yellow heads to her. Owning these things makes "her part of the world" and "the world a part of her" (47-48) until she believes that she has acquired the bluest eyes.

What Pecola does not own are the blue eyes that Morrison uses as a synecdoche for the larger framing device of her novel: the quiet but inescapable presence of a safe, comfortable, and "very pretty" green and white house with a "red door" where Jane lives with her family, her cat, and her dog (3). In her framing device, Morrison brings together two icons of a dominant white culture—the physical attributes of a particular type of property and the physical features of a girl's body—in a way that anticipates what Pecola conflates in her own mind—the house that represents "a world of clean comfort" and love and the blue eyes that Pecola believes would make such a world accessible to her (50). Morrison depicts Jane's house and body as the powerful assertion of a dominant white culture that defines all worth in terms of images reproduced in Dick and Jane primers, Mary Jane candy wrappers, Shirley Temple cups, and big blue-eyed baby dolls.

It is this world of comfort and love that Pecola tries to swallow when she drinks three quarts of milk from a Shirley Temple cup at the MacTeer house where she goes after her father tries to burn down their rented storefront. The adoration that Pecola and ten-year-old Frieda MacTeer feel for Shirley Temple separates them from the younger Claudia MacTeer who explains that by age nine she had not yet "arrived at the turning point" in her "development" that "would allow" her "to love" Shirley (19). In *The Bluest Eye,* Morrison links the ages of ten and eleven to the time when the psyches of her fictional girls are especially vulnerable, just as Geta LeSeur identifies ten as the "age of darkness" in her study of the black Bildungsroman, and sociologists Jill McLean Taylor, Carol Gilligan, and Amy Sullivan notice in remarks made by slightly older adolescent girls more uncertainty about themselves and less willingness to be assertive.[8] Morrison links the milk that Pecola drinks from the Shirley Temple cup and the Mary Jane candies that she swallows to the question that she circles around until she is raped by her father: "[H]ow do you get somebody to love you?" (32). Morrison associates the rape of Pecola with her father's sense of his daughter as property, "his own pot of black dirt" (6), and with his movement back to the place of origin. The image of Pecola standing at the sink washing dishes as she rubs the back of her leg with her other foot takes Cholly back to his first attraction to Pauline's disfigured foot, as well as to his own rape at thirteen by the beam of a flashlight that white hunters shine on him during his first sexual experience with his cousin Darlene. The disinterested violence of the hunters who take over this experience become part of Cholly's psyche, which leads him to rape his daughter at the moment he feels affection for her.

However, it is not Cholly Breedlove but Claudia MacTeer who defines the disinterested violence that all of Morrison's fictional girls confront within the spaces of their girlhood. Claudia's resistance to the worth that "all the world" confers on the icons of white culture begins long before she is nine in her act of dismembering a "big, blue-eyed Baby Doll" in order to discover the secret of its value and beauty that seems to elude only her (20). Finding nothing of value within the doll, Claudia describes her longing to dismember white girls: "The indifference with which I could have axed them was shaken only by my desire to do so" (22). Her words identify qualities of "the thing" in Morrison's novels that coexist rather than cancel each other out: the combination of power, desire to harm, and indifference in the white men who sexually violate Sethe in *Beloved*; burn the cane fields and cabins of Vienna, Virginia, and torch the childhood home of Dorcas in *Jazz*; initiate the joke and control the economic system in *Sula*; and proliferate images of worth that exclude those who live outside the boundaries of middle-class life and who have features that are more African than Anglo-Saxon in *The Bluest Eye*. As Claudia points out, "[t]he *thing* to fear was the *thing*" that makes Maureen Peal "beautiful, and not us" (74). A similar blend of power, desire, and indifference is reflected in the gaze of Sula Peace and in the violent behavior of Cholly Breedlove toward his wife and daughter. Not only does Claudia MacTeer illuminate the disinterested violence in Morrison's portrayal of girlhood, but she also explains the metaphysical condition shared by some of Morrison's fictional girls. According to Claudia, the "real terror of life" is something she calls "outdoors" and describes as "the end of something, an irrevocable, physical fact" analogous to death in its finality and similar to the threat of annihilation that awaits Denver outside the yard of her house at 124 Bluestone Road in *Beloved* (17). Outdoors is a physical danger that threatens everyone who is "a minority in both caste and class" (17), a metaphysical terror that awaits Claudia outside her "old, cold and green" house (15), and a condition that she figures in her circular metaphor of *moving* "on the hem of life, struggling to consolidate our weaknesses and hang on, or to creep singly up into the major folds of the garment" (17).

As the hem marks a circle at the bottom of a dress, so the "metaphysical condition" of Morrison's fictional girls places them at the border of the terrifying physical condition of being outdoors (17). Outdoors is the place where Eva Peace of *Sula* finds herself with her infant son Plum in 1895 when she goes to the privy in the stinking shed to open his bowels, and the condition that prompts her to leave her three children with a neighbor and sacrifice her leg in order to build her labyrinthine house. Outdoors is the place where the fires of klansmen send Joe Trace of *Jazz* in 1893 and where the fires of white rioters would have consigned Dorcas in 1917 if Alice Manfred had not taken her to Harlem. Outdoors is also the source of what Claudia sees as the hunger to own "a porch" and "a yard," which are metonyms for property that represent part of Morrison's figuring of the space of girlhood in her novels.

Set on the outskirts of a Michigan town, the girlhood home of Hagar Dead in *Song of Solomon* also represents the margin of existence, but it seems far removed from the failed commercial enterprises of the rented storefront property where Pecola Breedlove lives as well as the dominant economic and social systems that consign her and her family there. Hagar's "narrow single-story house" that seems "to be rising from rather than settling into the ground" like a plant and that opens only to the woods in the yard is rooted in nature (27). The house is not connected to either electrical or gas lines because Hagar's grandmother Pilate Dead "would not pay for the service" (27). Coal and wood serve as their sources for heat and cooking, and water comes from a well. At night, the house is lit by "candles and kerosene" lamps, and since "[t]here were no street lights" in the part of town where the house is located, "only the moon directed the way of a pedestrian" (28). According to Hagar's great-uncle, Macon Dead II, the three women of the house—Pilate, her daughter Reba, and her granddaughter Hagar—live "as through progress was a word that meant walking a little farther on down the road" (27).

The interior of Hagar's home and the activities that engage the women and the girl in it also suggest alternative traditions of living. The large room that serves as the kitchen and communal living area contains almost "no furniture" other than "a rocking chair, two straight-backed chairs, a large table, a sink and [a] stove" (39). From the ceiling hangs "a moss-green sack" containing the bones of a dead man whom Pilate thinks her brother Macon killed and for whom she feels responsible. The walls are covered with "newspaper articles and magazine pictures," and the house smells of pine from the trees outside and "fermenting fruit" for the wine-making business that Pilate directs (39). In the evenings, the women and the girl sing together, Pilate "leading" in "her powerful contralto," Reba "building on" Pilate's phrases with her "piercing soprano," and Hagar adding her soft girlish voice while each of them completes a task: Pilate sways "like a willow" over her stirring pot, Reba cuts "her toenails with a kitchen knife or a switchblade," and Hagar braids "her hair" (29-30). In this household so deliberately set apart from a dominant culture and so guided by Pilate, Hagar seems safe from the force of an economic and social system that defines her as worthless.

Yet the same force that makes Pecola embrace what is most antithetical to her sense of herself insinuates itself into Hagar's girlhood home. The signs of this force are evident in the bedroom where Hagar sleeps in a "little Goldilocks'-choice bed" (314) and keeps the gifts that she asks her cousin Milkman to buy for her: "a navy-blue satin bathrobe," "a snood," "patent-leather pumps," "White Shoulders cologne"—things that are "quite out of place in her household" (92). These things that Hagar owns suggest not only the greed, possessiveness, and self-interest that she shares with the fairy-tale Goldilocks, but also her vulnerability to a construct of white feminine beauty that Morrison reflects in the brand names of the bed and the cologne, and in the image that negates Hagar's sense of her body and her self-worth: the sight of Milkman with his "arms around the shoulders of a girl whose silky copper-colored hair cascaded over the sleeve of his coat" (127).

Morrison represents Hagar's exile from herself in her circular movements in a place far removed from the door and the yard of her girlhood home—the cosmetics department of a store where she turns "[r]ound and round the diamond-clear counters" like "a smiling sleepwalker" who believes that "she could spend her life there among the cut glass, shimmering in peaches and cream, in satin. In opulence. In luxe. In love" (311). The sensuous qualities of the satin bathrobe and the shiny patent-leather pumps that Hagar owns are magnified in this commercial display as is the sense of the richness and desirability of skin the color of "peaches and cream." The reflective surfaces and cut glass around which Hagar circles recalls Pecola's state of mind at the end of *The Bluest Eye* as well as what Morrison calls "the form as well as the content of [that] novel": "[t]he visual image of a splintered mirror, or the corridor of split mirrors in blue eyes" ("Memory" 338). Although Pecola's permanent belief that she has acquired the bluest eyes that make her lovable differs from Hagar's temporary belief in love among the display of cosmetics, her circling shows that she has turned away from her self. Her last words are a lament about the difference between the "silky hair" that Milkman loves and her own that he is "never going to like," a lament that Pilate can only answer with the word "Hush" as her thirty-six-year-old granddaughter dies in her "little Goldilocks'-choice bed" (315-16).

The tropes of Morrison's novels show how central space is to her portrayal of girlhood. The dominant trope of her most contemporary narratives is property that links the things that Hagar Dead and Pecola Breedlove own and do not own to an economic and social system that defines them as worthless and unlovable because their houses and their bodies do not fit the paradigms of white culture. In Morrison's novels set within the era of World War I and the Harlem Renaissance, her tropes are connected to the powers of her defiant "new" fictional girls—Sula Peace and Dorcas Manfred—who dare to cross boundaries and court fire. In her novel of the mid- to late-nineteenth century, Morrison's trope is the trauma and the terror of violations that confine Denver within the spatial boundaries of the closed back door and the dangerous front yard, as well as the counterforce of her grandmother's teachings that enable her to move beyond them. Within the figurative space of the closed back door and the dangerous front yard, Morrison's fictional girls confront and "swallow" forces that make them knowledgeable, vulnerable, or both. The kind of space that her fictional girls occupy is simultaneously enclosed and open to physical dangers and metaphysical terrors that lead them toward or away from a sense of self.

The girl is a key figure in the composition of Morrison's novels because the powerful and contradictory forces that she confronts define the milieu in which she is placed. That Toni Morrison thinks of her fiction in terms of spatial composition and milieu is clear in her essay "Memory, Creation, and Writing," which turns on her affinity with ideas about composition as expressed by the painter Edvard Munch in his spatial metaphors of a stone "tossed at a group of children," their responsive scattering, and their "action" of "regrouping" (385). These spatial metaphors are also resonant for Morrison's representation of girlhood. Each of her novels includes the sense of a tossed stone as it is seen, felt , and interpreted by one of the children, a girl, who has been scattered or stood her ground or felt the weight of the stone or tossed the stone herself. The vision of each of Morrison's fictional girls is clear whether it is large and profound or so narrowly constricted that there is no room for her own body in it. And her response to the action of a metaphorical "tossed stone" is charted fully and precisely in her movements through space or in spatial metaphors that reveal her sense of herself. The curves implicit in the idea of a stone, if not always in its actuality, as well as the turns inherent in the idea of scattering and regrouping, suggest the circular movements and metaphors that Morrison links to her fictional girls.

Notes

1. The scholarship devoted to "Bildung" traditions that I found most helpful for my study of Morrison's fiction includes *The Voyage In: Fictions of Female Development*, eds. Elizabeth Abel, Marianne Hirsch, and Elizabeth Langland; *The Female Bildungsroman in English: An Annotated Bibliography of Criticism* by Laura Sue Fuderer; "Race, Sex and Self: Aspects of *Bildung* in Select Novels by Black American Women Novelists" by Sondra O'Neale, and *Ten is the Age of Darkness: The Black Bildungsroman* by Geta LeSeur. I wish to thank my colleague in the English Department at Skidmore College, Dr. Charlotte Goodman, for sharing this scholarship with me.
2. I deliberately omit *Tar Baby* from my essay because Toni Morrison includes only one scene from Jadine's girlhood in that novel. In this scene, Jadine watches the couplings of a female dog in heat with a pack of males. At that moment, Jadine decides that no man will ever do that to her. Although Jadine's sense of her own sexuality is central to the novel, it has no direct correlation to the space of her girlhood.
3. A number of scholars have written and spoken about the trope of memory and rememory in Morrison's fiction, including W. J. T. Mitchell who presented a paper called "Memory, Narrative, and Slavery" at the 1993 Narrative Conference in Albany, New York, to which I responded. His paper, which included remarks about the topos of the storehouse of memory, was dedicated to Hortense J. Spillers whose exemplary work on narrative and slavery includes her essay "Changing the Letter: The Yokes, The Jokes of Discourse, or Mrs. Stowe, Mr Reed," in *Slavery and the Literary Imagination*, 25-61.
4. Pamela E. Barnett's article "Figurations of Rape and the Supernatural in *Beloved*," is a fine analysis of Morrison's treatment of rape in *Beloved* and draws on the scholarship of Trudier Harris.
5. Although Morrison gives Beloved one section of the novel in which she "speaks," she never narrates a particular story about the past of Sethe or Denver.
6. Morrison does not identify the exact moment when Dorcas Manfred swallows fire. This is my conclusion. Since Dorcas is dead in the present time of the novel (1926), her girlhood is re-created from the principle narrator's imaginings and from the scattered stories told by some of the characters including

Dorcas herself. Thus, her girlhood does not "unfold" in any way but must be "reconstructed" from beyond the grave (so to speak).

7. Houston Baker gives a careful Freudian interpretation of this scene of sexual initiation in his essay, "When Lindbergh Sleeps with Bessie Smith: The Writing of Place in *Sula*." I am especially indebted to this article for my own analysis of *Sula*.
8. Trudier Harris has written an extensive analysis of the ways that Toni Morrison draws on folklore in her fiction in a book called *Fiction and Folklore: The Novels of Toni Morrison*.
9. The study by Jill McLean Taylor, Carol Gilligan, and Amy Sullivan is *Between Voice and Silence: Women and Girls, Race and Relationship*.

FIVE

Dizzying Possibilities, Plots, and Endings

Girlhood in Jill McCorkle's Ferris Beach

ELINOR ANN WALKER

Writers in the Bildung tradition have long used the narrative to comment on the possibilities available to their protagonists. Women writers, in particular, often construct both figurative and literal ways to document a female character's struggle to achieve a satisfactory ending to her story, one that allows her to reintegrate the disparate parts of herself or redefine the limited roles available to her. A writer's deliberate manipulation of plot, image patterns, and shifts in point of view can even reflect a protagonist's alienation—from herself, or from the society in which she lives. For example, from a distant and disembodied perspective, Zora Neale Hurston's Janie Crawford *(Their Eyes Were Watching God)* observes one self sitting under a shady tree and one self serving Joe Starks. Sylvia Plath's Esther Greenwood *(The Bell Jar)* sees herself reflected strangely in mirrors and at times masquerades as Elly Higginbottom. Josephine Humphreys' Lucille Odom, the first-person adolescent narrator of *Rich in Love* (1987), speaks of herself in the third person when she dons a Halloween costume of her mother's, and Jill McCorkle's Jo Spencer, the anorexic narrator of *The Cheer Leader* (1984), speaks in an increasingly fragmented voice, slipping also into a third-person rendition of her story before she emerges as an "unbounded" self. In each of these instances, the writer makes the narrative reflect the protagonist's own split from herself and her ensuing disorientation. As critics such as Rachel Blau DuPlessis and others have demonstrated,[1] the "plot," and particularly the ending, may also comment on the protagonist's choices of social identity or inner selfhood. In *Ferris Beach* (1990), McCorkle uses another adolescent female narrator, Kate Burns, to probe the ambiguities and multiplicities of growing up female and the accompanying cultural prescriptions of female roles. In this text, McCorkle deftly and often humorously appropriates plots from biography and autobiography (of Helen Keller and Anne Frank) and nineteenth- and turn-of-the-century British and American literary traditions (works by Thomas Hardy, Nathaniel Hawthorne, and Kate Chopin) to create frame narratives that vie for Kate's "ending."

Kate (or Kitty, as she is nicknamed) describes herself to the reader at least in part in terms of a physical feature, a birthmark "the color of wine" (5)[2] on her left cheek. Introduced so early in the novel, Kitty's birthmark sets the stage for three accompanying subtexts or stories about female identity (or the lack thereof), two of which are framed in the novel, and one that is an allusion. The first, mentioned on page one of the book, is Kitty's preoccupation with Helen Keller and her teacher Annie Sullivan. Kitty's own birthmark makes her identify with Helen's blindness so much that she pretends to be blind, bumping secretly about in her upstairs bedroom, but so noisily that her mother cannot help but hear her and be dismayed. Kitty's new best friend Misty and her mother Mo (whom McCorkle characterizes in stark contrast to Kitty's own mother Cleva) become the sources of the second narrative, the tale of Themista Rose Allen, Misty's namesake, who dies for her beloved, and thus sets up an idealized female paradigm of romance. Although the allusion is not acknowledged explicitly in McCorkle's text, the third narrative evoked by Kitty's birthmark is Nathaniel Hawthorne's tale of the beautiful yet scarred Georgiana and her scientist husband Aylmer, who is so determined to rid her of the one tiny blemish on her beauty (significantly located on her left cheek, as Kitty's is) that he kills her. The Helen Keller game, the Themista Rose Allen tale, and the allusion to Hawthorne's "The Birthmark" set up the conflicts among competing cultural prescriptions of women's roles in McCorkle's *Ferris Beach*.

When I taught *Ferris Beach* in an undergraduate contemporary women's fiction class, most of my female students agreed that the Helen Keller story is a source of fascination for young women. This preoccupation would seem reasonable, since there are relatively few strong female heroines in children's stories. The fact that Helen's story is true makes it more powerful, like the Anne Frank story, another narrative to which many students were drawn as young adults and another "real life" story to which McCorkle alludes. In both cases, a young woman overcomes tremendous odds and escapes either a literal or figurative silence, demonstrating that language and the ability to write and speak it, provide a woman with a kind of freedom that she would not otherwise have.

Furthermore, Helen Keller's story actually gives its readers not one heroine, but two, since Annie Sullivan plays such an instrumental role. Sullivan is the consummate woman, able to nurture *and* make a difference through her profession as teacher. She is not simply a schoolmarm, however, because in her role of language-giver she assumes almost deitylike power; she names things and Helen is able to understand. Interestingly, Sullivan also gets the best of both worlds in her "daughter" who is not really a daughter; Helen respects Sullivan, experiencing a kind of gratitude and love for her that she does not necessarily feel for her own mother.

It is not surprising, then, that Kitty is fond of this story, or that when she has acted out the narrative, she has cast herself in both roles, as Helen and Annie Sullivan. This pretense allows Kitty to reconstruct her own mother-daughter story. As she tells the reader when her tenth-grade class studies the play *The Miracle Worker,* "I knew all of Annie Sullivan's lines" (107). Kitty's private reenactment of Helen's blindness takes place in her bedroom, when she is younger. She locks her bedroom door and blindfolds herself, telling the reader that she is surprised by how quickly the familiar is transformed into the unfamiliar, how her hands, while feeling for the fabric of her chenille bedspread, strike "only air" (20). She becomes overwhelmed: "It seemed the more I tried to find my way, the harder it became, the harder to breathe, like the panic that comes suddenly in deep water. . . . The frustration of it all was overwhelming and left me feeling dizzy and tired" (20). Both literally and figuratively disoriented, Kitty no longer recognizes her room, and the images of water too deep to navigate, suffocation, dizziness, and spinning out of control will recur throughout the novel. In this instance, Kitty's performance is not as private as she imagines, despite her locked door; her audience, ironically, is her mother, who overhears her as she bangs around upstairs. Her mother's response is typical of her communication with her daughter. She blames Kitty for "making a game out of a horrible thing" (20). As Kitty acknowledges, Helen would not have been able to hear anyone calling up the stairs to her, and this awareness of her extreme isolation overwhelms Kitty.

Significantly, it is Cleva's voice in her head that has prompted Kitty to identify with Helen Keller in the first place, to "see" what it would be like to be blind and imagine how such an existence would feel. Cleva has told her, "What if YOU were this way or that way . . . , then YOU would realize that a little birthmark is NOT the end of the world" (20). To her mother, Kitty's "little" birthmark is insignificant, and her daughter's self-consciousness nothing more than silly adolescent vanity. Her attitude conveys no sympathy, no remembrance of the ways that adolescent girls become suddenly objectified on the brink of their womanhood. Thus Cleva utterly misreads her daughter's effort to "be" Helen. But to Kitty, outgrowing the Helen Keller simulation is more significant than her mother's perception of the game would imply; as the novel begins, she remarks that these days are drawing to a close. She can imagine what it would be like to be Helen Keller, but finally she cannot *be* Helen,[3] a fact Kitty recognizes with relief; at the same time, however, she is overwhelmed by the obstacles—the panic-inducing isolation, the literal strangeness of her room—that she encounters as she tries to be like someone else whose life, finally, will not ever be hers. No longer able to cast herself as Helen or Annie Sullivan, Kitty struggles to figure out who she can become.

Through this subnarrative, McCorkle illustrates Kitty's dissatisfaction with what her mother Cleva represents: the educated woman who nonetheless vacuums the floor in pearls and attends afternoon teas and DAR functions; the woman who could do the advertising for appliances as clean and glistening and passionless as her own surface is. Cleva wants her daughter to cultivate the same stoicism; Kitty should accept what she looks like, birthmark and all, and make the best of it. From Boston and a graduate from a girl's school in Virginia, Cleva is fascinated by history, proud that their home was built in the 1800s, proud to have ancestors who fought on both sides during the Civil War. Cleva encourages Kitty to join the Children of the Confederacy, and she is quick to judge her neighbors by their homes. Even Cleva's name is clipped and harsh, as Kitty puts it, "tight-lipped with teeth clenched on that long *e*" (4)—perhaps the reason that Kitty prefers her nickname to her given name, Kate, which she also describes as a "short sharp bite" (4).

McCorkle characterizes Cleva as prim, fastidious, distant, and controlling, and her reaction to Kitty's cousin Angela would almost suggest jealousy.[4] Kitty's own obsession with Angela springs in part from her frustration with her mother. Angela is mysterious, young, and a little wild; Kitty's father is her uncle and her closest living relative, and she would occasionally stay with Kitty's family before Kitty was born. Kitty first meets Angela when Kitty is five, her father having taken her on a visit to Ferris Beach for that very purpose and without telling Cleva that they will see Angela. When they arrive at Ferris Beach, Angela asks her uncle, Kitty's father, "How's the general?" (16), referring to Cleva. As Kitty matures, she nurtures her memory of this trip, identifying Angela and the shimmering lights of Ferris Beach with everything that Cleva is not. Instead, she "attach[es] to Angela everything beautiful and lively and good; she was . . .

the waves crashing on Ferris Beach as I spun around and around because I couldn't take in enough of the air. . . . She was energy, the eternal movement of the world, the blood in my veins and the wind in the bare winter branches that creaked and cried out in the night like tired ghosts in search of home" (5). Again McCorkle uses the act of spinning, this time to capture Kitty's euphoria, but even in this ecstasy, Kitty cannot "take in enough of the air," and later she will learn that the romanticism that Angela embodies can be equally asphyxiating. For now, though, Kitty is a "tired ghost" herself, searching for a form, a shape, to fill.

Scholars and critics such as Adrienne Rich, Nancy Chodorow, Carol Gilligan, and Marianne Hirsch have suggested that a woman undertakes a complex psychological journey as she grows into and creates her own identity. Part of this process may even entail a rejection of her own mother. By choosing a completely different role model or by denying her mother's influence, an adolescent may seek to "other" her mother, to use Hirsch's terminology. Kitty seeks substitutes for Cleva in *Ferris Beach,* namely Angela and Mo Rhodes, her friend Misty's mother. Angela's mother died at the age of seventeen, in childbirth, and significantly Kitty identifies her—and Angela—with Themista Rose Allen, the subject of the story that Mo Rhodes tells the girls.

The Themista Rose Allen story centers upon a young woman from Ferris Beach, who, at the age of sixteen and in the year 1900, drowns while wading across an inlet to meet her beloved. So enthralled by her lover, she completely forgets about the rising tide, but she must return home or risk her father's wrath. In the process of crossing back to shore, she finds herself in water well over her head and drowns. The story sets up an idealized notion of love for Kitty and Misty, who treasure the tale for its romantic tone and neglect the fate of its heroine. Mo tells them the story over and over, and each time, Kitty says, it "got a little bit better" (29). Mo's eventual behavior suggests that she, too, has fallen prey to a certain romanticism, perhaps the very reason that she is willing to tell the Themista Rose Allen story to the girls so many times, and to name her children after figures whose own brief lives seem to glorify dying young. In addition to its resonance with Kate Chopin's *The Awakening,* the story of Themista Rose Allen elaborates upon different notions of love and desire—whether married, adulterous, or adolescent—in this novel.

Ferris Beach tells the story of Kitty's own awakening to sexuality through the conventions of a Bildungsroman and a metafictional acknowledgment of real and imagined narratives. The turn-of-the-century tale of Themista Rose recalls Chopin's novel of 1899, except that within the context of *Ferris*

Beach, Allen's story is "true," that is, it is assumed to be true by the characters, while the readers make the connection with the "real" source, Chopin's *The Awakening.* Critics differ in their interpretations of Edna Pontellier's final embrace of the sea, but regardless of what the sea and swimming symbolize—freedom, independence, maternal space, autoeroticism—Edna does die, and dying, even symbolically speaking, is dubious resolution for a young woman just beginning to know herself. Using characters rather than cultures as the basis for the dichotomy, McCorkle contrasts Cleva's aloofness (rather than Kentucky Presbyterianism) with the sensuality embodied by Mo and Angela (rather than Creole Catholicism). As critic Annis Pratt has observed, the female growing-up tale is just as likely to become a "growing down" tale as the possibilities for self-realization dwindle. McCorkle's appropriation of death by drowning in the Themista-Rose-frame tale yokes the brink of adulthood with life's end and finally keeps love—and sex—a rather abstract and rarefied phenomenon, an ideal for which the heroine dies a clean death in the sea because she forgets that the tide always rises. The heroine's failure to think about natural cycles of waning and waxing suggests three things: one, the heroine transcends present circumstance, even if just for a while, because love is such a giddy otherworldliness; two, the heroine is childlike and scatterbrained, doomed to die before she matures; or three, the heroine chooses not to worry about cycles, whether moon-driven or menstruation-driven. Not one of these options would seem to satisfy a critical listener to the tale, and, finally, Kitty's own troubles with love and sex are far less cleanly resolved. Once again, her life fails to render the story true.

McCorkle uses Mo's character to undercut established narrative expectations of the romantic heroine. At first, however, she sets Mo up *as* a romantic heroine, and in this role, Mo is very different from Cleva. She "was the youngest mother" (28) that Kitty has ever known. She fixes s'mores in the stove for Kitty and Misty on rainy afternoons, plays Buddy Holly and Elvis Presley songs, sings along, dances in the kitchen, wears purple earrings, and converts her front yard into a Japanese garden, much to the neighbors' curiosity and disapproval. As Kitty and Misty become best friends, Kitty spends as much time as possible at Misty's house; unlike Cleva, Mo relaxes with the girls and talks to them about love and love songs. In keeping with her impetuous nature, Mo runs away with another man on the Fourth of July, taking the youngest, six-month old Buddy (named after Buddy Holly), with her, abandoning Misty, her brother, and her father quite publicly at the field where the town fireworks are displayed. In a parody of some nineteenth- and early twentieth-century novels,[5] Mo's eventual death in a car accident comments upon her infidelities, and McCorkle wryly points out that Mo, like Themista Rose, is actually returning penitently home when the accident occurs, making the whole episode rather naturalistic. Like many romantic heroines, Mo pursues her dreams but ends up dead and exposed to public scrutiny. To Misty, Mo's daughter, Mo's departure and death are certainly not romantic, though were they to be described to her in a story, or a love song, she would be apt to perceive them as such.[6]

McCorkle's characterization of Mo juxtaposes Cleva's aloofness and controlling love even as McCorkle proves that too much youthfulness may simply be immaturity, something that Kitty is too young to see. In fact, Mo never really becomes an adult; like Themista Rose Allen, she is stunted in girlhood, incapable of making good decisions, caught in a process of "growing down," as it were. Her end suggests that romantic love, especially sexual love, is a risky basis for identity; furthermore, by her death in the car, she is forever trapped in that moment of transit, inconsistency, departure, regardless of whether she is going or coming.

Kitty cannot help but compare Mo's flamboyance to her mother's reticence, Mo's willingness to give all for love to her mother's discomfort in her husband's embrace if Fred hugs her in front of Kitty. Kitty believes, "for every animated move my father had, [my mother] had composure and reserve" (2), and her parents seem so incongruous that sometimes she imagines that Cleva is not her real mother. It is her father to whom she ascribes a romantic sensibility. Fred, in fact, becomes the embodiment of all things Victorian. Named Alfred Tennyson Burns after the poet, he tells Kitty stories that Cleva then revises. For example, according to Fred, Kitty's grandmother (his mother) was "a brilliant lady, a poet's soul buried in a tough little shell" (3), but Cleva tells Kitty that her grandmother was "a poor sad woman who lost her mind" (3). Also a Thomas Hardy fan, Fred wants to name Kitty "Arabella" when she is born, but Cleva tells Kitty that she wouldn't let him, because Arabella "sounded like something you'd better hope not to get in pregnancy" (3). Time and again, Fred constructs the romantic possibility only to have Cleva deconstruct it; to Kitty, this behavior testifies to her mother's coldness. The reader, however, may recognize that Cleva is carefully, even humorously, reminding Kitty of reality, a reality that is not gentle and that Kitty will have to face. When Fred dies later in the novel, Cleva's independence, sense of humor, and strength will keep her from the fate of the mourning romantic heroine.

Kitty, however, continues to reject Cleva's revision of her father's stories. She thinks that the name "Arabella" is lovely; it, too, connotes all that her mother is not. Kitty confesses that she used to whisper the name over and over to herself: "Just the movement of the mouth to sound the word was sexy, its open-mouthed ending coming with a shallow, quickened breath. . . . I could say 'Angela,' and my mouth would form the same shape" (3-4). Convinced that having another name would alter her whole destiny, Kitty pines to be called Arabella. But if she cannot be called such a name, she may still be able to embrace a romantic existence, a quickening of heartbeat, pulse, breath, and body. Because of these longings, Kitty considers Mo and Angela paradigms for female selfhood—which is closely yoked with being desirable (or *bella*) and capable of desire—evocative of sheer "energy," to use the word that Kitty assigns to Angela. Such energy, however, may be destructive.

The Thomas Hardy reader will recognize Arabella as a character from *Jude the Obscure.* She is, in fact, Jude's wife whom he disdains for being a country girl, though he is merely of artisan class. To lure Jude into marrying her, Arabella leads him to believe that she is pregnant. In despair over his mistake of marriage, Jude begins to drink, and Arabella, perhaps sensibly, leaves him. Arabella's story, then, is hardly romantic. At first, the element of being swept off one's feet into a potentially better life suggests fulfillment, but reality commands otherwise, namely because romance cannot exist in a vacuum, without a partner's accord and the common vision of what the life together should be. Arabella's name, though pleasant on the tongue, does not determine her destiny. Finally, she must depend upon another who rejects her on the basis of her social class. As the Hardy reader knows, Jude's lot does not improve much over the novel's course either, and he comes from a line of ancestors whose marriages go awry. His great-aunt tells him, "The Fawleys were not made for wedlock" (70). Significantly, Jude's mother has drowned herself because of differences with his father, and the endings of suicide and death comment upon the characters' failures to reconcile intellect and desire, spirit and flesh, mind and body. McCorkle's allusion continues to set up the pieces of the romance plot, the plot that Kitty believes she wants as her own, and Arabella's story introduces the possibilities of confused male desire, lustful and sometimes cruel.

Ironically, Kitty, like Jude, will become involved with someone of a lower social class. Her first sexual relationship involves Merle Hucks, whose family is both socially and economically inferior to Kitty's own. Nonetheless, she has known Merle most of her life; as a boy he hid under her porch and called "Meow" over and over again, teasing Kitty about her name. Despite the class differences, Merle's home and her own exist very close to each other geographically. Significantly, Kitty has watched Merle and the Huckses for years from her own sleeping porch, at once playing voyeur and vicariously participating in that family. The Huckses's home, which is a "light blue house with a tar paper roof" (26), is located across the cemetery from the Burns's property, but it fails to embody the standards set by the rest of the neighborhood. According to Cleva, the "houses were thrown up right after the Depression" (26), in contrast to their own 1800-era dwelling, and Cleva complains that the houses are "eyesore[s] and she wished they'd move elsewhere" (26). Kitty tells the reader that Cleva and her friend Mrs. Poole (who hosts the neighborhood teas) "talked about all the families who lived back there and how ours was the last 'nice' street before the town *fell*" (26).

Perhaps in rebellion against these judgmental responses, and perhaps seduced by class and sexual tension bound up together in the tradition of Lady Chatterley, Kitty falls for Merle, and they consummate their relationship in the neighborhood's bastion of propriety, the Poole home. In no way is Merle the absent and perfect lover of the Themista Rose Allen tale or the simple and animalistic gardener of Lawrence's novel, but he provides support for Kitty after her father dies suddenly, and the two of them establish an honestly communicative relationship. Kitty confesses that as a child she was scared of Merle, and he responds, "The bottom line is that you were scared of me because I was a Hucks" (221). Recognizing the truth of his claim, Kitty defies her mother and Mrs. Poole by growing closer and closer to him. Mrs. Poole, who rather paternalistically provides for whose who have less than she, even as it remains clear that she still considers Merle not of her social class, hires Merle to help her around her house and yard. In a fitting defilement of "sacred" spaces, Kitty and Merle's final sexual encounter takes place in Mr. Poole's room, a private place where he was rumored to "get away" from Mrs. Poole, and where he has also kept a cot. These separate sleeping quarters suggest some coldness between the Pooles, and Kitty and Merle's naked "fumbling" (257) is real intimacy by comparison. Indeed, their coupling yields such "absolute peace" (258) that the two fail to hear Kitty's mother calling for Mrs. Poole and then coming up the stairs only to discover them. Secret and hidden love has been delightfully taboo to Kitty, but in fact she has experienced a rather gentle version of lust and its satiation.

Before she and Merle become involved, Kitty has taken her predilection for voyeurism several steps closer than her vantage point of the sleeping porch. One night, she sneaks outs so that she can "spy . . . and see what it looked like inside of that house" (172). What she witnesses will dispel some of the romanticism associated with young love. From the safe height of a tall tree, where she has climbed to get a good look, Kitty at first becomes fascinated by watching Merle's brother Dexter and his girlfriend, Perry, even titillated by the sight of Perry "stretched out on the grass, her hair loose and falling over one shoulder as she beckoned to whoever was standing in the darkness" (173). Kitty watches, her "heart pounding" (173), as Perry and Dexter lie together on the grass, but the scene turns ugly when Dexter's friends show up and Dexter gets one of them to hold Perry's arms. Kitty sees Perry's "stark white" face, her "white lacy bra with a little pink rosebud in the center" (174), all details that make Perry little girl-like, innocent, and afraid. Kitty sees Merle there, too, and he tries to stop his brothers from their rape of Perry, but he is outnumbered. Kitty finally cannot "shake the picture of Perry, her muffled screams as hands and mouths stifled and probed her, her body held and pinned, naked and helpless, an experiment, a specimen" (176). In looking hard into another life, Kitty is left with another picture, but this picture is violent and inescapable. The Pre-Raphaelite images evoked by the Themista Rose tale are replaced by things "dark red, blood red" (176), and Kitty sees firsthand, almost, what it is to be an objectified, undressed, violated, and discarded female self. The provocativeness of "Arabella" over the tongue, "splendor in the grass,"[7] and other such imaginings may lead to this objectification. This is not the first time that Kitty feels overwhelmed by what it means to be female. As she tells the reader when she is watching Perry, she cannot close her eyes for fear of the "dizziness [that] would have caught up with [her]" (176); again, projecting herself into a different world of femaleness leaves her literally reeling. She must keep her eyes open to dispel her dizziness, however, because if she falls out of the tree, she will also literally find herself like Perry, surrounded by boys who will rape her.

Kitty's watching reflects her continuing desire to escape her own circumstances by imagining what someone else's life is like. She is obsessive about this watching, just as she has been obsessive about her Helen Keller game, or the Anne Frank diary that replaces the Helen Keller biography as the source of her pretending. She has imagined Anne Frank so many times that she can conjure her up in her head, not even needing an actual photograph to project her own need of what Anne Frank should be: "Just as I had imagined . . . Annie Sullivan and even Angela, I could close my eyes and see [Anne] there in her pinafore, thick, dark hair clipped on one side . . ."[8] (54). In "seeing" Anne Frank, Kitty can also re-create herself, imagine her own role changing, as she says, "hearing her 'Dear Kitty' as an endearment of myself. I read the letters so often . . . that sometimes I almost believed that I *was* her Kitty, and that she was still very much alive and writing her letters, and sometimes I caught myself suddenly filled with hope for her salvation and future" (54). Kitty is dissatisfied by the real story's ending—one that renders Anne Frank's growth and her adolescent love for Peter, an aspect of the story that fascinates Kitty, finally and simply stopped by her death.

At the same time, however, Kitty responds to the metaphysical presence of Anne Frank, or as she puts it, "someone out there for me" (54). This desire in turn prompts her own willingness to become "out there" herself, so that if there were "someone out on a sleeping porch crouched and shivering while the world spun back around to day, someone who would wonder what purpose there could be to it all, . . . I could, with the breath of a weeping willow, . . . lean down, and whisper an answer as soft as ducks' down" (54). Again, a "spinning" world seems too much, and the witness to such a universe needs to be spared from isolation. But Kitty's desire to be taken up into a starry universe herself just so that she could provide comfort to some other lonely girl is also problematic. Kitty is flesh, not spirit, and must remain so while alive. Being taken up into the night, capable of whispering with the breath of a weeping willow, sounds too close to becoming one with Edna Pontellier's sea. On the other hand, such thoughts allow Kitty to rewrite the real-life ending to the Anne Frank story so that Anne lives on and plays the role of comforter, of isolation-dispeller, just like Annie Sullivan, something that Kitty very much desires from her mother but is denied. As Kitty's story continues, her relationship with her mother deteriorates. Cleva's anger and Kitty's inability to communicate with her after being discovered naked with Merle in Mr. Poole's cot further estrange daughter from mother. But Kitty pushes her mother away only to discover that she cannot replace her.

Kitty turns to Angela after the scene with Merle. Believing that Angela, who has fearlessly pursued men, will sympathize with Kitty's feelings for Merle, who is to move away, Kitty wants to go and live with her. The moment of Kitty's departure is a painful one, not because she will miss Cleva, but because both Cleva and Angela say hurtful things. McCorkle has reminded the reader periodically of the rift between Angela and Cleva. For example, Angela has told the family that she is married and on her honeymoon via a postcard from Memphis, "with Elvis on the front" (201), and Cleva has been hurt that Angela did not introduce the family to her fiancé. The reader also knows that after the death of Angela's mother Cleva has tried to take care of Angela, an endeavor that yields only resentment because Angela rejects Cleva's interest. As Kitty is poised to leave with Angela, Cleva accuses Angela of her own failure to commit to the family. "Tell Kate that you don't want her to come" (263), Cleva dares her. Angela denies having run away from home, and McCorkle writes that she "spat the word [home] as she narrowed her eyes" (263). Angela goes so far as to suggest that maybe Cleva's house is not Kitty's home either, and finally Cleva lets out a torrent of words addressed to her daughter: "'I guess I could say something to make it easier. I could say that I wish . . . you had never been born? . . . . Or better . . . I could say that I wish I had died in childbirth so that you could have taken your chances elsewhere.' She waved a hand toward Angela" (263). Cleva acknowledges Kitty's own romanticization of Angela's life, her "failure" to die so that Kitty, too, could live the vagabond life of an orphan and be mysterious, unlocatable. Also significant is Cleva's use of the adult name "Kate," rather than the more childlike "Kitty," in this conversation. Angela's behavior has been erratic, unpredictable, and not adult in any sense, and Cleva strives to treat her daughter like an adult, not a child who needs easing into reality. Just as Cleva has refused to let Fred mislead his daughter by casting family stories in a romantic light, so she must clarify Angela's choices in front of Kate. In this scene, McCorkle seems to suggest that Cleva also must let go of her own romanticized notion that she can "mother" Angela; she must instead spend her energy on Kate, her real daughter, the one who needs her more.

Nonetheless, Kitty departs with Angela for Ferris Beach, site of Themista Rose's untimely death and, appropriately, Kitty's own disillusionment: "There were dishes in her sink, sparse furnishings with sandy, threadbare upholstery, a floor-to-ceiling lamp with adjustable lights like some kind of insect; a square of lime green shag carpet covered the center of the floor" (267). The apartment turns out to be dimly lit; Angela's husband has disappeared; she doesn't seem to have a job; she says insensitive things about Kitty's birthmark, and she invalidates Kitty's feelings for Merle, saying "'Now, I know you think you're in *love*.'" Kitty thinks, "Just the word in her mouth sounded like a disease" (266). Increasingly uncomfortable in Angela's space, Kitty calls her mother to come and get her; "the words were barely out of my mouth before she said, *Yes, I will,* and hung up the phone" (271). Although it takes some time for Cleva and Kitty to heal from their respective hurts, Kitty realizes her mother's worth. Cleva may not be the most imaginative or warm person, but she is mature, reliable, and consistent, three words that fail to apply to Mo or Angela. Kitty's imperfect mother is the role model with whom McCorkle leaves her.

Kitty loses her notions of romanticism along with her virginity, and she approaches adulthood with few of her prior ideas about femininity intact. She cannot be blind and deaf, like Helen Keller, or captive, like Anne Frank. She has witnessed the awful consequences of adultery via Misty's bereavement, the terrifying immediacy of male lust and female objectification via Perry's rape, and the hollowness of an enervated life that she perceived to be exciting, sheer "energy," via Angela's barren existence and dirty apartment. Her father and biggest fan, Alfred Tennyson Burns, has died a sudden death. Her first love moves away. She is left with her mother and herself in uncomfortable union. Nothing has been the way she thought it would be.

McCorkle makes repeated use of the discrepancies between the exterior or appearance of a situation and the interior or reality of it. Kitty's birthmark becomes a useful symbol in this context. On one level, McCorkle uses the birthmark to develop, not Kitty's character, but her mother's. Cleva constantly tells Kitty not to "whine" about her appearance, but to be thankful for what she has; in short, she is not very sympathetic at all to Kitty's adolescent insecurities. Furthermore, the birthmark epitomizes how much of a woman's life is bound up in her appearance. Finally, Kitty's preoccupation with it and her constant imagining of its effect on other people link her to Hawthorne's Georgiana, whose birthmark is made hideous to her only because she internalizes the revulsion of her husband Aylmer, its beholder. The raped Perry is also like Georgiana; that is, she becomes, to use Kitty's words, "an experiment, a specimen" (176).

Although many critics initially read Georgiana's birthmark as a sign of original sin and Aylmer as a sort of tragic hero prey to his own hubris, feminist critics have interpreted "The Birthmark" as a text concerning female sexuality, power, and male idealization of the female form. *Ferris Beach* may elaborate upon these interpretations by McCorkle's attention to male manipulation of a woman's life or story and female resistance to such control. For example, the rape of Perry, Cleva's deconstruction of Fred's stories, the reference to the name "Arabella" and its associations with Jude, whose expectations negate his marriage, and the allusion to Hawthorne's "The Birthmark" all imply tension between male and female conceptions of desire. To Kitty, her own birthmark contradicts "beauty," and as more contemporary and cultural criticism has attested, the politics of beauty grow out of what is labeled desirable. Furthermore, these politics are backed by a corporate machine in American society, a machine that promotes preadolescent figures, blank stares, flat chests, and skin-revealing baby doll clothes on models. "Beauty," in short, deconstructs Bildung. It is not surprising that a woman must work to accept who she is and how she looks in the face of competing, and almost impossibly perfect, images and mirrors, and *Ferris Beach* acknowledges this contemporary concern.

Kitty turns outward for signs of femininity, for images and mirrors of beautiful female adulthood, but the romantic plots she embraces will not help her grow. Cleva, however, will. As Kitty has voiced, she is frustrated by her mother's lack of empathy, and by the repeated phrase of "lots of people have birthmarks" (44). Kitty confesses, "I always wanted to say that if it was a *birthmark* it must be *her* fault" (44). McCorkle depicts the ambivalence and tension between mother and daughter accurately: the daughter's longing to throw off the mother's influence; the mother's fatigue and frustration as she alone tries to control the household while her husband remains friends with their child; the ensuing isolation of both mother and daughter.

Nonetheless, it is Cleva who embodies adulthood. But what informs Kitty's fascination with Angela and Mo is that their lives signify romance and desire; ironically, Kitty objectifies these women who differ so much from her mother, seeing them only on the surface and remaining ignorant of their real lives. Angela and Mo are romantic experiments whose results are disappointing, and their stories, their plots, leave Kitty longing for home, for her mother. Finally, she is forced to recognize her mother's strengths as she rejects Angela and Mo as role models. Cleva, however, never quite achieves the status of a "likable" character, a fact that raises other questions. Are "good" mothers doomed to be unlikable? What ending can Kitty choose if every single female after whom she has modeled herself is unhappy, distant, or dead? In this novel, the crux of the mother/daughter story—and of the romance plots as well—seems to be that women are only human, prey to their own frailties, insecurities, desires. McCorkle suggests that becoming an adult requires an acceptance of imperfection in both self and other.

In Jill McCorkle's *Ferris Beach*, each internal narrative figures into Kitty's own story as she attempts to achieve her own identity, and at the novel's ending, she rejects the romance plot for a more realistic story, knowing full well that realism may also yield disappointment. In this novel, McCorkle appropriates historical figures and literary references, images, and story lines to develop her characters and dramatize their choices and the consequences thereof. The competing plots and textual allusions exemplify some of the perils that confront girls on the brink of womanhood, namely the search for a role model and life in a culture that bombards women with impossible female ideals. By setting up, and then undercutting, the beautiful romantic heroine, McCorkle reveals Cleva's strengths even as she honestly assesses the difficulties between fictional mother and daughter. Cleva is not perfect, and perhaps Kitty begins to realize that she does not have to be, either.

Ferris Beach does not end with exclusive focus on Kitty's future. Kitty has turned her story away from herself and instead attempts to predict, with hope, what awaits her best friend, Misty, imagining "a whole world of possibilities spinning around her" (278). As other moments in the narrative have shown, a spinning world makes balancing difficult. Despite the book's apparently upbeat ending, *Ferris Beach* depicts a world rife with danger and betrayal, and other subplots of death, adultery, and rape contradict the title-inspired images of beach frolics and other such adolescent antics. The spinning world of possibilities is often disorienting, at best, as any adult woman knows. Kitty's final projection for Misty suggests a departure from her previous self-consciousness, an act resonant less of self-consumed adolescent awkwardness and more of a newly discovered confidence, a step from girlhood to womanhood and all its dizzying choices.

Notes

1. I refer mainly to DuPlessis's *Writing Beyond the Ending: Narrative Strategies of Twentieth Century Women Writers,* published in 1985. Critics including Nina Auerbach, Elaine Showalter, Sandra Gilbert, and Susan Gubar discuss the ways in which fictional strategies may mirror social concerns of their authors and comment upon issues of a heroine's "morality" or position in society. Duplessis herself cites Nancy K. Miller's work on the eighteenth-century novel as an important precursor to her own (*The Heroine's Text: Readings in the French and English Novel, 1722-1782*), as well as the theoretical paradigms of Fredric Jameson (*The Political Unconscious: Narrative as a Socially Symbolic Act*) and Julia Kristeva, which establish narrative as a site of political and social discourse and ideology.
2. Jill McCorkle, *Ferris Beach* (New York: Fawcett Crest Books, 1991). All subsequent references to *Ferris Beach* come from the 1991 Fawcett Crest paperback edition, published by Ballantine Books in arrangement with Algonquin Books of Chapel Hill.
3. Nor can Kitty be another Helen, the fairest, upon whose beauty civilizations rise and fall.
4. The reader, however, later learns that Cleva's ambivalence has grown out of the fact that she has tried to mother Angela, who rejected Cleva's concern. This experience seems to influence Cleva's behavior with Kitty.
5. George Eliot's *The Mill on the Floss* or Theodore Dreiser's *Sister Carrie,* for example.
6. Misty "can quote every single line of 'The Ballad of Bonnie and Clyde'" (33), for example.
7. These lines are the 19th-century British poet William Wordsworth's, but the 1961 film by the same title and starring Natalie Wood and Warren Beatty deals with tense family relationships in the wake of young love.

8. Though Kitty is heterosexual, her strong feelings for Angela, Annie Sullivan, and Anne suggest a crushlike enthrallment again common in romance plots; her attraction to these women arises from imagined versions of their personalities, not real ones.

SIX

"I Ain't No FRIGGIN' LITTLE WIMP"

The Girl "I" Narrator in Contemporary Fiction

RENEE R. CURRY

The title of this essay comes from a line spoken by Earlene Bean at the end of Carolyn Chute's novel, *The Beans of Egypt, Maine.* Earlene, like two of her counterparts in contemporary fiction—Ruth Anne Boatwright from *Bastard Out of Carolina* and Annie John from the novel, *Annie John*—declares execratively what her "I" is not. She is not a sissy, jellyfish, pansy, milksop, milquetoast, pantywaist, weakling, dotard, coward, chicken, baby, or mollycoddle. She is nothing that signifies frailty. She knows what she "ain't." Earlene is an "I," and she speaks her "I" proudly. Earlene, Annie, and Bone, as girl "I" narrators, are not in the process of becoming. They are not dreaming about who they will become. These girls already are, and they "ain't no friggin' little wimp[s]."

Research on girls as speakers or narrators involves both psychological studies of live girls as well as theoretical studies of fictional representations. Rather than make rigid distinctions between these disciplinary studies and their subjects, I explore the complex interweavings that inform adult perceptions of girl "I"s both lived and fictional. Cultural studies scholars Michelle Fine's and Pat McPherson's concept of girl bodies as "unclaimed territories"[1], literary critic Alison Donnell's thoughts on "cultural ventriloquism"[2], Feminist critic Carolyn Heilbrun's discussion of "female impersonation"[3], and Fine's and McPherson's recognition of "occluded truths"[4] all provide frameworks that allow us to access and read the girl "I" narrator as trustworthy, persuasive, and, above all, neither innocent nor tragically suffering from loss of innocence.

"Innocence," when used to characterize the condition of girls collectively, assumes a monolithic definitude. Girls equate with innocence, and innocence is equivalent with girls. This homology between girls and innocence deems young females to be blameless, faultless, virtuous, spotless, pure of heart, irreproachable, unimpeachable, inculpable, chaste, guiltless, guileless, harmless, simple, naïve, unsophisticated, artless, unknowledgeable, and free from responsibility. The innocence position demands that girls inhere to all of its attributes. To be "Girl" is to be innocent. This essay argues a rift in this monolithic homology. The girl "I" narrators under discussion are not naive, unknowledgeable, irreproachable, or free from responsibility. Nor do they wish to represent themselves as such. However, they are, by virtue of age and law, blameless and guiltless in the face of actions perpetrated upon them. Too often we, adult women and men, demand silence from girls about perpetrations and knowledge so that we may maintain our romantic ideals about the milksopish purity of girls. Enforcement of silence and maintenance of romantic ideals permits us to sustain an ongoing irresponsibility toward girls in our lives. These girls are neither innocent of the knowledge that life experience grants them, nor are they mere victims of such experience. They are vitally involved in their lives and in the profoundly responsible work of consecrating truths about girls. Authors Jamaica Kincaid, Carolyn Chute, and Dorothy Allison write these girls into their art with the hope that we will come to recognize them in fiction, and in life.

The research on girls is inadequate. Therapist Mary Pipher, author of *Reviving Ophelia,* ascribes this lack of information to the secretive and internally oriented behavior of girls, themselves (21). She remarks upon the difficulties inherent in researching reticent human subjects. Cultural critic Angela McRobbie claims that studies in youth culture predominantly cover boys and that "the absence of girls from the whole of the literature in this area is quite striking and demands explanation" (35). At first glance, contemporary women fiction writers such as Kincaid, Chute, and Allison appear as if they write to remedy the paucity of information about girls. They seem to agree that the girl's sense of self must be engaged before she becomes reticent. A cursory glance at the work of these writers suggests that they are familiar with the psychological literature that espouses (through the mouths of girls themselves) that profound selfhood is lost at preadolescence: "One girl said, 'Everything good in me died in junior high'" (Pipher 20). A casual reading of Kincaid, Chute, and Allison suggests an alliance with Hillary Carlip, author of *Girl Power,* who also claims that girls have a tendency to go inward, shut down, lose their confidence, become self-conscious, and "no longer speak freely, editing their communications" (1).

However, Kincaid, Chute, and Allison are not about the work of Pipher and Carlip. They do not herald an adult female authoring agenda that will recuperate the voices of the so-called voiceless girls. Like Fine and McPherson, these three writers propose girl "I"s who know full well that adult women prefer either silence or discourse about "shutting down" and "going inward" from the mouths of girls. These girl "I" narrators recognize that adults do not want to hear about incest, sexual activity, sexual desire, masochistic desire, and other "unladylike" language, but these girls, like their authors, no longer wish to fake their innocence, nor to preserve the innocence of the surrounding adults. Fine and McPherson descry that feminist writings have "ignored, indeed misrepresented, how well young women talk as subjects" (178). Furthermore, their research suggests that "our"—feminist scholars'—commitment has been to the representation of adolescent girls as victims of patriarchy to the detriment of their representation as strong young women who are passionate about themselves and others and who relish in their "capacities to move between nexus of power and powerlessness" (178). In other words, girls are continuously resisting both patriarchy's constraints as well as the constraints of feminist portrayals of them as victims.

In her introduction to *School Girls,* journalist and former editor of *Mother Jones* Peggy Orenstein expresses astonishment at how "consistently articulate and insightful" girls are when given the opportunity (xxv). Astonishment such as Orenstein's occurs because we—predominantly white, educated, middle-class adult women—have constructed an image of girls in life and in literature as silent, absent, innocent figures. Fiction writers Kincaid, Chute, and Allison bring new girl "I"s to life in fiction. Their texts do not struggle to capture a fabricated adolescent "I" before it goes inward; rather, they struggle to give accurate voice to the girl "I" as she speaks.

Interestingly, psychologists, feminist scholars, and fiction writers do agree that the girl "I," if we are to know her, is best evidenced on paper. Carlip quotes a passage from one of the girls whom she studies: "Sometimes paper is the only thing that will listen to you" (343). Carlip's work demonstrates clearly that, when presented the opportunity "to safely put on paper what they wouldn't dare say aloud," girls do write, and "something dramatic" occurs (2). Kincaid, Chute, and Allison write the girl "I" narrator because it is in writing that the slippage between public facade and private truth occurs. As Angela McRobbie tells us, girls use silence as a tactic in public when in fact, in private, with each other, or with their own writings, girls can be quite articulate.

In her research on working-class girls, McRobbie notes that "Talking was their favorite activity" (49). By enacting fictional narrations that capture girls involved in their favorite act, Kincaid, Chute, and Allison locate a moment of dual nostalgia: nostalgia for the innocent girlhoods that never existed and nostalgia for the girl voices denied a hearing. Whereas Carlip suggests that girls shut down out of fear for what life might bring (1), I argue that they already know what life has brought and that the language prescribed as suitable for girls will not let them tell what they know. Girl "I" narrators of the contemporary fiction under discussion speak with an always already wisdom that profoundly disturbs adult readers because of reader desire for genuine (or, at least, rhetorical) innocence and optimism on the part of girls—regardless of the girls' fictional or lived lives.

If you want to hear that your daughter loves you wholeheartedly, sweetly, innocently, and willingly, listen to Annie John; she will lie her love for you in the exact tone and with the exact bodily gestures you desire. Jamaica Kincaid published *Annie John* in 1983. The book opens with a hint of Eden. The ten-year-old Annie John's seemingly innocent existence consists of feeding animals and conversing with her parents (3). She appears to be sheltered from anything "unnatural" and from any "unnatural" relationships. Her world consists of animals, Mom, and Dad—a virtual paradise for children. And yet, for some reason, Annie feels compelled to lie. The innocence position is demanding, and this girl "I" narrator already knows that as an innocent, she must lie about who she really is. And who is Annie John? She is a girl who steals. In narrating her ability to steal, she says, "I was always successful, because casting suspicion away from me and putting on an innocent face had become a specialty of mine" (55). Even by the end of the novel, Annie John experiences the same old pressure to exhibit disingenuous feelings. In particular, she feels compelled to smile at her mother when she has no desire to do so: "We looked at each other for a long time with smiles on our faces, but I know the opposite was in my heart" (147). Annie John must leave her mother because her mother, and the whole world, insists that Annie enact innocence.

Women and girls occlude the truth in cultural ways. Adult determination to adorn the site of the adolescent girl with innocence constitutes just such participation in occluded truths. Occlusion, by definition, means both to be stopped and to be absorbed. An interesting phonetic phenomenon defined as "occlusion" is "a momentary complete closure at some area in the vocal tract, causing stoppage of the breath stream and accumulation of pressure." The occluded truths of girls figure as a complex site that is both cultural and phonetic. The innocence position is one which culture first enforces by "stopping" an other, more precise, language. The girls then "absorb" fictions of innocence, and a truthful, non-innocent voice actually responds to the cultural and physiological conditioning by stopping certain articulations right in the vocal tract. In a sense, Kincaid, Chute, and Allison reach into the figurative throat of girls and allow the accumulated pressure of innocence to release. Jamaica Kincaid has Annie John narrate the occlusion experience—before release—for us: "I knew that in my fifteen years a lot of things had happened, but now I couldn't put my finger on a single thing" (111-12). Kincaid vibrantly reveals the cost to girls of having to occlude their truths: inability to speak of (or to know) the occurrences in their own lives.

Annie reveals this burden as an "unbearable" one that she wishes she could drown: "I wished I could reduce it to some small thing that I could hold underwater until it died" (128). Kincaid makes sure that we readers understand more than does Annie's mother. She wants us to know that Annie lies with every movement of her body as a result of having to feign innocence. The entire body site screams, "I lie." Annie John proclaims, ". . . my untruthfulness apparatus was now in full gear" (63). For her, the territory of being a girl operates as a highly complex machine that requires all manner of "apparatus" to keep its lies in place. If young girls such as Annie have no innocence to speak of, and yet the only permissible voice for them to occupy is one of innocence, "we" then deny them their realities, and we deny ourselves anything like a truth about girls. The "we" here is significant because it reminds adult feminist scholars that if we do not read carefully what the girl "I"s are telling us, then in fact, we participate in keeping them quiet. For instance, if we read in *Annie John* a coming-of-age story that tells of a young girl who distances herself from her mother as she comes into her own sexuality, we participate in the silencing of young girls just as Annie John's mother does. Annie John knows about sexuality, and she knows that her mother is sexual. Her mother's wanting her to be "nice" and maintain a quietude about sex, relationships, passion, fornication, friendship, intimacy, love, affection, and regeneration is effective only in forcing Annie to lie. Her mother's projection of innocence onto Annie via the pressures of silence does not make Annie innocent. Annie is not innocent of sexuality; she is, rather, disdainful of the cultural pressure to pretend to be so. If we read the text as a tragic, but perhaps necessary, separation between mother and daughter, we promote an irresponsible reading, one that refuses to see that what came between Annie and her mother was untruthfulness about sexual knowledge and sexual being.

In *At the Bottom of the River*, a set of short prose pieces in which Kincaid expresses the pain experienced by girls and women who are continuously silenced, Kincaid lyrically warns us about the power of silence to seduce and erase the voice: "Living in the silent voice, I am no longer 'I.' Living in the silent voice, I am at last at peace. Living in the silent voice, I am at last erased" (52). In this excerpt Kincaid warns us that silence seduces. Its offers a surface of seeming peacefulness and serenity; however, its real power is in its ability to erase one's being. Kincaid suggests that we risk erasing girls if we refuse to hear the chaos of their positions. Peace sounds seductive, but peace expunges the "I" because it does not depict an accuracy of experience.

In postcolonial terms, literary critic Alison Donnell insists that we must stop encouraging just such voicelessness because "voicelessness not only condemns writers to dismal and oppressed self-defining narratives but burdens readers with a baggage of unresolved cultural sensitivities, and critics with a tireless round of congratulations and careful critiques" (102). Donnell argues that to read postcolonial texts that feature mothers and daughters as uniformly allegorical of colonizer/colonized relationships is narrow and prescriptive. She argues that to read all silences in postcolonial texts such as *Annie John* as uniformly reflective of the dominance of the English language in colonial situations is repetitive and lacking in complexity. Donnell critiques Kincaid harshly for writing texts that can be easily misread as postcolonially allegorical and postcolonially voiceless. I read Kincaid's texts as more complex in that she does transgress the typical allegorical narrative by rendering Annie specifically. Kincaid, Chute, and Allison successfully enact narrative girl "I"s who not only speak to colonialism, but also about the atrocities, the vibrant sexualities, and the lived experiences of girls. The girl narrators in these texts are not merely allegorical figures of wider political issues (and, therefore, permitted to have been endowed with surprising wisdom); they are also ordinary girls with unsurprising wisdom.

If you want to hear some unsurprising wisdom from a girl who accurately tells what it is like to "sleep" with her daddy, then listen to Earlene Bean. Carolyn Chute published *The Beans of Egypt, Maine* in 1985. Earlene Bean, the girl we watch grow from seven years old into early adulthood, invites us into her life through an "I" who admittedly has nothing to do but look out from her prefabricated ranch home at the most rugged people alive in Egypt, Maine: the Beans (3). When we meet her, she already knows about discrete differences in levels of poverty. She knows how to inflict a judgmental gaze upon others, and she knows what it feels like to be gazed upon. Earlene grows up to marry one Bean, and by the end of the novel, she seems about to marry another. She only ever looks at Beans; thus she becomes what she has always already gazed upon. She becomes the "I" we met at the beginning of the text. In an interview with Ellen Lesser, Carolyn Chute expresses frustration at critics' and readers' inability to understand Earlene's non-upwardly mobile sensibilities: "People talk about breaking the cycle and escaping all this crap. Escaping what? Your family? Your roots? . . . How come we have to leave our homeland and our people to have a good life?" (177). Chute argues that staying with one's people is not an innocent nor an ignorant position, that it actually is a decision.

Fine and McPherson claim that young girl bodies constitute "unclaimed territories" (180), territories that adults battle to claim as psychological or literary sites of lost innocence. Adults either invest these body sites with a type of mourning for lost innocence and too early knowledge of femaleness as constraint and liability (Orenstein xiv), or we acknowledge the body site as one of astute awareness of its cultural position. Either case forces us to recognize the so-called innocent girl "I" as a site of desire and nostalgia. In other words, we, living and reading adults, participate in teaching and enforcing lessons of girl silence in our efforts to insist on their bodies as sites of innocence (Orenstein xxvii).

In the opening pages of *The Beans of Egypt, Maine,* Chute writes a scene that many critics have read as an incestuous one based on assumptions about the position of Earlene's body. Earlene's grandmother discovers that Earlene's father sleeps with his daughter, and the grandmother quickly decides that something wretched has been occurring. In response to her accusations, Earlene's "I" narrates: "Daddy's eyes go wild. 'But Mumma! It don't mean nuthin'. She's just a baby!' 'I ain't a BABY!' I scream" (6). Chute makes way for the enactment of multiple "unclaimed territories" by rendering this scene. Within the text, the grandmother claims Earlene's body as innocent (although she will then punish Earlene for having "slept" with her father); Daddy claims Earlene's body as that of a baby; and Earlene emphatically reclaims her own body as not BABY. Outside the text, from the readers' points of view, Earlene's body becomes the now familiar territory of incest victim. Carolyn Chute expresses astonishment at reading Earlene's body in this way: "I think a lot of people just assumed it was incest because these characters are poor, and that made me really mad, too" (Lesser 171). Trusting a girl "I" narrator means that we trust what she claims is going on and what she claims is not going on. Carolyn Chute asks us to resist any sense that Earlene is innocent of what occurs between her and her father.

Earlene is not a baby and not a wimp. When Earlene's Dad enters her room, even after having been confronted by the grandmother, Chute wants us to believe what Earlene's "I" tells us: "In the middle of the night Daddy finally comes in my room. . . .We sleep" (8). Allowing the girl "I" narrator to claim her own body and her own territory means that we must believe that

Earlene and her Daddy simply sleep together. Hillary Carlip writes that it's tragic what girls have been through (2). I argue that it's equally tragic to assume and enforce innocence. Earlene Bean knows a sleeping father when she sees one. Chute asks us to trust that she would know an incestuous one.

If you want to understand how a twelve-year-old girl survives incest, survives the mother who cannot love her, and develops masochistic sexual desires, then Bone can voice her truth. Dorothy Allison published *Bastard Out of Carolina* in 1992. Ruth Anne Boatwright (Bone), the twelve-year-old girl "I" narrator of *Bastard Out of Carolina,* introduces herself to us with incredible surety: ". . .and there I was—certified a bastard by the state of Carolina" (3). No insecurity, no exclamation. Ruth Anne knows who the culture says she is, and by the end of the novel, she knows who she has been all along: "I wasn't old. I would be thirteen in a few weeks. I was already who I was going to be" (309).

Unlike Earlene, Ruth Anne is an incest survivor. Part of claiming her "I" is acknowledging and telling this part of her story. Dorothy Allison has suffered criticism due to Bone's recognition of her sexuality and her sexual experiences. In an interview with Michael Rowe, Allison describes this aspect of the critical response to her work: "These people totally flipped out . . . probably because I was acknowledging that this little girl, who is a victim of sexual abuse, also had sexual desire. And that her desire is profoundly masochistic" (8). When asked why she thinks that readers become upset in the face of child sexuality, Allison says, "I think because it's anarchy, and probably more perverse because it's raw" (8). Allison views the sexual territory to which young girls would lay claim (should adults permit it) as far from innocent. These knowledgeable, noninnocent girls are deliberate constructions.

In *Two or Three Things I Know For Sure,* Dorothy Allison talks about the deliberateness of crafting a girl "I" narrator for the purpose of capturing story. She would articulate girl "I"s for her sisters in order to "make story out of us" (1). Furthermore, Allison writes that she concocted these girlhood storytelling "I"s with incredible awareness of exactly what she was doing: "I walked, I talked—story-talked, out loud—assuming identities I made up" (2). She talks about remaking the "I" as a deliberate task undertaken in the lived experience of a girl's life; this ability to craft and recapture such an "I" also eases into her art.

Always the sense exists that the girl "I" has much to say, but that cultural occlusion and insistence on innocence have erased a place for this saying. Allison insists that she carries a girl child inside her, one who needs voice, one who is "always eleven years old" (71). For Allison, telling these stories from this deliberate girl "I" perspective is an act of love, self-love, and love of others: "Two or three things I know for sure and one of them is that telling the story all the way through is an act of love" (90). The choice not to impersonate an innocent girl is an act of trust and love that may not always be appreciated or reciprocated by readers because reader desire has been set up as a desire for innocence on the part of girl "I"s.

As readers and as adults, we desperately want our girls to have innocent lives. Our adult desire for demonstrated innocence or at least articulated innocence is an immense pressure on girls. In an interview with Carolyn E. Megan, Dorothy Allison explains why she has Bone express an angry "I." She claims that she, herself, was unable to express anger until she was in her twenties. Bone's anger emerges at thirteen, which enables her to claim an "I" and to hold others responsible for their actions (73). Girls do not live innocently, and they do not narrate the world innocently when they are allowed to narrate. Furthermore, they will point to the lack of innocence in others.

Kincaid, Chute and Allison provide their girl "I"s with voices that seem strangely adult to us. These writers give voice to girls who always had to sound like adult women. This type of ventriloquism serves to recapture simultaneous agency for the young girl and for the adult woman (Donnell 113-14). Readers typically enforce an enactment of innocence that discourages writers from allowing girl "I"s to tell what they know. In some of Carol Gilligan's more recent research, she notes that a young adolescent girl is "cautious, more aware of what it means to know what she knows, more willing to silence herself rather than to risk loss of relationships and public disagreement" (81). As readers, we often succumb to the idea that girls with knowledge must either be silenced or disbelieved. We label them "untrustworthy narrators," and we doubt the stories they tell.

Any girl with the wisdom and the courage to tell a story seems, according to the codes of innocence, to be impersonating an adult woman: "to be without the conventional story of female becoming—can be a deeply frightening experience, since it is to be without a model and thus to potentially be on one's own, confronting the responsibility for authoring one's life" (Gilligan 72). Kincaid, Chute, and Allison refuse to permit this storylessness. They subvert the conventional story of female becoming and claim space for anti-impersonation in contemporary fiction. Donnell calls for a new agency in fiction, a change in literature that mimics a change in perspective about innocence. Lyn Brown, who researches self-authorization as a form of resistance in girls, suggests that "For a girl . . . to tell a story true to her rich and varied experiences of childhood relationship—to stay with what she knows in the face of pressure to not know—would be to engage in an act of resistance, an act of moral courage in the face of potential risk to her body and her psyche" (84). Chute, Allison, and Kincaid enact this risk for the young girl "I" narrators. The girl "I" is a deliberate, and a trustworthy, choice. The girl narrator of contemporary literature defies our definitions of twentieth-century fragmentation and alienation. She occupies a self-aware "I" who speaks of the past, present, and future as if it were always already occurring. This girl "ain't no friggin' little wimp," not in the face of rape, not in the face of incest, not in the face of poverty, not in the face of her own developing desires, nor in the face of leaving a country. Dorothy Allison expresses astonishment about the resilience and fragility of these kids: "there are incredible myths in this society about kids. In this society we're always talking as if they are more fragile and ignoring where they are strong" (79). The girl "I" narrators of contemporary fiction exhibit just such resilience. They grow into the people they were in their youths. Each knows her "I" at an early age, and by offering readers her story, each claims the non-innocent girl "I" as worthy of trust and of love.

Notes

1. Fine and McPherson claim that young girl bodies constitute "unclaimed territories" (180) in so far as "we," adults, are all battling to claim these bodies either as psychological sites of lost innocence or literary sites of voices of lived experience. They state, "At this moment in social history, when the tensions of race, class, and gender couldn't be in more dramatic relief, social anxieties load onto the bodies of adolescent women. . . . Struggles for social control attach to these unclaimed territories" (180).
2. In Alison Donnell's essay "She Ties Her Tongue: The Problems of Cultural Paralysis in Postcolonial Criticism," she argues that the naive child's speaking voice is a fake. She explores the politics and the ethics of postcolonial texts by reading "what lies beneath" the false surface. She claims that such a voice is a "consummate work of ventriloquism that deploys a whole series of voices in order to debate the values and limitations of the cultural discourses and positions associated with postcolonialism" (107).
3. In Carolyn Heilbrun's *Writing a Woman's Life,* she discusses the concept of "female impersonation" as a role that young women enact and a discourse in which young women partake in order to comply with the culture's expectations of who young females are. In other words, girls impersonate females.

They know who they are supposed to be and how they are supposed to speak, and they do so.

4. In Fine and McPherson's essay, "Over Dinner: Feminism and Adolescent Bodies," the authors discuss a series of dinners they shared with adolescent girls in order to "hear" the adolescent girl voices. However, they realized that in the discussions "no one of us told the whole truth. We all 'occluded the truth' in cultured ways. The conversation was playful and filled with the mobile positionings of all of us women" (201).

SEVEN

Coming-of-Age in the Snare of History

Jamaica Kincaid's The Autobiography of My Mother

DIANE SIMMONS

The literary career of West Indian author Jamaica Kincaid can be seen as one long meditation upon the way in which the young woman manages to forge a life in the face of colonial oppression, how she manages to stay psychically alive when, as Craig Tapping has put it, "the self is faced with extinction by the very processes of acculturation which all who nurture the child commend" (53). In Kincaid's earlier work, her girls Annie and Lucy still believe they can free themselves from the power relationships into which they were born. They still seek a form of love and nurture—even if it is only self-love and self-nurture—that does not, finally, erase them, replacing the self with a set of characteristics that define the deepest levels of subjugation. But with Kincaid's novel, *The Autobiography of My Mother,* Kincaid's girl no longer hopes for the freedom to build an authentic self. In a work that reviewers have called "inhuman," and "almost unbearable" (Schine), "bitter" and "repell[ant]" (Kakutani), Kincaid portrays a world in which the coming-of-age girl is hopelessly trapped in history. There is nowhere to turn but to revenge, nothing to nurture but a heart that is cold and closed.

Though colonial oppression has always been at the heart of Kincaid's work and the primary influence upon her growing girl, it was possible to read her first, coming-of-age novel, *Annie John,* as a statement of universal adolescent malaise with Kincaid's Annie as a black, West Indian version of J. D. Salinger's Holden Caulfield. *Annie John* could also be compared to coming-of-age stories told by other West Indian women writers, such as Merle Hodge in *Crick Crack, Monkey*. In all of these works adolescence both disrupts the certainties of childhood and challenges the compromises of adulthood. Even Kincaid's early work, however, departs from the conventions of adolescent angst that Salinger portrays, suggesting that for West Indian girls coming-of-age in the 1940s and '50s, the onset of maturity is particularly difficult to negotiate.

In Salinger's book, maturity is presented as hypocrisy, a "phoniness" that allows adults to pursue success and status without recognizing that they have lost their souls in the process. Though Holden has the luxury of rejecting the adult world, at least for a time, it is always there waiting for his embrace, waiting for him to take his place in the successful and confident—if "phony"—world of upper-middle-class white males. For him, the route to successful, acceptable maturity is never really blocked. For Annie John however, and for Tee, Hodge's young protagonist, the route is not blocked; rather there seems to be no such route. For these black, West Indian girls, acceptable, successful maturity appears not to exist.

Annie John comes of age under her mother's rule, which mirrors the attitudes of English colonial rulers. Here the child is not asked, as in Salinger's book, merely to submerge the individual point of view in order to negotiate successfully the compromises of adulthood. Rather, the girl is required to understand that for a person like herself there can be no individual point of view. What Annie's mother, Annie senior, senses, if she does not consciously know it, is that any authentic point of view held by black Antiguans would be so antithetical to the British beliefs by which colonial society is ordered, that the two cannot be allowed to coexist. The colonial schoolchildren in Annie's world are not taught, as Holden is, the value of sophisticated hypocrisy, but something quite different, to "proudly [witness] against themselves from a British perspective" (Tiffin 32). They can successfully mature in this environment only by defining themselves as eternal bad children, forever inferior to their British rulers.

Annie senses that in coming-of-age she begins a struggle to avoid the death of her spirit, signaled by her obsession with death and particularly the death of little girls. For Annie, however, death is not associated directly with colonial power, but with her own mother, who is often present when someone dies, and who seems to carry death on her hands. For, as she copes with her child's impending maturity, the mother appears to have internalized Kipling's characterization of colonized peoples, seen in his poem "The White Man's Burden," as "half devil and half child." It follows that if Annie is no longer part child, she must be all devil. The mother who had adored her perfect, innocent infant, now sees the growing girl as a thief, a liar, and slut who must, for her crimes, be expelled from the paradise of love into the living death of a loveless hell. Earlier Annie's mother had spent a great deal of time looking over and caressing the tiny garments and other mementos of her daughter's life, a process that is, for Annie, a feast of love. But this feast ends with puberty as Annie grows tall, develops a different smell, and finds herself thinking her own thoughts. Now, rather than luxuriating in a celebration of self, the girl is sent out to numerous lessons designed to make her a "young lady," an effort which the mother is certain will fail.

In *Crick Crack, Monkey,* Hodge portrays the same change in the way the child is treated as she moves from infancy to girlhood. While Kincaid shows the mother changing, turning on the girl in betrayal, Hodge splits the maternal function between two different aunts. The girl, Tee, is taken from the happiness of her early childhood, where she lives with her loving, self-knowing Aunt Tantie, and put as an adolescent to live with her anxious, striving-to-be-white Aunt Beatrice. Like the mother of Annie's adolescence, Aunt Beatrice seems to know neither herself nor the child. She assesses value in terms of "lightness" of skin, and the ability to emulate British speech and manners. While Annie's mother accuses her daughter of being "sluttish," that is adhering to the stereotype, internalized by the mother, that colonized peoples have the uncontrollable sexual drives of animals, Aunt Beatrice's favorite epithet is "niggeryness," by which she means any characteristics that have been attributed to blacks by colonial authority. Tee tries to cope with the charge of "niggeryness" and the requirement that she be as British as possible, by inventing a double, Helen, an English girl exactly her age and height. So perfect is this Helen, that once invented she is perceived by Tee as her true self, "the Proper Me. And me, I was her shadow hovering about in incompleteness"(Hodge 62). For her part, Annie tries to deal with her mother's sense that she is dirty and bad, by playing out this role as thoroughly as she can. With the aid of the wild Red Girl, she attempts to be as bad as her mother seems to think she is. For neither girl, however, do these efforts wipe out the sorrow of loss.

While both Kincaid and Hodge write of a lost paradise, and while both reject the mother figures who seem bent upon turning the paradise of childhood into a hellish adulthood, both, at the same time, find a source of hope and strength in magical grandmother figures, who continue to inhabit a still-enchanted "African cosmology" (Timothy 242). These grandmothers know what and who they are, are comfortable in their skins, and have not been hypnotized by what Kincaid has elsewhere called the "fairy tale of how we met [the English], your right to do the things you did, how beautiful you were, are, and always will be" (*Small Place* 42). In *Crick Crack, Monkey,* Tee's grandmother, Ma, who lives up in the hills, inhabits "an enchanted country" that calls up "the days when Brar Anancy and Brar Leopard and all others roamed the earth outsmarting each other" (14). The grandmother has offered the girl another identity than that of "niggeryness," on one hand, or of becoming an "incomplete" English girl on the other. Rather she gives Tee the hope that she will inherit her own indomitable spirit (19). A similar figure is Annie's Ma Chess, who still knows ancient magic. Through a symbolic rebirthing, she cures Annie of the mysterious illness that has been produced by the grief of adolescence. Recovering, Annie still feels the loss of the childhood joy, but is no longer paralyzed, and can begin her search for another world (*Annie John* 126).

At the end of *The Catcher in the Rye,* Holden is seen debating whether to "apply himself" in school. The option of joining the adult world is still very much open and beckoning to him. Both stories of West Indian girlhood, however, close with the young protagonists painfully turning their backs on everything they have ever known. Annie, toward the close of *Annie John,* has the clear sense that she must leave the world as she knows it. She, like Tee, departs for England, both girls leaving with a sense of great loss. For Tee, everything in her childhood home has become "unrecognizable, pushing me out" (110). For Annie, the sensation of leaving is one of emptiness: The ship bound for England "made an unexpected sound, as if a vessel filled with liquid had been placed on its side and now was slowly emptying out" (148). Neither girl sees this departure as a triumph or even an opportunity, but as a necessary relief from the pressures of colonial society. Neither girl has a vision of what will be accomplished in the new setting; there are no particular hopes or dreams. Still both authors allow the reader to hope that the girls will manage to free themselves in a new environment, and that in their freedom an authentic self may be discovered.

However, in Kincaid's novel *The Autobiography of My Mother,* set on the Caribbean island of Dominica, there is no such hope. The possibility of magical rebirth, of paradise regained, is only a cruel hoax, one through which Kincaid's girl, Xuela, sees with her earliest awareness. In *Annie John,* the child is often betrayed by those who seem to provide nurture, who seem to love selflessly. Still, nurture and love may be found, if only in the magical—and perhaps imaginary—figure of Ma Chess. For Annie, further, there is the hope of beginning again in a new environment. But in Kincaid's *The Autobiography of My Mother,* there is no escape and no saving magic. There is an angelic mother, but she dies at Xuela's birth, symbolizing the world of loss that, Kincaid suggests, is the black, West Indian child's birthright. With the mother dies any hope that the child might experience selfless care and love. All that remains of such love is a recurring dream, and even here love is painfully and ultimately elusive. In the dream Xuela, standing below, sees her mother eternally descending a ladder, but never arriving.

Motherless, Xuela experiences from birth a brutal world in which there is no genuine nurture, no selfless love. Here every apparent invitation to love and trust is actually an invitation to be possessed and used. For Xuela that which masquerades as love and that which the girl knows to be hate are so intertwined that though she "tries to tell the difference between the two [she] cannot, because often they wear so much the same face"(22). For her, love and hate are, horribly, the same thing. While Annie believes, at least for a time, in the "paradise" in which she lived (25), Xuela always knows that she was born into a "false paradise"(32). The hope that one will find the freedom to know the true self, no longer exists in "the prison of history" that is Xuela's universe. Kincaid's girl is completely trapped because she sees that in this prison her deepest self has been formed in response to the needs of those in power. Even the child's first words demonstrate the way in which everything about her, even her innermost being, has been determined by British power: "That the first words I said," Xuela remarks, "were in the language of a people I would never like or love is not now a mystery to me; everything in my life, good or bad, to which I am inextricably bound is a source of pain"(7).

In such a world there is no hope that the individual will magically transcend her situation. Now the self-loving, self-knowing guardian grandmother of *Annie John* is replaced by the brutal, self-hating Ma Eunice, with whom the child is put to live. Ma Eunice treats Xuela as she does her own children, which is to say with the thoughtless cruelty that "in a place like this . . . is the only real inheritance" (5). Kindness and nurture, Kincaid says, simply do not exist in the colonial environment. All are caught in the "manichean allegory" of colonial societies in which, as Abdul R. JanMohamed has described, "the dominant model of power- and interest-relations . . . is the manichean opposition between the putative superiority of the European and the supposed inferiority of the native" (82). If those of European descent are noble and powerful, intelligent and good, then those of African descent must necessarily be the opposite, and must learn to treat themselves and one another as such.

Ma Eunice, in her own humble way, plays her part in this manichean scenario, seeing everything in her own world as despicable, everything English as superior, even divine. For her the adored "fairy tale" of England is represented by her prized possession, a china plate with a picture painted on it of beautiful fields "filled with grass and flowers in the most tender shades" and a sun "that shone but did not burn bright" (8). The picture is labeled, "Heaven." "Of course," Xuela says, "it was not a picture of heaven at all; it was a picture of the English countryside idealized. . ." (9).

Ma Eunice is not an entirely unknown figure to readers of Kincaid, as she may be read as a coarser, simpler version of the maternal figure in both "Girl," (*At the Bottom of the River*) Kincaid's first published story, and in *Annie John*. These earlier maternal figures insist that the girl become a "young lady," which is to say she they must become as much like an English girl as possible. In both "Girl" and *Annie John,* the girl struggles to comply with the mother's desire to play out through her child her own fantasy of being English and perfect. But Annie senior will never be able to see her girl child in this light, for the mother is in thrall to another, even more powerful fantasy furnished by the English, that of the oversexed, inherently uncivilizable African. Annie's mother, therefore, is certain that no matter how the girl is taught, she will end up a "slut," thus smashing the image of English perfection that the mother is struggling to create.

Ma Eunice has none of the beauty, grace, and commanding presence of Annie's mother; nor does she have the capacity to care and hope for the child that Annie's mother possesses during the short period of her daughter's infancy. Ma Eunice does not manage, as does Annie's mother at least to bolster her own self-image by projecting her negative feelings onto the growing girl. Rather Ma Eunice is mindlessly, totally trapped in the English worldview, despising everything about herself and her environment, adoring, with animal stupidity, the heavenly England painted on a plate. And no longer is there a moment of grace for Kincaid's girl. While Annie as a small child adores her powerful mother, unable to fathom what is to come, Xuela is never under the illusion that the invitation to love can be trusted. She hates the false, fantasy English heaven as completely as Ma Eunice loves it, and, in her first independent act, breaks the cherished plate. Xuela, with no hope of real love, now instinctively refuses false substitutes, smashing the first gorgeous representation of false, entrapping love she sees.

The loss of the plate throws Ma Eunice into a frenzy of grief and rage. She weeps, curses, and then punishes the unrepentant girl by making her kneel in the broiling sun of the stone heap, holding bricks aloft in each hand. In this she forces the girl into her own vision of the world, a place where only humiliation and harshness remain once the heavenly fantasy of England is taken away.

Unlike Annie, who is grieved at the sudden harshness of the world that comes with puberty, Xuela uses the occasion of her punishment to demonstrate how thoroughly she understands the fact that in her environment any seduction—in this case the chance to adore a fantasy England—is always part of a bid for power. And we see Xuela begin to grasp the concept that once one develops an unsentimental understanding of the relationship between "love" and power, then even the weak and oppressed may use the offer of love as a trap. Xuela sees that she too may exchange the powerlessness of subjugation for the power to dominate, if on a very small scale. For, during her punishment, Xuela "falls in love" with three land turtles and later when she is released she captures and cages the turtles so that they are "completely dependent on [her] for their existence" (11). When they refuse to come at her call and otherwise fail to obey her wishes she "teaches them a lesson" by leaving them without air and water. When she returns, they are dead.

But Xuela has only begun by destroying the plate and killing the turtles. In her encounter with the La Battes, the couple with whom she is next put to live in early adolescence, Xuela most chillingly comes to understand what she must do to survive in this world. From the La Battes, another set of stand-ins for Xuela's missing parents, the girl experiences two grotesque parodies of love. By night the husband takes the girl into the room where he counts his money and wordlessly "makes love" to her; by day the wife treats her tenderly, apparently supplying the kindness and nurture that the girl so needs. For a moment it seems that Kincaid might be allowing the existence of something like true maternal care, and also the idea that those who have victimized may unite to help one another. But soon this too is revealed as a trap, for the woman, locked in a loveless marriage, only hopes to use Xuela to produce the child she herself has not been able to bear.

Understanding this, when Xuela becomes pregnant, she runs away to an abortionist. With this act, carried out in great pain, Xuela demonstrates to herself that she is proof against even the must fundamental of seductions, the invitation to love one's own innocent and helpless child. She knows that this child is the product of yet another power play; even more painfully she knows herself as one unable to truly love. For once, though, Xuela appreciates the enormity of what she has done, as she feels herself "eternally emptying out" (82). After destroying her own child she is changed, having demonstrated to herself her own ruthless will. She sees now that she has the ability to "carr[y her] own life in [her] own hands" (83). In this she is the tragic opposite of Annie, who managed to move forward, not after a child is killed, but after she herself has been symbolically reborn.

But however painful the process of emptying oneself of the hope and the desire for love, Kincaid here says it is better than succumbing to the cruel trap that a belief in love's paradise inevitably springs. Though Xuela indicts everyone in her world, including herself, with the inability to love selflessly, and the willingness to exploit those too innocent to know the score, Kincaid at the same time understands that all of these individuals have themselves been entrapped in the colonial embrace, have allowed themselves to be smitten by the image of a "fairy-tale" England, have been completely formed by the British attitude toward them, and have come to despise their own world and all those within it. Out of this self-hatred, Kincaid suggests, comes an utter inability to love selflessly. Rather every relation is, at root, an attempt to mimic the colonial rulers, to entice, to ensnare, to dominate, to enhance one's own sense of power and importance by taking advantage of those who are innocent or weak. Unable to get at the English, who are, Xuela says, "beyond our influence completely" (48), the black Dominicans can only vent their grief, rage, and sense of deprivation on one another: "to mistrust each other was just one of many feelings we had for each other, all of them the opposite of love, all of them standing in the place of love. It was as if we were in competition with each other for a secret prize, and we were afraid that someone else would get it; any expression of love, then would not be sincere, for love might give someone else the advantage" (48). Xuela, in her refusal to believe in the possibility of love, is fundamentally the same as those around her. She is only different in that, having never experienced even the semblance of the first, maternal care, she does not have even this memory to cling to. No one in this environment is able to love or be loved; Xuela is only different in that she sees this fact with eyes that are unclouded by nostalgia, fantasy, or illusion.

What then is life for the girl who renounces every hope of love and all possibility of nurture—whether received or given—and is confident in her ability to make the renunciation stick? How do you manage, as Xuela declares she will, to make a life for yourself in "an atmosphere of no love"? With whom or what do you join, when every connection will inevitably prove to be a betrayal?

Unlike Annie John and Hodge's Tee, Xuela does not leave for England. She understands that there are no new, different situations. In England, as well as the Caribbean, all are caught in the endless trap of history. And so, Xuela, acknowledging that the trap has closed and rusted shut, takes the only self-protective act available to her. She accepts the terms of her environment but manages, by an immense act of hard-hearted will, to reverse those terms. If every relationship is one of power, she will be the one on top.

Proof against love's illusion but expert in how that illusion works, Xuela is in a position to use another's desire for love as a weapon against him. Now it is the Englishman, Philip, a man for whom Xuela does not for a moment imagine feeling anything, who is ensnared, and who loses everything to a cold-hearted seduction. Like subjected peoples before him, Philip succumbs easily to Xuela's inexorable will to power. From the moment Xuela seeks to seduce him, he is lost, imprisoned by the "sound of [her] name," as those colonized have been imprisoned by the name of England. Enthralled, he is "not himself" and "never would be" when he is with her (153); he has been "erased" in the way, Kincaid has suggested, colonized peoples are erased by their rulers ("Seeing England" 14). With this marriage, Kincaid paints a tragic portrait of the ongoing relationship between the descendants of Europeans and the descendants of African whom they have enslaved and colonized. The colonial relationship and the legacy of slavery dictate the inner sense of self for both ruled and ruler. Turning the tables of domination is only a cold comfort, as both groups are still tragically cut off from themselves, locked into the destructive terms of their mutual history.

Xuela has chosen her time well, for Philip is a degraded version of the English conqueror, ripe to be conquered himself. Historically he is the victor, but he is also the dispossessed; an inheritance of conquest has placed him "at the end of the world" (148). With nothing to do but to play the assigned role of victor in a scenario of domination, he has become sterile. He, surprisingly like those who play the role of vanquished in the same scenario, is cut off from any authentic self. He is "empty of real life and energy, used up, too tired even to give himself pleasure" (211). For, as JanMohamed has written of European imperialists in general, Philip himself has been reduced to a term in a hierarchical system: "By subjugating the native, the European settler is able to compel the Other's recognition of him, and in the process, allow his own identity to become deeply dependent on his position as master" (85). So dependent is Philip upon this role that it has blotted out other aspects of himself. In the decline of imperialism he is man without a future, only a past. He, without fully realizing it, is no longer an actor, only a tired, passive place-holder in a drama, the terms of which were set long ago. Seeing that his identity has come to be based solely on his position in an artificial hierarchy, Xuela understands that in defeating her, he has defeated himself, and that "in my defeat lies the beginning of my great revenge" (216).

Understanding how fundamentally a man like Philip has come to depend upon those like herself, Xuela realizes that she has the power to dominate him, to take him even further away from everything he knows, moving him into her territory "into the mountains, into the land where my mother and the people she was of were born" (206). There Xuela, who may be read as a cruel and vengeful version of the magical Ma Chess, causes the Englishman to become utterly disoriented, stripping him of all that has formerly made him himself, reducing him to a degraded version of his former self so that he will never find the will to escape her trap. In so doing she reverse the terms of engagement between those of African descent and those of English. As black Dominicans have been taught to adore a magical Englishness they can never attain, Xuela denies the white Philip the love she has made him crave, denying him her magical self upon which, like a child, he now depends: "He grew to live for the sound of my footsteps, so often I would walk without making a sound; he loved the sound of my voice, so for days I would not utter a word" (218).

Philip, who cannot quite grasp that he is no longer in charge, still struggles ineffectually to organize and control his world. He cultivates odd plants, captures and observes animals, organizes and reorganizes his books. But, like Xuela, he has nowhere to go, no possibility of escape or rebirth. British colonial power has stolen first home, then freedom, then self-esteem from the descendants of African slaves; now Xuela takes these same things from Philip, denying him every avenue back to himself. His attempts to recall history do not bring him peace, for now "he lives in a world in which he could not speak the language" and Xuela, who must translate for him, "blocks off his entrance into all the worlds he had come to know" (224). When he begins to reminisce about the England of his childhood, Xuela cuts him short, ordering him onto his knees to please her sexually, always demonstrating that he exists only to serve her, and that even a nostalgic re-creation of identity will be crushed. Thus stolen from himself, he becomes "all the children" Xuela "did not allow to be born" (224). For she is sterile, too; her revenge upon him, her destruction of his world, is her only offspring.

And so, Xuela says, they live together in the "spell of history," which neither can escape though both long to do so. At the same time Xuela refuses to acknowledge—though this truth occurs to her at times—that he, too, is human, for to do so would be to cause her to feel too much anger. If he and the people he came from are human, she says, "where would that leave me and all that I come from?" (220). It is, Kincaid suggests, easier to see the English as monsters than to try to untangle the more complex web of events that have brought English and African together. Further, to acknowledge the Englishman's humanity won't undo the spell of history; rather, locked by history into a rigidly hierarchical system, she can only hope to turn the tables. History, Xuela says, will not allow them both to be happy at the same time, as it has dictated that white and black are on different sides, and that when one wins the other loses. Philip dies a "lonely man, far away from the place where he was born, far from the woman who might have loved him" (206). He has been reduced, in short, to the situation in which Xuela has found herself from the moment of her birth. At the end of Xuela's own life her body is "withering like fruit drying on the vine" but not "rotting like a fruit that has been picked and lies uneaten on a dirty plate" (225). In this scene there is some, sad triumph. She has not really lived, has never managed to love or be loved. Though she has aged she has not matured. Her only felt accomplishment is that, at least, she has not allowed herself to be used. Still, as she looks at the life she and Philip have led, and by extension all colonial relationships, she must ask, "Did so much sadness ever enclose two people?" (224).

In a vision that is unusually bleak, even among those who write about racial and colonial oppression, Kincaid seeks to trap her readers in the hell of a world based entirely upon power relations, refusing to offer the notes of hope and uplift found in her own earlier works. She does not create characters who rise above the harshness of their situations or who bond together for mutual nurture and support. Rather, Kincaid insists that all are trapped in a Machiavellian world of cutthroat power relationships, where absolutely the only way to avoid being dominated and destroyed is to dominate and destroy others. There are no new environments, Kincaid insists; there is no saving magic. Rather the maturing girl must face the hard facts of her history, and stand and fight, taking power in a world in which the only relations are power relations. But there is no joy in reversing this equation. A world made up of hierarchical relationships ensures only sadness and sterility for all.

A key to the apparent shift in Kincaid's thinking may be found in her reaction to reviews of her scathing 1988 essay *A Small Place,* in which she first speaks bluntly of racism and the aftermath of colonialism in her native Antigua. In an interview she described how reviewers were put off by its "anger," *The New Yorker* refusing to take the piece though it had published everything else she had written. She noted that one *New York Times* reviewer lamented that the "charm" of *Annie John* was nowhere to be found in the new work. This response pleased Kincaid, she said, for "when people say you are charming you are in deep trouble. I realized in writing that book that the first step to claiming yourself is anger" (Perry 132-33). With *The Autobiography of My Mother,* Kincaid has renounced charm, and appears to have decided never again to allow white readers to enjoy the West Indian exotica of her books, to skim past the true situation of the totally disenfranchised, like the oblivious tourists she shows vacationing in the Caribbean in *A Small Place.* Nor does Kincaid have much patience with what might be called black nostalgia, expressing her scorn for the Antiguans who, ignoring their present lack of opportunity, "speak of slavery as if it had been a pageant full of large ships sailing the blue water," which, despite its horrors, suddenly came to a glorious end with "emancipation" (*Small Place* 55). And she does not associate herself with any sort of back-to-Africa philosophy, declaring:

> I'm very much against people denying their history. There was an attempt, successful, by English colonization to make a certain kind of person out of me and it was a success. It worked; it really worked. . . . I do not spend my present time trying to undo it. I do not for instance spend my life now attempting to have some true African heritage. My history is that I came from African people who were enslaved and dominated by European British people. And that is it. (Simmons, unpublished interview)

In an interview given during the time she was writing *The Autobiography of My Mother,* Kincaid cast some light on how this process might work:

> I've now reached the point where I feel some sympathy . . . for the powerful, because I now can see how things change . . . the flux in human history. . . . This always tempers or should temper any feeling you have when meting out justice. That could be you. A sense of identification. . . if it's lost in human communication, that's where trouble begins, if you can never identify with anyone in the other position whether you are at the bottom looking up or the top looking down. (Simmons, unpublished interview)

This sad book, then, need not be read as an act of hopelessness. Rather it seems that Kincaid has a positive purpose for seeking to trap readers in this painful scenario. For she believes that it is only when we all—black and white—fully face the trap of history that continues to limit our understanding and our lives that we may finally understand that we are all equally ensnared. Only then may we begin to find a way out.

EIGHT

Subversive Storytelling

The Construction of Lesbian Girlhood through Fantasy and Fairy Tale in Jeanette Winterson's Oranges Are Not the Only Fruit

ISABEL C. ANIEVAS GAMALLO

Jeanette Winterson's *Oranges Are Not the Only Fruit* illustrates the subversive way in which contemporary women writers use storytelling to make sense of their own or other women's lives. Winterson's novel is explicitly about what it is like to grow up as a white lesbian while defying the legacies of expectation of a working-class Evangelical family in England. But it is also, and obviously, about storytelling as a way to relate to prevailing cultural ideologies and to achieve self-understanding and self-explanation in/and/or against them. Both the subject matter and the structure of Winterson's novel highlight the role of stories in the literary, as well as in the personal day-to-day, construction of girlhood. As a novel of girlhood, development, and growth, *Oranges* inscribes itself in the literary tradition of Bildungsroman, but its bold and original construction of lesbian girlhood defiantly problematizes and rewrites the genre, both in its content and its form. Winterson's novel subverts the ideological implications of the traditional Bildungsroman not only by questioning conventional images of girlhood and femininity, but also by challenging the cultural construction of heterosexuality and, ultimately, by providing alternative models of female identity. On a formal level, *Oranges* also departs from the traditional genre of formation and growth by emphasizing the role of storytelling in our personal and collective arrangement of experience, and by interweaving magical and fabulous narratives into the main realistic plot while overimposing a biblical framework on Winterson's first-person autobiographical account.

Winterson not only rewrites a literary genre that has been traditionally dedicated to the construction of boyhood *and* girlhood, she consistently challenges and relocates woman's position in the patriarchal realm of language. In Lacanian terms, this means that her work can be interpreted as an attempt to renegotiate the female subject situation in the male-oriented symbolic order and, consequently, to reformulate the young girl's process of socialization. French theorist Jacques Lacan argued that women's access to the symbolic realm of language is hindered and difficult. For Lacan, the social construction of gender is determined in the process of language acquisition. Therefore, language is what identifies us as gendered subjects, since it is precisely by entering what he calls "the symbolic order" (which inevitably privileges the masculine over the feminine) that we acquire identity, subjectivity and sexual difference. The "Law of the Father" will force the girl into the symbolic realm (694), where the "phallus" is the privileged signifier (692) and where, hereafter, she is doomed to become the absolute "other" (732). Following his insights, French feminists such as Luce Irigaray have persistently denounced the fact that women have no access to language except through and within "masculine" systems of representation (Waelti-Walters 88). Winterson's novel, however, exemplifies the ongoing process of female reappropriation of the symbolic realm that we are witnessing in contemporary women's literature. In her literary construction of lesbian girlhood, Winterson's storytelling engages in a literary project of self-creation and self-explanation that boldly rewrites the position of the female heroine in the patriarchal realm of language. She explores the bounds of traditional genres and crisscrosses the frontiers between autobiography, Bildungsroman, fantasy, romance, and fairy tale. Her risqué experiment convinces us that a young girl's access to language and representation does not have to be necessarily self-limiting and self-annihilating.

Winterson's storytelling aims to disrupt the straightforward immediacy of the predominantly realistic mode of the Bildungsroman. The novel opens in a realistic tone, with a first-person account of Jeanette's childhood and adolescence. However, and within the framework of this conventional genre, Winterson does not hesitate to include biblical and fairy-tale-like stories with the odd quest hero adventure recovered from chivalric romance. Commenting on the layout and overall design of *Oranges,* Winterson states in her introduction to the second edition of the novel: "I don't really see the point of reading in straight lines. We don't think like that and we don't live like that. Our mental processes are closer to a maze than a motorway." However, the structure of *Oranges* does not resemble a maze, but has a rather complex, albeit clear and consistent, set-up. Following a linear and straightforward biblical pattern from Genesis to Ruth, the autobiographical material of *Oranges* progressively unfolds its subversively original construction of lesbian girlhood in Northern working-class England. Not even the disruptive fantasy and fairy-tale episodes come to stage at random, but, instead, they are carefully selected to lay stress on the most crucial moments in the girl's development as a female subject and as a lesbian.

Significantly, the first chapters of the novel deal with the central and determinant mother/daughter relationship, a key element in the female Bildungsroman. In the manner of many other female protagonists that preceded her, Jeanette will have to grow against an overwhelmingly strong and powerful mother figure. Analyzing different female Bildungsroman, Mary Ann Ferguson concludes: "These works show the need for a powerful mother figure who provides an either positive or negative impetus and guidance for the psychic journey" (232). Many female heroes, Ferguson adds, are motivated primarily by their mother's lives, even if only (and often) as one they must flee (235). This key relationship with a powerful mother figure echoes the equally determinant and equally conflictive connection of the male hero with his father so characteristic in the literary construction of boyhood in the tradition of male Bildungsroman (see Buckley 17-19). It also simultaneously confirms feminist sociologist Nancy Chodorow's influential revision of psychoanalytic arguments and her insistence that women's sexual difference stems primarily from their identification with their mothers (and not with their fathers, as is the case with boys [164]).

Symbolically, the title, apart from making a playful intertextual gesture by pretendedly quoting a suggestive historical figure, Nell Gwyn—the vital and irreverent seventeenth-century actress who started as an "orange girl" and ended as Charles II's favorite—contributes the unmistakable impression that the whole book is constructed as an assertion and rebellion against this powerful mother figure and her favorite motto: "oranges are the only fruit" (Winterson 29). "Oranges are the only fruit" is her mother's one, single, and only answer to Jeanette's problems and interrogations, and stands as a metaphor for her severe single-mindedness and her limited, rigid, and absolutist worldview. Her mother has taught her that there is only one right "reading" and interpretation of the world, but Jeanette's answer is to contest it by writing and rewriting as many as she can.

Other commonplace themes associate *Oranges* with the conventional and traditionally male Bildungsroman, evidencing several coincidences in the typical pattern of literary construction of boyhood *and* girlhood. Among the most relevant are her isolated childhood, her dissatisfaction at school ("at school there was only confusion" [41]), her complicated confrontation with the outer world ("the daily world was a world of Strange Notions, without form, and therefore void" [48-9]), the record of her first stumbling steps in the process of her "literary education" (her mentor, Elsie, initiates her into poetry by reading Blake and Yeats to her) together with some direct allusions to the literary tradition of Bildungsroman in which Winterson is consciously inscribing her novel—notably Jane Eyre: "who faced many trials and was always brave" (28). Certainly, we are not so far off the archetypal plot of the Bildungsroman, as formulated by humanist critic Jerome Buckley in his by now "classical" definition of the genre that includes the "child of some sensibility" who grows up in the country or in a provincial town, "where he finds constraints, social and intellectual, placed upon the free imagination," a family, especially the father (Buckley is defining the typical plot of the Bildungsroman exclusively in male terms) "who proves doggedly hostile to his creative insights or flights of fancy," a first "schooling experience" that, "even if not totally inadequate, may be frustrating," and at least "two love affairs or sexual encounters, one debasing, one exalting" (17). The main denouement in the plot comes from the hero´s journey away from home (typically into a main city), and the climax will be provided by his eventual return to this home once his initiation is complete. Thus, we could add, the narrative formula of the Bildungsroman comes close to the *rites of passage* and echoes myth and archetypal critic Joseph Campbell's famous stages of the hero's adventure, namely, separation-initiation-return, since, by virtue of its depicting a hero who is embarked both literally and metaphorically in a journey of self-discovery, the typical quest-motif plot becomes, ultimately, not more and not less than an initiation story.

The strong autobiographical element of *Oranges* connects the novel, once again, to the tradition of Bildungsroman. Traditional Bildungsroman critic Francois Jost states that there is hardly any Bildungsroman that is not, in reality, a barely disguised autobiography (100). In fact, most of the critics dealing with the genre have agreed on its common and distinctive autobiographical quality. Buckley goes even further in his speculations by declaring that it is usually a first or second book in which the novelist is still too close to the lived experience to achieve an adequate perspective (24). If Winterson's first novel is, indeed, highly autobiographical and certainly dwells in not very distant personal experiences, her way of handling this autobiographical material with different "detachment" techniques, mainly humor, irony, and parody, recalls again Buckley's definition of the Bildungsroman's author: "usually a younger man, nearer in time to his initiation, self-protectively more ironic, still mindful of the growing pains of adolescence" (25). Nevertheless, and as tends to be the case with most Bildungsroman, the "autobiographical pact," as established by autobiography critic Philip Lejeune, is not made explicit in the text, and the work is ultimately presented as a piece of fiction and not as an *autobiography proper.*

Winterson's literary construction of girlhood not only aligns itself with a traditional genre such as the Bildungsroman, it also partakes of a more subversive version of it, the "Coming Out" novel, which, as feminist critic Paulina Palmer succinctly puts it, includes a number of recurrent motives such as the intelligent but inexperienced protagonist who feels confined by the narrowness and pettiness of her provincial surroundings, her discovery of her lesbian orientation through a first love affair, the subsequent punishment inflicted by her community, and the loss and/or betrayal by her lover who often reverts to heterosexuality (100). The typical Coming Out story line is, after all, a revised version of the plot of the traditional Bildungsroman (in other words: lesbian girlhood versus heterosexual boyhood), and it is also significant and representative of the ideological change the genre has undergone in the twentieth century and its progressive displacement from the center to the margins of the literary and cultural discourses.

The attribution of *Oranges* to the Coming Out genre is essential for the ideological appraisal of the novel and determines its potential to bring about social change (instead of reinforcing social conformity as the traditional bourgeois Bildungsroman would typically do). The mainstream interpretation of it, however, has insisted on seeing it mainly as a story about a child growing up within an Evangelical set, thus compromising its nonapologetic lesbian content in a successful way, as feminist critic Hilary Hinds suggests, to secure its "high cultural status"(161). Hind argues that lesbianism has been dismissed in the critical appreciation of the *Oranges* (156-57) and that decentering lesbianism has become part of the "official" reading of the novel, downplaying, in this way, its resistance to the dominant culture. Many critics choose to ignore the lesbian element in *Oranges* in favor of a more "universal" reading, despite the fact that there is enough evidence in the novel to suggest its importance and centrality. In fact, the handling and selection of narrative materials leave little doubt, as I will now try to prove, that the construction of the protagonist's sexual identity is one of the main points at stake in this Bildungsroman.

Lesbianism is not a mere accident in Winterson's construction of girlhood. On the contrary, the search for a sexual identity shapes and orients her literary project. The first events concerning Jeanette's sexual identity come up strategically early in the story. Already in the first chapter ("Genesis") we have an old gypsy woman's prediction: "You'll never marry . . . not you, and you will never be still" (7). The crucial importance of this event on the hermeneutic level is reinforced by its immediate connection with the story of the two women who "didn't have husbands at all" and who "dealt in unnatural passions," which, for the young and inexperienced focalizer of the autobiographical narration, seemed to mean simply that "they put chemicals in their sweets" (7). From here on, lesbianism will be an issue throughout the narration that is increasingly marked with the confusion and curiosity of a young girl's slow process of "finding out" about lesbian relationships, first through others (May and Ida) and eventually through her own experience.

The central chapters of the novel are significantly and strategically dedicated to the construction of her sexual identity. "Numbers" opens with her recurrent dream of marriage, unveiling her fear and rejection of heterosexuality. Her dreams, her "beast" theory, and her repulsion of close and "affectionate" male characters such as Uncle Bill, are carefully selected autobiographical materials that point toward the construction of a lesbian identity, while implicitly rejecting prevailing and conventional images of girlhood as a state of passive and narcissistic romantic brooding. Jeanette consciously ponders over and defiantly rejects the cultural myths available for the growing girl:

> There are women in the world.
> There are men in the world.
> And there are beasts.
> "What do you do if you marry a beast? Kissing them didn't always help"
> And beasts are crafty. They disguise themselves like you and I.
> Like the wolf in "Little Red Riding Hood." (72)

Jeanette's first "love story" is preceded by a display of all the "wrongs" of marriage and married men, together with scattered allusions to other women's homosexuality and the social rebuke of it (76-77); whereas, significantly enough, the day she takes Melanie to their church the sermon is dealing with the "dreadful sin" of "Unnatural Passions"(85). After having been so carefully and strategically announced, the actual representation of lesbian sexuality and eroticism in *Oranges* will probably take few readers by surprise. In any case, and by means of her lyrical and suggestive decoding of sexual practices that are generally silenced by dominant literary and cultural discourses, Winterson undoubtedly succeeds in subverting heterosexual constructions of sex and gender. From this point in the narration, lesbianism emerges as a growing awareness of the sensual power of the female body, and Jeanette's active, intense, and nonapologetic sexual desire becomes integrated as an irrenunciable part of her identity.

The reaction of the community and the punitive treatment of this first love story is presented in "Joshua" and coincides with two other key moments in the young protagonist's Bildung: her psychological acceptance of uncertainty and her emotional detachment from her mother: "She burnt a lot more than letters that night in the backyard. I don't think she knew. In her head she was still queen, but not my queen any more, not the White Queen any more" (112). The definitive emotional separation from the mother will also mark Jeanette's ideological detachment from her and the rejection of her whole worldview and system of values. This progression is symbolically marked by her contesting of her mother's favorite motto: "It was a bowl of oranges. I took out the largest and tried to peel it. . . . What about grapes, or bananas?" (113), which signals the outset of the complex process of "shedding" and "unlearning" necessarily involved in lesbian education.

Similarly, Winterson's subversive use of humor and parody can be placed within this tradition of the Coming Out story (or lesbian Bildungsroman), as Paulina Palmer points out, thus rejecting the commonplace claim among critics that *Oranges* is unprecedented in its subversive style of humor: "The comic scenarios which Winterson creates, inventive though they are, develop a tradition of lesbian humor which, having originated in the 1970s, has increased in wit and sophistication and finds expression in the 1980s and 1990s in a variety of cultural forms" (80). The subversive significance of laughter has been appropriated by lesbian writers before as a means to invert and problematize the perspective of the dominant culture, which aligns Winterson's text with the emerging lesbian comic fiction that has been developing from the 1970s on. As several critics have pointed out, the use of humor is a covert way of dealing with personal and potentially painful issues (O'Rourke 66-67), especially her conflictive and unresolved relationship with her mother: "I had been brought in to join her in a tag match against the Rest of the World. She had a mysterious attitude towards the begetting of children: it wasn't that she couldn't do it, more that she didn't want to do it. She was very bitter about the Virgin Mary getting there first. So she did the next best thing and arranged for a foundling. That was me" (3).

Laughter becomes, in this way, a useful maneuver of detachment to handle autobiographical material, but it also remains a politically subversive weapon that challenges conventional standards of perceiving and writing the world: "Now and again, my mother liked to tell me her own conversion story, it was very romantic. . . . One night, by mistake, she had walked into Pastor Spratt Glory Crusade. . . . He was very impressive. My mother said he looked like Errol Flynn, but holy. A lot of women found the Lord that week" (8). Winterson's text parodies and mimics authoritative and righteous patriarchal discourses, from romance, fable, and myth, to the sacred language of the Bible, and her laughter thus becomes carnavalesque, powerful and irreverent, deeply subversive but always sympathetic to human frailty.

Winterson's construction of girlhood through fantasy, myth, and fairy-tale challenges expectations about the conventional novel of growth and development while defying and unsettling any final interpretation of her own text. As Winterson herself declares, her aim is to "challenge the way people think, not just about big things but about little daily things as well, to free them for a time from gravity" (13). And it is this effort to free the reader "for a time from gravity" that accounts for her use of fable and fairy tales as a potentially subversive, and deeply destabilizing, autobiographical device. By her interweaving of fabulous narratives, Winterson manages to build up a parallel and alternative plot that replicates and complements, while simultaneously problematizing, the realistic coming-of-age story. These fantastic tales comment on, explain, displace, condense, and/or allegorize some of the crucial elements displayed in the linear progression of realistic events, subverting the possibility of a single authoritative reading of her fiction.

The aim of Winterson's use of fantastic storytelling is to illustrate personal and psychological conflicts and to point out possible solutions or alternative explanations for them. According to psychologist Bruno Bettelheim, fairy tales "depict in imaginary and symbolic form the essential steps in growing up and achieving an independent existence" (73). Fairy tales, Bettelheim suggests, illustrate the conflicts of growing up at the conscious, unconscious, and preconscious levels (6), and play a crucial role in the attempt to master the psychological problems that emerge in the process of growing into maturity. As he points out, the characters and events of fairy tales not only personify inner conflicts, crisis, and dilemmas, but they also hint possible answers and solutions to them (26).

Winterson's magic fairy tales are ultimately tales of Bildung, which is not so surprising if we believe, as historian of religions Mircea Eliade suggests, that fairy tales are almost always translated into initiatory tales. According to feminist critics Sandra M. Gilbert and Susan Gubar, fairy tales make cultural statements with greater accuracy than do more sophisticated literary texts (36). Their ability to do so is based on their potential to reduce the complex process of socialization to a simple and essential paradigm. Feminist critic Ellen Cronan Rose will argue that it is precisely this quality of fairy telling that allows us to *discuss* these stories as "tales of Bildung, narratives of growth and development" (209). This is certainly the case in *Oranges,* where the scattered mythical, biblical, or folklike stories build up a parallel narrative of growth and education that incorporates, in a creative and original way, the use of the bizarre, the fabulous, and the magical in the midst of a personal, intimate, sometimes lyrical and sometimes humorous, but otherwise realistic, coming-of-age story. Winterson is, thus, moving between autobiography and myth, and is getting close to what African American poet Audre Lorde would call "biomythography."

Winterson continuously emphasizes the role of stories in our personal and communal understanding, apprehension, and representation of reality. As folklorists, anthropologists, sociologists, and psychologists have figured out, traditional narrative, namely, fairy tales, folktales, legends, and religious teaching stories, can play an important role in the rearrangement of experience. Folklorist James Roy King, among others, points out the fact that, in fairy and folktales, basic human experience is often pushed beyond the limits of logicality or plausibility into the bizarre and improbable as a way of conveying a certain knowledge and understanding of the world (199). The implicit function of these narratives would be, therefore: "alerting readers and listeners in highly personal ways to *other* arrangements and interpretations in the stuff of experience" (3). Obviously, the suspension of disbelief and the challenge of a rational perspective plays a major role in this process of representation and rearrangement of reality in order to offer *that* particular understanding of the world. Winterson's autobiographical mythmaking is also a "world-making" process that offers different alternative and simultaneous "arrangements of the stuff of experience," thus challenging our stable and logical knowledge of the world.

While discarding a single, autonomous, unitarian model of subjectivity, Winterson also conveys a clear awareness that experience—even autobiographical experience—cannot be explained or legitimized by a single overarching narrative and that there is no one single established and accepted path through experience. Consequently, in Winterson's text we can find no reliable or unique pattern, historical, linguistic, or otherwise, but are forced to remain painfully aware of the instability and lack of finality of any narrative we construct. Since the act of storytelling itself is the most basic of all techniques for establishing an identity, the self becomes a constantly shifting entity, a product of language and narratives, and ultimately, a narrative in itself.

The main reflection on storytelling ("Deuteronomy. The last book of the law") is not placed at random, but is strategically situated right in the middle of the novel, and immediately after the account of Jeanette's first sexual encounter. By this means, Winterson clearly refuses to impose a single meaning either on her own narrative process or on her own personal experience. She hereupon sets herself to deconstruct the dichotomy: history/story ("people like to separate storytelling which is not fact from history which is fact" [93]), denouncing its complicit ideological function: ("They do this so that they know what to believe and what not to believe . . . knowing what to believe had its advantages. It built an empire and kept people where they belonged" [93]). Winterson not only attempts to expose the extent to which the project of establishing one particular narrative as "official History" becomes a strategy to impress and reinforce dominant ideological discourses, but also underlines the fact that both language and memory inevitably reshape the past, "pretending an order that does not exit, to make a security that cannot exist" (95). According to her, this "arranging" and "reshaping" of experience is, precisely, the role of History, and also the role of stories, since official History—or biblical History even—is nothing more (or less) than another type of "story."

Throughout the novel Winterson repeatedly uses her magic storytelling as a way to displace and externalize inner conflicts, undertaking in fabulous terms a parallel and alternative narrative that echoes and reenacts her more autobiographical voyage of self-discovery. One example of how the interweaving of multiple narratives suggests alternative readings to the main autobiographical account is the way in which her mother's conversion, presented in the first chapter of the novel ("Genesis") is echoed and allegorized in the subsequent story of the "brilliant" and "beautiful" princess who, "in danger of being burned by [her] own flame" (9), needs to take on a number of duties and responsibilities in order to channel her energy and resourcefulness. This pattern of fabular reenactment of the autobiographical events will recur again in the novel.

"Stories give shape to lives," asserts Carol P. Christ (1), and in *Oranges* Winterson is actually giving multiple shapes to her life. Jeanette tells of her childhood and adolescence basically through the stories that others tell her and through the stories that she, herself, tells the reader. "Stories helped you to understand the world," Elsie tells the young and confused protagonist (29) and from then on fantasy becomes a means to survive and explain outer reality. At school, Thetrahedron metamorphizes itself into an emperor living in a palace made completely of elastic bands. And her adolescent insight on perfection, in theological (and ontological) opposition to what she is being taught in her church, materializes in a fairy-tale story about a prince in search of a perfect woman. The prince's philosophy on perfection is parodied, downplayed, and finally discarded as "an exhortation to single-mindedness," and so is, implicitly, the religious discourse on perfection. Thus, while maintaining a key role in the process of construction of the young protagonist's consciousness, fantasy also helps to illustrate her new insights in relativism and her growing disagreement with Evangelical fundamentalism.

Some critical moments in the narration, such as her inner struggle to accept her lesbianism, are rendered exclusively in fabulous and allegoric tones. Fantasy overtakes the "Joshua" chapter while Jeanette's "orange demon" (a fairy-tale-like figure) explains to her what will happen is she accepts her sexual difference:

> "What sex are you?"
> "Doesn't matter, does it? After all that's your problem."
> "If I keep you, what will happen?"
> "You'll have a difficult, different time."
> "Is it worth it?"
> "That's up to you." (109)

In the last two chapters ("Judges" and "Ruth"), storytelling becomes more and more crucial in the structure of the novel, coming very close to a total disruption of the realistic mode of the narration. The moment of separation, arguably the most determinant point in the protagonist's Bildung, is echoed by two main stories: the tale of Winnet and the sorcerer and the chevalier romance of Sir Percival. The long and continued story of Winnet and the sorcerer rewrites and reenacts Jeanette's relationship with her mother in fairy-tale magical terms. Significantly enough, the story is fraught with gender reversals since the mother figure is played by a male sorcerer that tricks the young and inexperienced Winnet into believing him her father whereas her lover is rendered as a young boy who unwillingly provokes Winnet's expulsion from the sorcerer's castle. Winnet's story becomes an allegory of Jeanette's painful separation from her mother, her home, and her Evangelical community, while allowing her to express feelings of sorrow and homesickness, as well as a growing sense of foreigness and exclusion that is, for the most part, concealed or overlooked in the main autobiographical and "realistic" narration. It is also in the Winnet's story that we hear of the mythical "sacred" city (presumably Oxford) that becomes Jeanette's dream, in a clear echo of Jude the Obscure's quest for Jerusalem the Golden (arguably, another reference to a well-known Bildungsroman in the English tradition).

The second continued narrative that is chosen to translate into fantastic and fabulous tones both the experience of separation and her final, though tentative, return to her parents' home is the story of Sir Percival. Here the gender role reversal is complete, since Jeanette is choosing to identify herself with a male hero from the chivalric romance tradition. The errant Knight is an old image who traditionally represents the man in search of self-knowledge. And Jeanette is, significantly enough, comparing her plight with that of Sir Percival, the wandering hero who, having been forced to leave King Arthur's court, where he was the favorite, has to face the darkness lying both outside and within himself. Impelled by a vision of "perfect heroism" and "perfect peace" (166), he leaves in search of himself "for his own sake, nothing more," though his journey, may seem at times "fruitless, and himself misguided" (173). "I seem to have run in a great circle, and met myself again on the starting line" (173), says Jeanette at the close of her story. Sir Percival's quest illustrates the circularity of Jeanette's developmental process, her unresolved conflicts, her fluctuations between identification with and separation from her mother, and her mourning of her lost past.

Although the use of storytelling serves a destabilizing purpose in Winterson's text, the subversive potential of the fairy tale remains a problematic question for the feminist critic and/or writer, since, despite Marxist allegations of politically subversive value, it is undeniably obvious that fairy tales and folk stories have traditionally offered different (and unequal) paradigms of maturation for men and women. For the most part, feminist critics have tended to see fairy tales as a source of negative and limiting female stereotypes, ever since the early studies of Simone de Beauvoir (1953) and Betty Friedan (1963), who both denounced the negative effects of myths like "Cinderella," "Snow White," or "Sleeping Beauty" on women's lives. Radical feminist Mary Daly's defiant argument, "Patriarchy perpetuates its deception through myth" (44), succinctly summarizes contemporary feminism's attitude toward fairy tales.

Winterson seems to be echoing all these arguments when she meditates and reconsiders stories like "Beauty and the Beast" or "Little Red Riding Hood." While reflecting on the deceptive nature of these fairy tales, she openly rejects the roles offered to the female protagonists, foreseeing that only disappointment can come from them. After reading "Beauty and the Beast" her young protagonist reflects: "I wondered if the woman married to a pig had read this story. She must have been awfully disappointed if she had. And what about my Uncle Bill, he was horrible, and hairy, and looking at the picture transformed princes aren't meant to be hairy at all" (72).

Winterson's conclusion echoes Mary Daly's: "Slowly I closed the book. It was clear that I had stumbled on a terrible conspiracy. . . . Why had no one told me? Did that mean no one else knew? Did that mean that all over the globe, in all innocence, women were marrying beasts?" (73).

Nevertheless, the folk and fairy tale are not inherently or necessarily patriarchal, as Winterson's novel has proved. Critics such as Jack Zipes emphasize the way in which, from the feudal and early capitalist period on, educated writers engaged themselves in the appropriation of the traditional folktale with the aim of transforming it in a cultural and ideological discourse directed to the children of the European upper classes. Part of this transformation, Zipes explains, involved the replacement of the earlier matriarchal mythology of oral folktales by more patriarchally oriented patterns of socialization (7).

Since the rise of the bourgeoisie and the triumph of the industrial revolution, fantasy and fairy tale have been used to reinforce the cultural construction of girlhood and the clearly differentiated processes of socialization for males and females: "That the rise of the fairy tale in Western Europe should have been coincidental with the rise of the bourgeoisie in the 17th and 19th centuries comes now as no surprise. The increasing conditioning of little girls (seen not heard!) and the inflexibility of rules for women are two aspects of the same repression" (Waelti-Walters 88). From the outset of the industrial revolution, traditional fairy tales underwent a process of ideological rewriting in order to clearly convey and spell out the duties of a bourgeois girl while, at the same time, reinforcing the cultural discourses that supported the capitalist division of labor between the sexes. As Zipes himself points out, the Grimm Brothers' tales are a good example of this process. In their rewriting of a traditional story such as "Snow White" they have an entirely different socialization process in mind, which reflects the sex role ideology of the bourgeoisie: ". . . the growing notion that the woman's role was in the home and that the home was a shelter for innocence and children belonged to a conception of women, work, and child-rearing in bourgeois circles more so than to the ideas of the peasantry and aristocracy" (53).

Contemporary feminist authors like Winterson are, however, currently engaged in utterly re-inverting the process. As we have seen, in many of the stories of *Oranges* gender roles are reversed, patriarchal values are questioned or problematized, and images of girlhood and femininity are challenged, subverted, or interrogated. Rejecting conventional gender hierarchies and challenging the cultural construction of heterosexuality, Winterson's storytelling becomes a source of alternative models of female identity.

Oranges's fairy tales are inhabited by wise, resourceful, and brave heroines who make assertive choices instead of enduringly and self-sacrificingly staying at home, sweeping hearths and awaiting a charming prince. Winterson is undertaking the bold enterprise of rewriting the traditional tale in order to reinvent the position of women as gendered subjects in the patriarchal discourse of myth, romance, and fairy tale.

Winterson's story of rebellious and unconventional coming-of-age builds on the legacy of a tradition of twentieth-century women writers who are using storytelling to formulate their own personal process of socialization. In England, other writers had attempted this task before. The Merseyside Women's Liberation Movement in Liverpool started with the aim of subverting the traditional and patriarchal values embodied in the old fairy tales and argued firmly that "Fairy tales are political" (6). Similarly, Angela Carter has deliberately set out to tell old stories "differently" in her collection *The Bloody Chamber* (1980), where she consciously appropriates and subverts some of the traditional myths and fairy tales that have explained and ratified women's marginal position for centuries. Carter's baroque collection of highly stylized tales tells the "other" side of the story of such well-known popular folk narrations as "Beauty and the Beast," "Little Red Riding Hood," or "Snow White," but also includes her own fully original versions of the tradition.

When used as an instrument of political subversion, the function of storytelling is not exclusively personal, individual, and psychological anymore, but becomes also, and *mainly*, social. Traditional narrative has always played an important social (and arguably political) role. As feminist critic Karen E. Rowe points out: "fairy tales fulfill basic psychic needs for both the individual and society" (69). Marxist critics have been most interested in this subversive potential and have long agreed that even when, for the most part, folk and fairy tales have been part of the ideological discourses determined to legitimate the prevailing cultural, sociological, and economical status quo, they also contain original elements that can be subsequently used with subversive "revolutionary" purposes. Consequently, storytelling can have a countercultural intention, which, as Jack Zipes points out, is made manifest through alternative techniques that "no longer rely on seductive, charming illusions of a happy end as legitimization of the present civilizing process, but make use of jarring symbols that demand an end to superimposed illusions" (179). *Oranges* readily supports Zipes's arguments. Loaded with a clear countercultural intention, Winterson's oblique and creative use of the folk- and fairy-tale tradition, her display of gender ambiguity, her disruption of the seductive happy endings of heterosexual romantic plots, and her offering of alternative models of female identity provide good evidence that storytelling is becoming an instrument of political subversion in contemporary feminist fiction.

Myth, folktales, and fairy tales, however, are not the only kind of traditional narrative that Winterson sets herself to subvert. Another key extended metaphor in *Oranges* is provided by the biblical framework of the narration. Apart from providing the overall structural design for the novel—from Genesis, the book of origins, to Ruth the story of the foreigner—its overwhelming presence is continuously felt, since many of the interwoven narratives share this religious-biblical story tone. Jeanette's adoption at the beginning of the novel, for instance, is presented in visionary, biblical terms, as a replica and a parody of the finding of Jesus by the Three Wise Men (10). Biblical parody and pastiche recur in the narration, which quite often adopts a mythopoetical biblical style, especially in its suggestive, allegorizing speeches where, in full Old Testament fashion, time and place are left undefined, and thoughts and feelings unexpressed, while Jeanette's mother establishes herself as the bearer of the divine will: "We stood on the hill and my mother said, 'This world is full of sin.' We stood on the hill and my mother said, 'You can change the world'" (10).

The female protagonist repeatedly identifies herself with (mainly male) biblical figures: "I scrambled up and went inside, feeling like Daniel" (41). And the actual *reading* of the Bible will play a key role in her educational and formation process: "I developed an understanding of Historical Process through the prophecies in the Book of Revelation" (17). Learning to read from the Book of Deuteronomy will give her a visionary taste for the dark and the "exotic" and a deep-rooted conviction to be "right," which will cause a severe conflict between her inbred evangelical worldview and her more "liberal" formal schooling: "If it had not been for the conviction that I was right, I might have been very sad" (43). This crash with the outer world, the sharp confrontation of values, and her inability to fit in, is again presented in biblical terms, in the chapter entitled "Exodus," which will elaborate on the story of the children of Israel leaving Egypt, "guided by the pillar of cloud by day, and the pillar of fire by night." But the pillar of cloud becomes a log, and the protagonist is left in confusion and perplexity, unable to understand "the ground rules" and doomed to a continual rearranging of "their version of the facts" (49). Biblical certainty and absolutism are no longer possible. If nothing else, her experience of formal schooling has been a lesson in relativism and contextualizing, which suggests that the possibility of a "master text" that can provide a single, authoritative reading of reality has to be finally deconstructed.

Oranges' biblical and fairy-tale-like storytelling ultimately deals with the way we endeavor to make sense of experience and attempt to interpret, represent, and name reality, thus exploring and widening the possibilities offered by the cultural and ideological discourses available to us. "Naming is power," insists Winterson, "that is the way with stories; we make them what we will. It's a way of explaining the universe while leaving the universe unexplained" (93). In *Oranges,* as we have seen, storytelling is a means not only to represent and explain experience, but also to write and create the female subject. In that process of self-writing, both memory and language play an essential part since they reinvent and re-create the past "to fit it, force it, function it, to suck out the spirit until it looks the way you think it should" (93-94). Language not only explains, but inevitably reshapes reality, underlining the multiplicity of meaning and the instability of the process of signification: "Everyone who tells a story tells it differently, just to remind us that everybody sees it differently" (93).

In her own lesbian coming-of -age story, Winterson, as we have seen, audaciously explores the crosslines of genres such as the chivalric romance, the biblical parable, the traditional Bildungsroman or the folk-and fairy tale, reinventing them from their margins and renegotiating the position of the girl heroine as a gendered subject in the male-biased realm of language. *Oranges* decenters the male hero position in the patriarchal story in order to celebrate female identity and sexuality and to prove that the girl's access to the symbolic order is not necessarily as doomed by her subjection to "the Law of the Father" as Lacan has suggested. She can still reclaim a space of her own within the linguistic realm from which to spin her personal and subversive yarn. Ultimately, and by means of the multilayered self-portrait that she chooses to write, Winterson denies the possibility of a single overarching narrative or a single official "History" that could be allowed to impose a final authoritative reading on the self.

NINE

But that Was in Another Country

Girlhood and the Contemporary "Coming to America" Narrative[1]

ROSEMARY MARANGOLY GEORGE

> Coming of age in Antigua—so touching and familiar . . . it could be happening to any of us, anywhere, any time, any place.
>
> —*New York Times Book Review*[2]

BECOMING AMERICAN

This essay takes as its focus the trope of "coming to America" in three contemporary literary texts written by women of color in the United States and published from the late 1980s to 1990s. Novels and autobiographies such as *When I was Puerto Rican* by Esmeralda Santiago (1993), *Lucy* by Jamaica Kincaid (1991), and *Jasmine* by Bharati Mukherjee (1989) rely, for the most part, on a similar narrative: the coming-of-age of girls or young women whose growth is calibrated by the stages in which they discard their associations with the places they belonged to *prior* to their coming to the United States. I will examine the ways in which these three minority texts weave the coming-to-America narrative into the coming-of-age plot and discuss the ideological discourses that frame their reception in the U. S. classroom as much as among the general readership. My intention is to contribute to the larger ongoing discussion that considers the multifarious tasks performed by "minority literatures" within the U. S. academy.

Each of these texts could be described very loosely as a narrative that records the growth of the protagonist from a diffident young girl into a young woman who authorizes or writes her own story. What interests me, in these and similar texts, is the degree to which these narratives problematize this logic of progression even as they move their protagonist simultaneously into adulthood and into the United States. This second journey that piggybacks on the first also implies a journey into the English language and into the "ethnic" narrative of successful progress that becomes *in itself* a sign of acculturation and assimilation *as minority* into the mainstream. The goal in these narratives is not only to take the protagonist to the threshold of adulthood but also to make her authorize the "minority text" in English, which becomes the standard sign of arrival onto the literary center-stage that is available to the immigrant writer. The "America" that is the destination of these journeys is the imagined nation signified by a unifocal patriotism, a monolingual tongue (English or rather, American English) and a determined assimilation of all difference into this national story. The texts that I consider in this essay engage in some degree of resistive negotiations with this America, but these narratives are also severely shaped by the slot that is prepared for the generic coming to America experience in the national imagination. Clearly, this slot is under reconstruction at all times in all (but the most formulaic) coming to America tales. However, I will argue, that unlike the *many* other stories told through minority cultural productions in the late twentieth century, the straightforward coming-of-age to America plot remains almost wholly overdetermined by dominant expectations of the appropriate posture to be adopted by those immigrants who wish to partake in *the* American grand narrative.[3]

While these stories register crossing over and into the geographical boundaries of the United States, what is symbolically being established is the entry into a mythic America. Hence my inclusion of Esmeralda Santiago's autobiographical text *When I was Puerto Rican* in this discussion is not an oversight. Santiago's text and its reception signals that a certain America is the final destination of these narratives, which a place like Puerto Rico cannot satisfy despite being U. S. territory. In its review of *When I was Puerto Rican,* the *Washington Post Book World* takes the liberty of calling it "the American story of immigration, this time with a unique Latin flavor." The fact that Puerto Rico is U. S. territory is insignificant: only certain geographic locations in the United States can carry the weight of the symbolic. Leaving Puerto Rico for New York City parallels the multilayered movements made by immigrants into this metropolis, except for the detail of citizenship.

Is there a certain irony implied in the title of Santiago's text? Does becoming American require not actively being Puerto Rican? This sense of "un-belonging" is woven into the very texture of narratives that claim belonging. The title suggests that to be Puerto Rican is to be foreign or un-American and yet this is the very premise of the coming to America plot.

These narratives both exploit and transform a very rich seam of the Western cultural understanding of itself in relation to the rest of the world by superimposing travel to the West onto the more familiar narrative of traveling to adulthood. The novels suggest that both journeys—to the United States and to adulthood—are indeed the final and logical destination for young subjects who are deemed *worthy* of literary or biographical attention. So that if little Esmeralda, the narrator of *When I was Puerto Rican*, had stayed on in Puerto Rico there would have been no story to tell and no travel to plot with all due literary embellishments. In the progress that we as readers make through the plots of these texts, the two journeys are equated and posed as equally inevitable. This progression relies on hierarchies that have been pervasive at least for three centuries and buttressed by Western discourses of the self and other. For example, in his *Philosophy of History*, Hegel posits a global growth chart of the "historicity" of continents: hence, the African continent and its inhabitants at best equal the darkness of the womb, that is, civilization at the fetal stage; the Orient (namely China and India) represents the childhood of man; Greece and Roman civilization marks the youthful era of mankind; but for the adult man who has reached *his* full human potential we need to look toward the European or "Germanic" man. The logic underlying this worldview has become naturalized to such an extent that it becomes hard to find succinct "citations" that expose the ideologies that circulate within these pervasive racial/geographic discourses.

Of course, as the autobiography demonstrates, Esmeralda grows up and does move out of this past tense, but "becoming American" in New York without continuing to be Puerto Rican (a label that resonates differently in New York City than it would in Puerto Rico) is the location that the author Esmeralda Santiago tries to establish by the end of the novel. She does this through her account of getting admission into a mainstream acting school and then, nurtured by the white women she trains under at the school, going on to Harvard. Yet does this attempt to write herself into the American mainstream also serve to underline the minority citizen's distance from the national norm? These stories insist on a singular national norm even when such singularity would seem anachronistic. In a curious yet predictable fashion, the narrative of the young girl or woman of color who makes it to Harvard University, serves primarily to reconfirm the value of preexisting and hitherto exclusive routes to American success.[4] In a similar fashion, the mythic America requires the consent and cooperation of those it "contains" in order to substantiate itself. And these narratives of "making" Harvard or learning English and so on, provide this substantiation.

Working with the nationalist leader and theorist of the French Revolution Abbé Sieyes's distinction between "passive" and "active" citizens, diaspora studies scholar Vijay Mishra has recently suggested that, "[i]n the cultural sphere active citizens represent the nation-state (in films, fiction, etc.) while passive citizens can participate but not offer themselves as models of the nation" (435). It could be argued that through the very act of writing the minority woman's American Bildungsroman these writers move such citizens from the category of passive to active, or better still expose the irrelevance of such categories in the context of the United States, where the vast majority of the population has a history of immigration in its recent or distant past. Abraham Verghese's best-selling medical autobiography, *My Own Country: A Doctor's Tale,* could be marshaled forth to make this point. In this compelling book, Verghese, a South Asian doctor (with an African childhood), narrates the story of his journey from India to becoming the local AIDS expert in small-town Tennessee. Verghese's text provides a skillful example of immigrant writing of oneself into the national narrative of the United States, to the extent of claiming it as "my own country." "Within a nation-state citizens are always unhyphenated, that is, if we are to believe what our passports have to say about us," writes Vijay Mishra (433). And yet, in actual and symbolic ways, as Mishra immediately acknowledges, "the pure, unhyphenated generic category is only applicable to those citizens whose bodies signify an unproblematic identity of selves with nations" (433).

In a recent essay on ethnic identity in the United States, cultural critic Ruth Hsu interprets "America" as an "ideological construct [which] is designed to maintain and buttress the values and interests of the dominant group, and to do so in such a way as to remove all but the most banal signs of the center's rule" (38). "A crucial element of this discourse of domination" Hsu stresses, "is the concept of ethnicity, which is itself constituted of cultural narratives that undertake to emplot immigrants and other 'ethnics' into the existing socio-ideological framework of national narratives"(38). Ruth Hsu goes on to develop her complex thesis around what she calls the "rehabilitative concept of ethnicity" and the ways in which this is "intimately bound up with the myth of the [American]

Dream." She notes ". . . in the cultural narratives of ethnicity, 'America' is the unquestioned hero, haven to the 'huddled masses,' the poor and the persecuted of the world. In this story, immigrants are drawn to these shores by the American Dream; in turn, it is their belief in this Dream and their hard work that gets them the rewards that they desire. *The rehabilitative concept of ethnicity functions first as proof that America works, that its principles and beliefs are well-founded.* In short, the cultural narratives of ethnicity bolster the discourse of 'America'" (emphasis in original, 38-39). Hsu's formulation of the "rehabilitative concept of ethnicity," when read in light of the coming-of-age/to America narratives, suggests that such rehabilitation is not solely imposed from above but, in some instances, is produced in collaboration with ethnic subjects themselves. Thus the coming-to-America narrative, while it allows for self-representation by minority writers and allows for the minority citizen's entry into the universal, also serves to fix their participation through well-traveled, familiar routes.

But it is the very *familiarity* of the plot that erases the resistance to dominant ideologies that each novelist offers in the novels under discussion. Hence, in *Lucy*, the novelist genre that Jamaica Kincaid references encourages us to read the young protagonist's constant state of rage as directed at the mother she has left behind in the Caribbean island of her past. So while *Lucy* makes trenchant critiques of white privilege in upper-class America, the novel's parallel preoccupation with this teenager's ongoing power struggle with her mother dims the potential of the less familial resistance proffered by the text.

Lucy's first-person narrative begins with her first day in the United States in 1968. Lucy Josephine Potter is nineteen when the novel begins and a Caribbean au pair in a U. S. metropolis. She hates and loves her name, her history, her mother, her home country, and the rich white family she works for. Yet despite the "vinegary" bitterness that Lucy carries over from the Caribbean to the United States, the novel maps her slow blooming into her own person in this new location. This inching toward happiness requires putting enormous space between her past, her mother, her colonial baggage. Despite the harshness of her criticism, the United States is acknowledged as a place where a crabby person like Lucy might find a contented *adult* life. Toward the end of the novel she recalls her past in telling terms: " I had begun to see the past like this: there is a line; you can draw it yourself, or sometimes it gets drawn for you; either way, there it is, your past, a collection of people you used to be and things you used to do. Your past is the person you no longer are, the situations you are no longer in" (136-37). And in the final pages, Lucy tells us: "I was alone in the world. It was not a small accomplishment. I thought I would die doing it. I was not happy, but that seemed too much to ask for" (161). The coming-of-age genre prepares us to read this as *no more* than a display of adolescent angst: the overly dramatic view on life, the carefully prepared presentation of being happiest when properly unhappy and alone.

The Bildungsroman plot has a distinguished literary history.[5] The question with which we have to come to terms with is simple: how do we mine the ironies of a text like *Lucy*, and read against the grain of the Bildungsroman plot as mapped onto geographic travel from the rest of the world to the West? Clearly, "growing up," however differently invested with social meaning, happens routinely to subjects the world over. Hence the effusive blurb from the *New York Times Book Review* on the cover of *Annie John* that serves as the epigraph to this essay, both speaks the truth and speaks it slant: "Coming of age in Antigua—so touching and familiar . . . it could be happening to any of us, anywhere, any time, any place." Embedded in this very quotation that urges the Western reader (implied by "any of us") to identify with Annie John, is the simultaneous erasure of difference. This kind of praise then performs the sleight of hand that cultural critic Palumbo-Liu and others have identified as a primary universalizing strategy in which the minor is hailed and then contained by the dominant.

The coming-of-age plot is especially captivating for young readers who are also in the process of grappling with their own burgeoning adulthood. Hence, whether it be novels popular with young readers around the world (one of the many byproducts of colonial educational systems) such as *Jane Eyre* and *Great Expectations,* or more recent texts like Jeanette Winterson's *Oranges Are Not the Only Fruit,* the coming-of-age plot grips the young imagination as no other generic narrative does. Mapped onto the coming to America narrative, the coming-of-age genre creates a certain level of readerly tolerance (and dismissal) of rebellion, subversion of authority, and loss of innocence. For instance, the title of Julia Alvarez's *How the Garcia Girls Lost Their Accents* is quite telling: here, the quiet humor operates at the level of equating the loss of accent with the loss of virginity, both of which are of concern to the Garcia girls and their family in the United States. In these texts produced by women of color, all anticolonial or oppositional resistance (as manifest through subversive questionings of racial and class hierarchies in a colonial or neocolonial situation) is rendered easily read as no more than a natural phase of suffering through "growing pains." The novels thus partake of and propagate a developmental narrative in which Americanization and the very American ideal of individualization plays a vital part in shaping and establishing the full adult. The texts then end when two thresholds are crossed: adulthood and Americanization. Hence, in *Jasmine,* in the last pages of the text, the protagonist, who has hitherto grown out of her childhood in short violent bursts, goes West (her version of "I light out for the territories") in the best-known American literary tradition.

HERE & THERE / THEN & NOW

Looking back on the work done by creative writers and scholars to expand the Western literary canon, there is much to celebrate. However, what has also become clear is that self-representation of minorities by minority writers is not an end in itself. In an essay that examines the connections between power, representation and resistance through comparative considerations of the movies *Coming to America* and Spike Lee's *Do The Right Thing,* cultural critic Tejumola Olaniyan makes some assessments that are helpful to the issues at hand. Writing about representations of African-Americans by African-Americans, Olaniyan argues that the focus should be on *how* dominated groups represent themselves, rather than simply celebrating the very act of such self-representation. As Olaniyan states in the conclusion to his paper, "Even as we struggle to wrest the means of self-representation, we also need to remain conscious of *how* we achieve it, of the ramifications of the kinds of dreams we encourage ourselves to dream, the types of worlds we invite ourselves to envision" (108). In the late 1990s, writing the coming to America narrative does allow the minority writer to create subject positions for her protagonists, but these positions are already overwritten by U. S. narratives of the proper "immigrant" mode of belonging via assimilation.

Today, such novels are regularly included in literature course syllabi for the best of reasons—to challenge us (as students and teachers) to read texts that are different from the usual canonical prescriptions and *thereby to learn to read differently.* And yet, a text such as *Jasmine* slips out of this well-intentioned pedagogical plan and falls right in line with a conventional reading of the rightness of a very narrow sense of Americanization. *Jasmine* urges us to applaud unquestioningly the young protagonist Jyotoi's transformation into Jasmine and then Jane—a renaming that parallels her equally applauded progression from innocence to experience—as she travels from rural Punjab in India to the American midwest. Hence, rather than present students in the high school or university classroom with textual dynamics that challenge or at the least trouble mainstream narratives on the necessity for all immigrants to "Americanize" themselves—an assimilation that requires a jettisoning of other languages, places, accents, and affiliations—a novel like *Jasmine* collaborates in this very limited yet hegemonic notion of the psychic and linguistic rejections that are necessary to proper Americanization.

In Santiago's *When I was Puerto Rican,* the title and the cover illustration record visually and verbally the parallel move out of childhood and Puerto Rico in evocative, nostalgia-drenched terms. (See Fig. 9.1.) Childhood, as well as the specific place (and language) in which it was played out, is that which must be discarded, moved beyond. This movement beyond is presented complete with its accompanying nostalgia and regret for the simple pleasures left behind—in girlhood—as much as in the Third World location of that childhood. The jacket design of Santiago's book is a carefully crafted testament to such sentiments. The placement of the little girl at the right-hand corner of the front cover serves as a tacit invitation to read, *through her,* this story about the evolution from the sepia- tinted place of thatch-roofed huts and palm trees and black-and-white photos of girlhood to the assertive, contemporary woman writer on the back cover whose very posture denotes the (author)ity of American adulthood. The ease with which a geographic location can be presented in the past tense is of course a logical interpretation of the plot that lies within the covers. This facile translation of space into time is further facilitated and naturalized by marking the "primitiveness" of the specific Third World location that is left behind. Further, the serrated edged border of the cover design for *When I was Puerto Rican* frames the front cover visual in a way that is immediately suggestive of a postage stamp. Clearly, Puerto Rico would not be issuing its own stamps; rather, this becomes a subtle way of stressing that the chronological distance is also a geographic distance.

The mainstream success of novels like *Jasmine* also results from the ease with which they can be read as affirming the suggestion that coming to America results in a modernized, "saved" woman, one who has grown to an individualized adult status and has correspondingly outgrown the childlike, even primitive, country of the past. Once again, this narrative on gender only serves to validate the stereotypes about global gender dynamics that are pervasive in the West: primarily, that women in the West are better off than women anywhere else in the globe with the implicit thesis being that this follows from the innate superiority of Western culture.[6] For instance, *The Baltimore Sun*'s review of *Jasmine,* elicits sympathy for the heroine on these "feminist" grounds: "The story of the transformation of an Indian village girl, whose grandmother wants to marry her off at 11, into an American woman who finally thinks for herself" (from the book jacket). Not surprisingly then, the blurbs on these novels are quite aggressive in pushing the reader to

Figure 9.1

ignore subtle and outright critiques of sexism in the West, of "gringo imperialism," of racial discrimination, or of white privilege. Instead, the reader's attention is repeatedly drawn to the familial; as in domestic themes such as mother-daughter battles or "a child's bittersweet loss of innocence" (from the *Miami Herald,* quoted on the jacket of *When I was Puerto Rican*).

The quotations from reviews that are reproduced on popular paperback editions of these novels demonstrate how this travel or rather the "rescue" into an adult Americanhood is immediately recognized as *the* feature of the text *most* worthy of the reader's attention. I have culled a few choice endorsements reproduced on the covers of these texts in order to demonstrate some of the arguments that I make in this essay:

- The blurb on *Jasmine* supplied by the *Kansas City Star* reads: "A Love Story, a thriller, a coming of age novel and an engaging documentary not only of the India her heroine leaves behind but also of the North America she discovers."
- The citation from *USA Today*'s review of *Lucy* is also illuminating: "what seems to be a story about a clash of cultures is actually about the ways a woman—any woman—must free herself from the past."
- Bobbie Ann Mason, quoted on Santiago's book, writes: "Generously,

Esmeralda Santiago shares with her reader her memories of her Puerto Rican childhood and her bewildering years of transition in New York City. I admire the courage it took to make that journey—and then to write about it with such a clear eye."

- The *San Juan Star* urges us to: "read her [Santiago's] book. . . . You will see how one particular woman's journey from a rippled metal shack in a Puerto Rican countryside barrio becomes a story rich in reverberations about all those who have made a transforming physical and spiritual journey in life."
- Finally, the publisher's blurb on Santiago's book: "How Esmeralda overcame adversity, won acceptance to New York City's High School of Performing Arts, and then went on to Harvard, where she graduated with highest honors, is a record of a tremendous journey by a truly remarkable woman." Note that this account of the book, which presumably had authorial clearance, frames it in terms that are quite compatible with the effusive praise it drew from reviewers.

My purpose in citing these snippets from reviews that are reproduced on the covers and on the initial pages is to point to *the force* with which both the text and its framing devices pressure us to read these narratives as fulfilling a progression toward Americanization (with all its linguistic and affiliative apparatuses). The very fact that one can write about the journey is a sign that the destination is reached—just as surely as one's childhood is past—and both can now become available only as nostalgically re-created narrative accounts.

Both *Jasmine* and *When I was Puerto Rican* begin with a brief chapter that dramatically cuts between origin (the past country of childhood) and final destination (the adult writer's present location in the United States). By using this similar technique, both narratives provide their readers with a map that shows up the vastly different terrain of the starting point and the final destination. Yet, in both texts, this initial chapter is enticingly secretive about this daunting journey between start and finish. This journey, the reader infers, will be the story that the text will leisurely narrate. Thus we are pulled into a narrative that we know will chronicle the dangers, heartache, and other difficulties of such travel. But this structural device also serves to quell any impulse to imagine a different destination at the end of this journey.

The short two-page initial chapter in *Jasmine* begins with a sentence that provides such an encapsulating narrative: "Lifetimes ago, under a banyan tree in the village of Hasnapur, an astrologer cupped his ears—his satellite dish to the stars—and foretold my widowhood and exile. I was only seven then" (1). The reader's introduction to this land of the protagonist's childhood that is now "lifetimes ago" proceeds at a rapid rate with all the violence and stench of the stereotypic, generic Third World. In the pace of two pages, the astrologer hits the seven-year-old Jyoti for resisting his prediction of widowhood and exile, causing a star-shaped wound on her forehead that makes her more docile sisters who are washing clothes by a nearby river shriek: "Now your face is scarred for life! How will the family ever find you a husband?" to which she sagely replies "it's not a scar it is my third eye. . . . Now I am a sage" (2). So saying, our young heroine goes for a swim in the river, where: "Suddenly my fingers scraped the soft water logged carcass of a small dog. The body was rotten, the eyes had been eaten. The moment I touched it, the body broke in two, as though the water had been its glue, and then both pieces quickly sank" (3). At this point in the narrative there is a significant break in the text that is marked by a visually effective blank space. The narrative then cuts to the present: "That stench stays with me. I am twenty-four now, I live in Baden, Elsa County, Iowa, but every time I lift a glass of water to my lips, fleetingly I smell it. I know what I don't want to become" (3).

In this brief first chapter, Mukherjee presents the reader with the sharp and shocking contrast between past and present: between the place of adulthood (age 24 in Baden, Elsa County, Iowa) which is the place of civilization and the old country fleetingly remembered through a stench of water (a glass of water raised to the lips). When Mukherjee ends this introductory section with "I know what I don't want to become," the exact referent is unclear.[7] What is suggested, however, is that the past erupts onto the present like a bad smell: as a reminder of what the 24-year-old in Iowa must constantly move beyond if she is to become what she *wants* to become.

When I was Puerto Rican opens, like *Jasmine*, with a short introductory chapter that sets the geographic and chronological parameters of the "journey" that is the subject matter of this text. In this two-page prologue, titled "HOW TO EAT A GUAVA," Santiago uses a more positively spun version of the same technique Mukherjee uses in her text; namely, fashioning a frame for the narrative that will follow from this presentation of a sharply contrasting past and present. Like the cover design, this prologue is a nostalgic lament of what must regrettably, and yet inevitably, be left behind in the country of one's childhood. The prologue that lovingly re-creates the many aspects of enjoying guavas in Puerto Rico ends with the following passage of the adult lingering over the fruit at a Shop and Save in New York City:

> Today I stand before a stack of dark green guavas, each perfectly round and hard, $ 1.59. The one in my hand is tempting. It smells faintly of late summer afternoons and hop-scotch under the mango tree. *But this is autumn in New York, and I am no longer a child.*
>
> The guava joins its sisters under the harsh fluorescent lights of the exotic fruit display. I push my cart away, toward the apples and pears of my adulthood, their nearly seedless ripeness predictable and bitter-sweet. (4, emphasis added)

There is, thus, in both these opening passages, a clear plot summary and interpretative device offered to the reader: with *here* and *there* signifying on several registers.

BEYOND THE PURELY LITERARY

In the late 1990s the radical edges of these texts by women of color risk being blurred (often despite authorial intentions) and instead are offered up as one more facet of the necessary growing pains attendant to becoming fully American. In this section, I will primarily offer suggestions for how we can teach these texts without further blunting the resistive edge of these fictions.

Texts such as these by Mukherjee, Kincaid, and Santiago provide great reading pleasure: they are engaging, fairly short, and easy to read. At the same time, however, they are very difficult to teach responsibly, that is with due attention paid to all the (literary and nonliterary) discourses in which they participate. The purely literary reading of these texts cannot do justice to the developments in the female protagonists' world that are mapped by the narrative.[8] In the late 1990s, the coming to America story, as presented in contemporary popular fiction must be read (and taught) alongside the very different immigration histories of various racial and ethnic groups. Even while these literary texts strive to represent minority experiences, we cannot expect literary works to single-handedly produce an awareness of the heterogeneity of reasons for and actual experiences of coming to the United States. It would be productive to teach these fictional and autobiographical novels alongside the whole spectrum of discourses on global economic relations, immigration and citizenship: from debates on bilingual education, present-day anti-immigrant legislation and mass hysteria about illegal (and legal) immigration to crossracial and crossethnic coalitions in the wake of such anti-immigrant moves. We need, for instance, to study and teach the impact of the exclusion laws in the late nineteenth century as much as the changes in demographics wrought by changes in immigration law throughout the twentieth century. In *Immigrant Acts,* cultural critic Lisa Lowe provides an exemplary demonstration of the kinds of economic and political analyses that must necessarily frame discussions on literary and other cultural productions. For example, Lowe suggests that the exclusions that have framed the lives of Asian-Americans in the United States, the U. S. wars in Asia, and the recruitment of labor and capital from Asia by U. S. interests, have together resulted in the situation where "in the last century and a half, the American *citizen* has been defined over and against the Asian *immigrant,* legally, economically, and culturally. These definitions have cast Asian immigrants both as persons and populations to be integrated into the national political sphere and as the contradictory, confusing, unintelligible elements to be marginalized and returned to their alien origins" (4). Within this understanding of Asian-Americans as available for integration and yet always alien (as "noncitizen labor"), Lowe's theorizing amply demonstrates the value of the pronouncement that cultural forms cannot be sifted out of the material circumstances by which they are produced.

Any examination of the coming to America narrative must consider the difference that issues of gender, class, and the historical moment of the writing makes to the reception of these texts. Over the past hundred or more years, several minority writers have rewritten the coming to America narrative that has been a staple of "ethnic" American literature from the nineteenth century onward.[9] This would include autobiographies like *Barrio Boy* published in 1971 under the auspices of the United States–Mexico Border Studies Project at the University of Notre Dame. *Barrio Boy* is Ernesto Galarza's autobiographical account of how he traveled from rural Mexico to Sacramento, California, with his impoverished mother and uncles to escape the upheavals caused by the 1911 Mexican revolution. The autobiography ends with his realization that he has found a vocation in organizing the migrant workers in California. *Barrio Boy* serves as a model for *When I was Puerto Rican* as much as it does for Richard Rodriguez's 1981 autobiographical collection of essays on growing up as Mexican-American in the United States, *Hunger of Memory.* Another powerful model from the 1970s is *The Woman Warrior: Memoirs of a Girlhood among Ghosts* by Maxine Hong Kingston. This rich and multilayered narrative recounts a young Chinese-American girl's journey from childhood to young adulthood. In their time, both texts by Galarza and Kingston made serious interventions in the white-black discourse of "being American."

For our purposes today the more crucial question is of the usefulness of this genre in challenging hegemonic notions of what it means to be or become American or to write American narratives from immigrant positions. We need to consider whether the radical interventions in mainstream discourses on immigration, equal opportunity, bilingualism, and acculturation that *Barrio Boy* and *The Woman Warrior* performed in the 1970s is possible through a similar narrative in the late 1990s. In the current moment when affirmative action and bilingualism bashing is in full swing, it is imperative that these coming-of-age/to America narratives not be read as simply prescribing assimilation as the proper destination of the fully developed immigrant. The conservatism of narratives such as *Hunger of Memory*, the writings of Dinesh d'Souza, and Mukherjee's 1996 diatribe against immigrants who are reluctant to submit to full Americanization (in citizenship, dress, American-accented English) already frames these novels and autobiographical accounts.[10] *Hunger of Memory*, Richard Rodriguez's 1981 autobiographical narrative, falls much too easily into arguments for abolishing affirmative action and bilingual education. Rodriguez himself posits these arguments by using the very Bildungsroman narrative that these later women writers employ. For instance, Rodriguez writes of his move from speaking Spanish to English as one from childhood to adulthood and from outsider to American. Of his success in newly learned English, Rodriguez writes: "At last, seven years old, I came to believe what had been technically true since birth: I was an American citizen." Or further on, ". . . the day I raised my hand in class and spoke loudly [in English] to an entire roomful of faces, my childhood started to end." In this text and in other writing Rodriguez takes his advocating against affirmative action and bilingual education to parodic levels. Despite the wide rift between the political stance occupied by Rodriguez and the women writers I consider in this essay,[11] the similarity in their use of literary techniques (the Bildungsroman narrative) facilitates the use of these texts in projects that are ultimately not immigrant-friendly.

It is also worth mentioning that in the late twentieth century, immigrants are not so unidirectional as these narratives make it seem. Cheaper and more accessible communications and travel has created scenarios in which there is no need to leave the other country entirely in the past. Immigrant affiliations are also more fluid than simply moving toward assimilation into the national body of America. Several scholars have noted how immigrants are able to maintain close ties with their countries of origin so that they form "transnational diasporas" rather than "immigrants." Anthropologist and cultural critic Arjun Appadurai calls this new distinction, the difference between reading the United States as "a land of immigrants and

[it] being acknowledged as being one node in a post-national network of Diasporas" (803). Appadurai has suggested that hyphenations should be doubled so that we have "African-American-Jamaican or Hispanic-American-Bolivian" (804). His point is that this would more accurately capture the affiliations that people carry with them. Furthermore, it has been noted that with the improved global networks (information and capital) that connect the United States to the rest of the globe, America travels to the Third World in multifarious forms: armies, foreign aid, AIDS, cultural products such as movies and music, and so on.

Hence, transnationalism is an important feature of international border crossing in the late twentieth century that must be brought to bear on these literary texts. Linda Basch, Nina Glick Schiller, and Christina Szanton Blanc, three scholars working on Haitian, Grenadian, and Filipino immigrants in the United States, independently observed similar phenomenon in these three communities and *Nations Unbound: Transnational Projects, Postcolonial Predicaments, and Deterritorialized Nation-States* documents their findings. They found that given the practices they observed in these communities, the very concept of the *immigrant* was outdated and instead the more accurate term to bring into usage would be: *transmigrants* or *transnationalists*. This follows from *transnationalism*, the term used by social scientists to refer to "the emergent migration process in which people live lives stretched over national borders"(4). Basch et al provide further elucidation of this distinction:

> The word "immigrant" evokes images of permanent rupture, of the abandonment of old patterns of life and the painful learning of a new culture and often a new language (Handlin 1973). The popular image of immigrants is one of people who have come to stay, having uprooted themselves from their old society in order to make for themselves a new home and adopt a new country to which they will pledge allegiance. Migrants on the other hand, are conceived of as transients who have come only to work; their stay is temporary and eventually they will return home or move on. *Yet it has become increasingly obvious that our present conceptions of "immigrant" and "migrant," anchored in the circumstances of earlier historic movements, no longer suffice.* Today, immigrants develop networks, activities, patterns of living, and ideologies that span their home and host society. (3-4, my emphasis)

In the second chapter of their book, Basch, Glick Schiller, and Szanton Blanc present four interrelated theoretical premises that "situate transnational processes within global history, make central the agency of transmigrants, and contextualize ongoing contention over the loyalty and identity of immigrants" (23). Of these four important premises, the first is most relevant to this discussion of literary/autobiographical texts: "Transnational migration is inextricably linked to the changing conditions of global capitalism and must be analyzed within the context of global relations between capital and labor" (23). I will insist that literary analyses of coming-to-America narratives cannot evade due consideration of such premises.

And finally, even as I point to the limitations of these texts in pedagogical situations that are not attentive to the nonliterary issues I have raised here, I do want to draw attention to a potentially generative by-product of my analysis; namely, that such analysis allows us to mark a genre (a literary tradition dare we say) that continues to be reinvented in the late twentieth century. This coming to America narrative is embroidered on by writers who are usually classified or categorized by their racial and geographic origins. Under this new rubric we could read Cristina Garcia (author of the Cuban- American novel *Dreaming in Cuban*) and one of her protagonists the young teenager Pilar alongside Rio, the girl protagonist of Jessica Hagedorn's *Dogeaters* (usually classified as Asian-American). *How the Garcia Girls Lost Their Accents* by Julia Alvarez and *No Telephone to Heaven* by the Caribbean-American writer Michele Cliff could also be brought into this discussion: we would need to determine the degree to which Clara Savage undoes this coming to America narrative by returning to her childhood home in Jamaica and the degree to which Alverez succeeds in her structural and thematic attempts to complicate her version of this story. In *Immigrant Acts*, Lisa Lowe writes of her intention to "thematize Asian American cultural productions as countersites to United States national memory and national culture"(4). It could be argued that texts such as those mentioned in this paragraph do indeed complicate the coming-of-age/to America story to the extent of creating "countersites" within their pages. These countersites are instructive in that they make explicit the incompleteness of such journeys and tacitly refuse to present normative Americanization as a singular, logical destination or safe haven.

Needless to say, there are many other plot-lines that minority cultural productions follow. Not all of them are as easily recuperated or "contained" within a mainstream understanding of difference. Nor are all minority cultural productions to be understood as aiming for integration into an America whose welcome to minorities is always suspect. We need to remind ourselves as teachers and as students of the different modes of resistance that are required in different locations. In a footnote to his essay on Murphy and Lee's films, Olaniyan provides a brief note on resistance that is very helpful here. He writes that "The important point is to have no illusions about the limits of the capacious jaws of hegemony but at the same time not to be paralyzed into inertia by it; to study the context of resistance carefully and not to dismiss aforehand gestures that are apparently too 'feeble' or too 'clearly overdetermined' by the dominant" (109). I began formulating the ideas in this essay when I decided (about two or three years ago) that I simply would not teach *Jasmine* in my undergraduate classes. However, in the course of writing this essay, I have learned that dismissing *Jasmine* and other such coming-of age/to America texts simply because they are "too 'feeble' or too 'clearly overdetermined' by the dominant," is the easy way out. Such texts provide us with the opportunity to meet creative writing with creative reading: to bear witness to the compromises as well as to the triumphs of minority cultural production.

Notes

1. This essay was first submitted to Ruth Saxton in February 1996 for consideration for a 1996 MLA panel on girlhood. I would like to thank Ruth, the other panelists, and a very attentive audience at that late night session at the Washington D.C. MLA, for their enthusiastic response to my work. I would also like to thank Ann duCille for valuable suggestions that have greatly benefited this essay.
2. This quote, reproduced here in its entirety, has pride of place on the front cover of Jamaica Kincaid's novel *Annie John*.
3. Critics like Lisa Lowe, David Palumbo-Liu, Arjun Appadurai, and Ruth Hsu have more fully discussed the dimensions of this normative America. These scholars are especially interested, as I am, in "how the aesthetic is a contested site of the minor's entrance into the universal" (Palumbo-Liu, 189).
4. See for example "Why I Took a Chance on Learning: From Community College to Harvard," an autobiographical essay by Cynthia G. Inda. In this essay published in the *New York Times* (3 August 1997), the young author writes of her journey from her California-based family of Mexican immigrant parents (a maid and dishwasher with the equivalent of a second-grade education) and five siblings (none of whom had attended college; most hadn't completed high school) to Harvard University. I would like to thank Indira Ganesan for this reference.
5. See Franco Moretti for an illuminating literary history of the Bildungsroman in Europe. Moretti reads this genre as the "symbolic form" of modernity

wherein youth, mobility, change, and interiority are showcased. Note that marriage provides the "logical" resolution in the protagonist's journey in most European Bildungsroman plots. Jane Eyre's "Reader, I married him" thus declares the suturing that provides satisfying narrative closure to the story. In the Bildungsroman texts that I examine in this essay, "America" is the final destination.

6. Non-Western, and increasingly, Western feminists have noted the fallacy of this viewpoint, even as they acknowledge that much work needs to be done to improve the status of women the world over. I am aware of the pitfalls of using large generalizations like "the West" and "the non-West" in scholarly writing., However, I find these terms accurate for the purpose of mapping popular feminism's generalizations on the status of women on a global scale.
7. I think that it is significant that the echoes of the line made famous by the U.S. Arrned Forces recruiting slogan ("Be all that you can be—Join the Army") that readers in the United States would hear in this sentence, does not deter Mukherjee from using it.
8. In her essay titled "One Mother, Two Daughters: The Afro-Caribbean Female Bildungsroman," Geta LeSeur provides just such a literary analysis of the coming-of-age plot. She finally concludes that "while the black American writer's Bildungsroman becomes a platform for protest, the West Indian's operates out of the child's consciousness, thus she is primarily apolitical"(27).
9. For example, Anzia Yezierska's autobiographical novel *Bread Givers: A Struggle between a Father of the Old World and a Daughter of the New,* is representative of the vast body of Jewish coming to America fiction. Also see Piri Thomas's autobiographical text, *Down These Mean Streets,* and Nicholasa Mohr's *Nilda.*
10. For a fuller discussion of these texts by d'Souza and Mukherjee, see essays by Rosemary Marangoly George, Kamala Visweswaran, and Susan Koshy.
11. Note for instance that Santiago's book was published simultaneously in English and Spanish, thus marking her refusal to give up bilingualism in the course of her quest for assimilation.

Works Cited

Abel, Elizabeth, Marianne Hirsch, and Elizabeth Langland, eds. *The Voyage In: Fictions of Female Development.* Hanover and London: University Press of New England, 1983.

Acker, Kathy. *Blood and Guts in High School.* 1984. New York: Grove Press, 1989.

———. *Don Quixote.* 1986. New York: Grove Press, 1989.

———. *Great Expectations.* 1982. New York: Grove Press, 1989.

Allison, Dorothy. *Bastard Out of Carolina.* New York: Dutton, 1992.

———. "Context." *Skin: Talking About Sex, Class and Literature.* Ithaca: Firebrand Books, 1994. 9-36.

———. *Two or Three Things I Know for Sure.* New York: Plume, 1996.

Alterers, Nanette. "Gender Matters in *The Sadeian Woman.*" *The Review of Contemporary Fiction* 14 (1994): 18-23.

Alvarez, Julia. *How the Garcia Girls Lost Their Accents.* Chapel Hill: Algonquin Books, 1991.

Anderson-Dargatz, Gail. *The Cure for Death by Lightning.* Toronto: Alfred A. Knopf, 1996.

Appadurai, Arjun. "The Heart of Whiteness." *Callaloo* 16 no. 4 (1993): 796-807.

Auchmuty, Rosemary. *A World of Girls.* London: The Women's Press Ltd., 1992.

Austen, Jane. *Northanger Abbey.* 1818. London: Everyman's Library, 1994.

Awkward, Michael. "Roadblocks and Relatives: Critical Revision in Toni Morrison's *The Bluest Eye.*" *Critical Essays on Toni Morrison.* Ed. Nellie Y. McKay. Boston: G. K. Hall & Co., 1988. 57-68.

Baker, Houston Al, Jr. "When Lindbergh Sleeps with Bessie Smith: The Writing of Place in *Sula.*" *Toni Morrison: Critical Perspectives Past and Present.* Eds. Henry Louis Gates, Jr., and K. A. Appiah. New York: Amistad, 1993. 236-60.

Bakerman, Jane S., and Mary Jean DeMarr. *Adolescent Female Portraits in the American Novel 1961-1981.* New York: Garland, 1983.

Barnett, Pamela E. "Figurations of Rape and the Supernatural in *Beloved.*" *PMLA* 112 no. 13 (May 1997): 418-27.

Basch, Linda, Nina Glick Schiller, and Christina Szanton Blanc. *Nations Unbound: Transnational Projects, Postcolonial Predicaments, and Deterritorialized Nation-States*. Amsterdam: Gordon and Breach, 1994.

Bausch, Richard. "Her Thoughts While Drowning." Review of *Black Water*. *New York Times Book Review*. 10 May 1992: 1, 29.

Beauvoir, Simone de. *The Second Sex*. New York: Alfred A. Knopf, 1953.

Berkley, Sandra. *Coming Attractions*. Illinois: Academy Chicago, 1988.

Bettelheim, Bruno. *The Uses of Enchantment: The Meaning and Importance of Fairy Tales*. New York: Alfred A. Knopf, 1976.

Birch, Eva Lennox. *Black American Women's Writing: A Quilt of Many Colors*. New York: Harvester Wheatsheaf, 1994.

Boose, Lynda E., and Betty S. Flowers. *Daughters and Fathers*. Baltimore: Johns Hopkins University Press, 1989.

Bordo, Susan. *Unbearable Weight: Feminism, Western Culture, and the Body*. Berkeley: University of California Press, 1993.

Bottigheimer, Ruth B., ed. *Fairy Tales and Society: Illusion, Allusion and Paradigm*. Philadelphia: University of Pennsylvania Press, 1986.

Brooks, Cleanth, and Robert Penn Warren. *Understanding Fiction*. New York: Appleton, Century, Croft, 1943.

Brown, Lyn Mikel. "Telling a Girl's Life: Self-Authorization as a Form of Resistance." *Women, Girls & Psychotherapy: Reframing Resistance*. Eds. Carol Gilligan, Annie G. Rogers, and Deborah L. Tolman. New York: The Haworth Press, 1991.

———, and Carol Gilligan. *Meeting at the Crossroads: Women's Psychology and Girls' Development*. New York: Ballantine Books, 1992.

Brownstein, Rachel. *Becoming a Heroine: Reading About Women in Novels*. New York: Penguin, 1984.

Brumberg, Joan Jacobs. *The Body Project: An Intimate History of American Girls*. New York: Random House, 1997.

Bryant, Sylvia. "Reconstructing Oedipus Through 'Beauty and the Beast.'" *Criticism* 31 (1989): 439-53.

Buchwald, Emile, Pamela R. Fletcher, and Martha Roth, eds. "Are We Really Living in a Rape Culture?" *Transforming a Rape Culture*. Minneapolis: Milkweed Editions, 1993. 7-10.

Buckley, Jerome H. *Season of Youth: The Bildungsroman from Dickens to Golding*. Cambridge, MA.: Harvard University Press, 1974.

Campbell, Joseph. *The Hero With A Thousand Faces*. Princeton: Princeton University Press, 1968.

Campion, Jane, dir. *A Girl's Own Story*. 1986. Films By Jane Campion. First Run Features, 1991.

Cantwell, Mary. "Jane Campion's Lunatic Women." *New York Times Magazine,* 19 Sept. 1993: 40+.

Carlip, Hillary. *Girl Power.* New York: Warner Books, 1992.

Carrington, Kerry, and Anna Bennet. "'Girls' Mags' and the Pedagogical Formation of the Girl." *Feminisms and Pedagogies of Everyday Life.* Ed. Carmen Luke. Binghamton: State University of New York Press, 1996. 147-66.

Carter, Angela. *The Bloody Chamber.* 1979. New York: Penguin, 1993.

Chesler, Phyllis. *Women and Madness.* New York: Avon, 1973.

Chodorow, Nancy. *The Reproduction of Mothering: Psychoanalysis and the Sociology of Gender.* Berkeley: University of California Press, 1978.

Chopin, Kate. *The Awakening.* 1899. Ed. Margo Culley. New York: Norton, 1994.

Christ, Carol P. *Diving Deep and Surfacing: Women Writers on Spiritual Quest.* Boston: Beacon Press, 1980.

Christian-Smith, Linda K. "Young Women and Their Dream Lovers: Sexuality in Adolescent Fiction." *Sexual Cultures and the Construction of Adolescent Identities.* Ed. Janice M. Irvine. Philadelphia: Temple University Press, 1994. 206-27.

Chute, Carolyn. *The Beans of Egypt, Maine.* New York: Ticknor Fields, 1985.

Cisneros, Sandra. *The House on Mango Street.* New York: Vintage, 1991.

Clark, Robert. "Angela Carter's Desire Machine." *Women's Studies* 14 (1987): 147-61.

Cliff, Michele. *No Telephone to Heaven.* New York: Vintage International, Random House, 1989.

Dalsimer, Katherine. *Female Adolescence: Psychoanalytic Reflections on Literature.* New Haven: Yale University Press, 1986.

Daly, Brenda. *Lavish Self-Divisions: The Novels of Joyce Carol Oates.* Jackson: University Press of Mississippi, 1996.

——— and Maureen T. Reddy, eds. *Narrating Mothers: Theorizing Maternal Subjectivities.* Knoxville: University of Tennessee Press, 1991.

———. "'An Unfilmable Conclusion': Joyce Carol Oates at the Movies." *The Journal of Popular Culture* 23: 3 (Winter 1989): 101-14. Rpt. in *Where Are You Going, Where Have You Been?* Ed. Elaine Showalter. New Brunswick: Rutgers University Press, 1994.

Daly, Mary. *Gyn/Ecology: The Metaethics of Radical Feminism.* Boston: Beacon Press, 1978.

Dane, Gabrielle. "Hysteria as Feminist Protest: Dora, Cixous, Acker." *Women's Studies* 23 (1994): 231-55.

DeMarr, Mary Jean and Jane S. Bakerman. *The Adolescent in the American Novel Since 1960*. New York: Ungar, 1986.

Dittmar, Linda. "'Will the Circle Be Unbroken?': The Politics of Form in *The Bluest Eye*." *Novel* 23 (1990): 137-55.

Doane, Mary Ann. "Ideology and the Practice of Sound Editing and Mixing." *The Cinematic Apparatus*. Eds. Teresa de Luretis and Stephen Heath. New York: St. Martin's Press, 1980. 47-56.

Donnell, Alison. "She Ties Her Tongue: The Problems of Cultural Paralysis in Postcolonial Criticism." *ariel* 26 no.1 (January 1995): 101-16.

D'Souza, Dinesh. *The End of Racism*. New York: The Free Press, 1995.

Duncker, Patricia. "Re-imagining the Fairy Tale: Angela Carter's Blood Chambers." *Literature and History* 10 (1988): 3-14.

DuPlessis, Rachel Blau. *Writing Beyond the Ending: Narrative Strategies of Twentieth-Century Women Writers*. Bloomington: Indiana University Press, 1985.

Eliade, Mircea. *Birth and Rebirth*. New York: Harper and Brothers, 1958.

Erdman, David V., ed. *The Complete Poetry and Prose of William Blake*. Berkeley: University of California Press, 1982.

Felski, Rita. *Beyond Feminist Aesthetics: Feminist Literature and Social Change*. Cambridge, MA: Harvard University Press, 1989.

Ferguson, Mary Anne. "The Female Novel of Development and the Myth of Psyche." *The Voyage In: Fictions of Female Development*. Eds. Elizabeth Abel, Marianne Hirch, and Elizabeth Langland. Hanover and London: University Press of New England, 1983.

Fetterly, Judith. "Women Beware Science: 'The Birthmark.'" *Critical Essays on Hawthorne's Short Stories*. Ed. Albert J. von Frank. Boston: G. K. Hall & Co., 1991. 164-73.

Fine, Michelle, and Pat McPherson. "Over Dinner: Feminism and Adolescent Bodies." *Disruptive Voices: The Possibilities of Feminist Research*. Ann Arbor: University of Michigan Press, 1992.

Friedan, Betty. *The Feminine Mystique*. New York: Dell Publ. Co., 1963.

Friedman, Ellen G. "Where are the Missing Contents? (Post)Modernism, Gender, and the Canon." *PMLA* 108 (1993): 240-52.

Fuderer, Laura Sue. *The Female Bildungsroman in English: An Annotated Bibliography of Criticism*. New York: Modern Language Association, 1990.

Galarza, Ernesto. *Barrio Boy*. Indiana: A Publication of the United States–Mexico Border Studies, University of Notre Dame, 1971.

Garcia, Cristina. *Dreaming in Cuban*. New York: Ballantine Books, 1993.

Gates, Henry Louis, Jr. "Review of *Jazz*." *Critical Perspectives Past and Present*. Eds. Henry Louis Gates, Jr., and K. A. Appiah. New York: Amistad, 1993. 52-5.

George, Rosemary Marangoly. "'from expatriate aristocrat to immigrant nobody': South Asian Racial Strategies in the Southern Californian Context." *Diaspora* 6, no. 1 (forthcoming).

Gerrand, Nicci. "The Prophet" (Interview with Jeanette Winterson). *New Statesmen Society* 2 (Sept. 1, 1989): 65.

Gilbert, Sandra M. "Life's Empty Pack: Notes Toward a Literary Daughteronomy." *Daughters and Fathers*. Eds. Lynda E. Boose and Betty S. Flowers. Baltimore: Johns Hopkins University Press, 1989. 256-77.

——— and Susan Gubar. *The Madwoman in the Attic: The Woman Writer and the Nineteenth-Century Literary Imagination*. New Haven: Yale University Press, 1979.

Gilligan, Carol. *In a Different Voice: Psychological Theory and Women's Development*. Cambridge, MA: Harvard University Press, 1982.

———, Nona P. Lyons, and Trudy J. Hamner, Eds. *Making Connections: The Relational Worlds of Adolescent Girls at Emma Willard School*. Cambridge, MA: Harvard University Press, 1990.

"'Grief, Fear, Doubt, Panic'—and Guilt." *Newsweek*, 4 August 1969: 22-31.

Grosz, Elizabeth. *Volatile Bodies: Toward a Corporeal Feminism*. Bloomington: Indiana University Press, 1994.

Hagedorn, Jessica. *Dogeaters*. New York: Penguin, 1990.

Hamilton, Jane. *The Book of Ruth*. New York: Anchor Books, 1990.

Hancock, Emily. *The Girl Within*. New York: E. P. Dutton, 1989.

Hardy, Thomas. *Jude the Obscure*. Modern Library Edition. New York: Random House, 1967.

Harris, Trudier. *Fictions and Folklore: The Novels of Toni Morrison*. Knoxville: University of Tennessee Press, 1991.

Hawthorne, Nathaniel. "The Birthmark." *The Celestial Railroad and Other Stories*. New York: Penguin, 1980. 203-20.

Heilbrun, Carolyn. *Writing a Woman's Life*. New York: Ballantine, 1988.

Heilman, Robert. "Hawthorne's 'The Birthmark': Science as Religion." *South Atlantic Quarterly* 48 (1949): 575-83.

Herman, Judith Lewis, with Lisa Hirschman. *Father-Daughter Incest*. Cambridge, MA: Harvard University Press, 1981.

Hinds, Hilary. "*Oranges Are Not the Only Fruit*: Reaching Audiences Other Lesbian Texts Cannot Reach." *New Lesbian Criticism: Literary and Cultural Readings*. Ed. Sally Munt. New York, London: Harvester-Wheatsheaf, 1992.

Hirsch, Marianne. *The Mother/Daughter Plot: Narrative, Psychoanalysis, and Feminism*. Bloomington: Indiana University Press, 1989.

Hodge, Merle. *Crick Crack, Monkey*. 1970. London: Heinemann Educational Books, 1981.

Hsu, Ruth. "'Will the Model Minority Please Identify Itself?' American Ethnic Identity and Its Discontents." *Diaspora* 5 no.1 (Spring 1996): 37-63.

Humphreys, Josephine. *Rich in Love*. New York: Viking, 1987.

Hunnewell, Susannah. "A Trusting Young Woman." *New York Times Book Review*. 10 May 1992: 29.

Hurston, Zora Neal. *Their Eyes Were Watching God*. 1937. New York: Harper & Row, 1990.

Inda, Cynthia G. "Why I Took a Chance on Learning: From Community College to Harvard." *New York Times*. 3 August 1997, education life section: 31, 40, 42.

Irvine, Janice M. "Cultural Differences and Adolescent Sexualities." *Sexual Cultures and the Construction of Adolescent Identities*. Ed. Janice M. Irvine. Philadelphia: Temple University Press, 1994. 3-50.

Jameson, Frederic. *The Political Unconscious: Narrative as a Socially Symbolic Act*. Ithaca: Cornell University Press, 1981.

JanMohamed, Abdul R. "The Economy of Manichean Allegory: The Function of Racial Difference in Colonialist Literature." *Race, Writing and Difference*. Ed. Henry Louis Gates, Jr. Chicago: University of Illinois Press, 1986.

Johnson, Mary Lynn. "Feminist Approaches to Teaching Songs." *Approaches to Teaching Blake's Songs of Innocence and of Experience*. Eds. Robert F. Gleckner and Mark L. Greenberg. New York: Modern Language Association, 1989. 57-66.

Jordan, Elaine. "The Dangers of Angela Carter." *New Feminist Discourses: Critical Essays on Theories and Texts*. Ed. Isobel Armstrong. London: Routledge, 1992. 119-31.

Kakutani, Michiko. "Loss in the Caribbean, From Birth On." *The New York Times* 16 Jan. 1996: E7.

Kappeler, Susanne. *The Pornography of Representation*. London: Polity Press, 1986.

Kaschak, Evelyn. *Engendered Lives: A New Psychology of Women's Experience*. New York: Basic Books, 1992.

Kincaid, Jamaica. *Annie John*. New York: Farrar, Straus, Giroux, 1983.

———. *At the Bottom of the River*. New York: Random House, 1985.

———. *The Autobiography of My Mother.* New York: Farrar, Straus, Giroux, 1986.

———. *Lucy.* New York: Penguin, Plume. 1991.

———. "On Seeing England for the First Time." *Harpers.* 283 (August 1991): 13-17.

———. *A Small Place.* New York: Farrar, Straus Giroux, 1988.

King, James Roy. *Old Tales and New Truths: Charting the Bright Shadow World.* Albany: State University of New York Press, 1992.

Kingston, Maxine Hong. *The Woman Warrior: Memoirs of a Girlhood among Ghosts.* New York: Knopf, 1976.

Koshy, Susan. "The Color of Whiteness." *Transitions* 73 (forthcoming).

Kristeva, Julia. *The Kristeva Reader.* Ed. Toril Moi. New York: Columbia University Press, 1986.

Lacan, Jacques. *Ecrits.* Paris: Editions du Seuil, 1966.

Lejeune, Philippe. *Le pacte autobiographique.* Paris: Editions du Seuil, 1975.

LeSeur, Geta. "One Mother, Two Daughters: The Afro-Caribbean Female Bildungsroman." *The Black Scholar* 17 no. 2 (March/April 1986): 26-33.

———. *Ten Is the Age of Darkness: The Black Bildungsroman.* Columbia: University of Missouri Press, 1995.

Lesser, Ellen. "An Interview with Carolyn Chute." *New England Review and Bread Loaf Quarterly.* 8 no. 2 (Winter 1985): 158-77.

Linkin, Harriet Kramer. "Isn't It Romantic? Angela Carter's Bloody Revision of the Romantic Aesthetic in 'The Erl King.'" *Contemporary Literature* 35 (1994): 305-23.

Lorde, Audre. *Zami: A New Spelling of My Name.* New York: The Crossing Press, 1983.

Lowe, Lisa. *Immigrant Acts: On Asian American Cultural Politics.* Durham: Duke University Press, 1996.

McCorkle, Jill. *The Cheer Leader.* Chapel Hill: Algonquin Books, 1984.

———. *Ferris Beach.* Chapel Hill: Algonquin Books, 1990.

McRobbie, Angela. *Feminism and Youth Culture: From "Jackie" to "Just Seventeen."* Boston: Unwin Hymen, 1991.

Mbiti, John S. *African Religions and Philosophy.* New York: Praeger, 1969.

Megan, Carolyn E. "Moving Toward the Truth: An Interview With Dorothy Allison." *The Kenyon Review* 16 no. 4 (1994): 71-83.

Meriwether. Louise. *Daddy Was a Number Runner.* New York: Pyramid Books, 1970.

Merseyside Women's Liberation Movement. *Red Riding Hood.* Liverpool: Fairy Story Collective, 1972.

Metzger, Michael M., and Katharina Mommsen. *Fairy Tales as Ways of Knowing: Essays on Marchen in Psychology, Society, and Literature*. Bern: Peter Lang, 1981.

Miller, Alice. *Thou Shalt Not Be Aware*. New York: Farrar, Straus, Giroux, 1993.

Miller, Nancy K. *The Heroine's Text: Readings in the French and English Novel, 1722-1782*. New York: Columbia University Press, 1980.

Mishra, Vijah. "The diasporic imaginary: theorizing the Indian diaspora." *Textual Practice* 10 no. 3 (1996): 421-47.

Mitchell, Sally. *The New Girl: Girls' Culture in England, 1880-1915*. New York: Columbia University Press, 1995.

Mitchell, W. J. T. "Memory, Narrative, and Slavery." Narrative Conference, Albany. 1993.

Mohr, Nicholasa. *Nilda*. 1973. Houston: Arte Publico Press, 1986.

Morretti, Franco. *The Way of the World: The Bilungsroman in European Culture*. London: Verso, 1987.

Morrison, Toni. *Beloved*. New York: Plume, 1987.

———. *The Bluest Eye*. 1970. New York: Penguin, 1993.

———. *Jazz*. New York: Alfred A. Knopf, 1992.

———. "Memory, Creation, and Writing." *Thought* 59 no. 235 (Dec. 1984): 385-90.

———. *Song of Solomon*. New York: Plume, 1977.

———. *Sula*. New York: Plume, 1973.

———. *Tar Baby*. New York: Plume, 1981.

Mukherjee, Bharati. *Jasmine*. New York: Ballantine (Random House) Books, 1989.

———. "Two Ways to Belong in America." *The New York Times* 22 September 1996: E13.

Oates, Joyce Carol. *Black Water*. New York: E. P. Dutton, 1994.

———. *Foxfire, Confessions of a Girl Gang*. New York: E. P. Dutton, 1993.

———. *I Lock My Door Upon Myself*. New York: Ecco Press, 1990.

———. "'Is This the Promised End?': The Tragedy of King Lear." *Contraries*. New York: Oxford University Press, 1981. 51-81.

———. "The Model." *Haunted: Tales of the Grotesque*. New York: E. P. Dutton, 1994. 99-144.

———. *The Rise of Life on Earth*. New York: New Directions Press, 1991.

———. *What I Live For*. New York: E. P. Dutton, 1994.

———. "When Characters from the Page Are Made Flesh on the Screen." *Sunday New York Times* 23 March 1986: 1, 21.

———. "Where are you going, where have you been?" *Where Are You Going, Where Have You Been? Stories of Young America.* Greenwich: Fawcett, 1984. 11-31.

———. "Why Is Your Writing So Violent?" *New York Times Book Review* 29 March 1981: 15, 35.

———. "Years of Wonder." *Where Are You Going, Where Have You Been? Stories of Young America.* Greenwich: Fawcett, 1984: 337-52.

Olaniyan, Tejumola. "'Uplift the Race!': *Coming to America, Do the Right Thing,* and the Poetics and Politics of 'Othering.'" *Cultural Critique* (Fall 1996): 91-113.

O'Neale, Sondra. "Race, Sex and Self: Aspects of Bildung in Select Novels by Black American Women Novelists." *MELUS* 9 no. 4 (Winter II 1982): 25-37.

Orenstein, Peggy. *School Girls: Young Women, Self-Esteem, and the Confidence Gap.* New York: Doubleday, 1994.

O'Rourke, Rebecca. "Fingers in the Fruit Basket: A Feminist Reading of Jeanette Winterson's *Oranges Are Not the Only Fruit.*" *Feminist Criticism: Theory and Practice.* Ed. Susan Sellers. New York, London: Harvester-Wheatsheaf, 1991.

Palmer, Paulina. *Contemporary Lesbian Writing: Dreams, Desire, Difference.* Philadelphia: Open University Press, 1993.

Palumbo-Liu, David. "Universalisms and Minority Culture." *differences* 7 no.1 (1995): 188-208.

Perry, Donna, ed. "Jamaica Kincaid." *Backtalk: Women Writers Speak Out: Interviews by Donna Perry.* New Brunswick: Rutgers University Press, 1983. 127-41.

Pipher, Mary. *Reviving Ophelia: Saving the Selves of Adolescent Girls.* New York: Ballantine, 1994.

Plath, Sylvia. *The Bell Jar.* London: Faber and Faber, 1963.

Pratt, Annis. *Archetypal Patterns in Women's Fiction.* Bloomington: Indiana University Press, 1981.

Quart, Barbara. "The Short Films of Jane Campion." *Cineaste* 19 no. 1 (1992): 72+.

Rapping, Elayne. "None of My Best Friends: The Media's Unfortunate 'Victim/Power' Debate." *"Bad Girls/Good Girls": Women, Sex, and Power in the Nineties.* Eds. Nan Bauer Maglin and Donna Perry. New Brunswick: Rutgers University Press, 1996. 205-25.

Redding, Arthur F. "Bruises, Roses: Masochism and the Writing of Kathy Acker." *Contemporary Literature* 35 (1994): 281-304.

Rich, Adrienne. *Of Woman Born: Motherhood as Experience and Institution.* New York: Norton, 1976.

Rimmon-Kenan, Shlomith. *Contemporary Poetics.* London and New York: Routledge, 1983.

Rodriguez, Richard. *Hunger of Memory: The Education of Richard Rodriguez.* Boston: D. R. Godine, 1981.

Rose, Ellen Cronan. "Through the Looking Glass: When Women Tell Fairy Tales." *The Voyage In: Fictions of Female Development.* Eds. Elizabeth Abel, Marianne Hirsch, and Elizabeth Langland. Hanover and London: University Press of New England, 1983.

Rosenberg, Ruth. "Seeds in Hard Ground: Black Girlhood in *The Bluest Eye.*" *Black American Literature Forum* 21 (1987): 435-45.

Rowe, Karen E. "Fairy-born and human-bred: Jane Eyre's Education in Romance." *The Voyage In: Fictions of Female Development.* Eds. Elizabeth Abel, Marianne Hirsch, and Elizabeth Langland. Hanover and London: University Press of New England, 1983.

Rowe, Michael. "We're as American As You Can Get." Interview with Dorothy Allison. *Harvard Gay and Lesbian Review* 2 no.1 (Winter 1995): 5-10.

Rush, Florence. *The Best Kept Secret: Sexual Abuse of Children.* New York: McGraw-Hill, 1980.

Salinger, J. D. *The Catcher in the Rye.* 1951. New York: Bantam, 1989.

Santiago, Esmeralda. *When I was Puerto Rican.* New York: Vintage (Random House), 1993.

Schine, Cathlee. "A World as Cruel as Job's." *New York Times Book Review.* 4 February 1995: 5.

Sciolino, Martina. "Kathy Acker and the Postmodern Subject of Feminism." *College English* 52 (1990): 437-45.

Shigekuni, Julie. *A Bridge Between Us.* New York: Anchor Books/Doubleday, 1995.

Sidel, Ruth. *On Her Own: Growing Up in the Shadow of the American Dream.* New York: Viking, 1990.

Simmons, Diane. An unpublished interview with Jamaica Kincaid. 12 June 1993; portions of which appeared in Simmons, Diane, *Jamaica Kincaid.* New York: Twayne, 1994.

Smith, Sidonie. "Identity's Body." *Autobiography and Postmodernism.* Eds. Kathleen Ashley, Leigh Gilmore, and Gerald Peters. Amherst: University of Massachusetts Press, 1994. 263-92.

———. *Subjectivity, Identity, and the Body: Women's Autobiographical Practices in the Twentieth Century.* Bloomington: Indiana University Press, 1993.

Soderlind, Sylvia. "Love and Reproduction: Plagiarism, Pornography and Don Quixote's Abortions." *Signs of Change: Premodern—Modern—Postmodern*. Ed. Stephen Barker. Albany: State University of New York Press, 1996: 247-59.

Spillers, Hortense J. "Changing the Letter: The Yokes, the Jokes of Discourse, or Mrs. Stowe, Mr. Reed." *Slavery and the Literary Imagination*. Eds. Deborah McDowell and Arnold Rampersad. Baltimore: Johns Hopkins University Press, 1989. 25-61.

Stone, Kay F. "Feminist Approaches to the Interpretation of Fairy Tales." *Fairy Tales and Society: Illusion, Allusion and Paradigm*. Ed. Ruth B. Bottigheimer. Philadelphia: University of Pennsylvania Press. 1986. 229-36.

Tapping, Craig. "Children and History in the Caribbean Novel: George Lamming's *In the Castle of My Skin* and Jamaica Kincaid's *Annie John*." *Kunapipi* 9 (1989): 51-59.

Taylor, Jill McLean, Carol Gilligan, and Amy Sullivan. *Between Voice and Silence: Women and Girls, Race and Relationship*. Cambridge, MA: Harvard University Press, 1995. 41-50.

Terr, Lenore. *Unchained Memories: True Stories of Traumatic Memories, Lost and Found*. New York: Basic Books, 1994.

Thomas, Piri. *Down These Mean Streets*. 1967. New York: Vintage Books, 1991.

Tiffin, Helen. "Decolonization and Audience: Erna Brodber's *Myal* and Jamaica Kincaid's *A Small Place*." *Span*. 30 (1990).

Timothy, Helen Pyne. "Adolescent Rebellion and Gender Relations in *At the Bottom of the River* and *Annie John*." *Caribbean Women Writers: Essays from the First International Conference*. Ed. Selwyn Cudjoe. Wellesley: Callaloo Pub., 1990.

Tolman, Deborah L. "Daring to Desire: Culture and the Bodies of Adolescent Girls." *Sexual Cultures and the Construction of Adolescent Identities. Ed. Janice M. Irvine*. Philadelphia: Temple University Press, 1994. 250-54:

———, and Tracy E. Higgins. "How Being a Good Girl Can Be Bad for Girls." *"Bad Birls"/"Good Girls": Women, Sex, and Power in the Nineties*. Eds. Nan Bauer Maglin and Donna Perry. New Brunswick: Rutgers University Press, 1996. 205-25.

Upchurch, Michael. "Unpleasant Dreams." Review of *Haunted: Tales of the Grotesque*. *New York Times Book Review* 13 Feb. 1994: 34.

Verghese, Abraham. *My Own Country: A Doctor's Story of a Town and Its People in the Age of AIDS*. New York: Simon & Schuster, 1994.

Vice, Lisa. *reckless driver*. New York: Plume, 1996.

Visweswaran, Kamala. "Diaspora by Design: Flexible Citizenship and South Asian in U.S. Racial Formations." *Diaspora* 6 no. 1 (forthcoming).

Waelti-Walters, Jennifer. *Fairy Tales and the Female Imagination*. Montreal: Eden Press, 1982.

Waugh, Patricia. *Feminine Fictions: Revisiting the Postmodern*. New York: Routledge, 1989.

Wells, Rebecca. *The Divine Secrets of the YaYa Sisterhood*. New York: HarperCollins, 1996.

———. *Little Altars Everywhere*. New York: HarperCollins, 1992.

White, Barbara A. *Growing Up Female: Adolescent Girlhood in American Fiction*. Westport: Greenwood Press, 1985.

Winterson, Jeanette. *Art and Lies*. New York: A.A. Knopf, 1995.

———. *Oranges Are Not the Only Fruit*. 1985. New York: The Atlantic Monthly Press, 1987.

Wise, Sue. "Sexing Elvis." *On Record: Rock, Pop, and the Written Word*. Eds. Simon Frith and Andrew Goodwin. New York: Pantheon Books, 1989.

Wolf, Naomi. *The Beauty Myth: How Images of Beauty are Used Against Women*. New York: W. Morrow, 1991.

———. *Promiscuities: The Secret Struggle for Womanhood*. New York: Random House, 1997.

Yezierska, Anzia. *Bread Givers, A Novel: A Struggle between a Father of the Old World and a Daughter of the New*. New York: Doubleday, 1925.

Zipes, Jack. *Fairy Tales and the Art of Subversion: The Classical Genre for Children and the Process of Civilization*. New York: Wildman Press, 1983.

Notes on Contributors

BRENDA BOUDREAU, a visiting Assistant Professor at McKendree College, Illinois, and a Ph.D. candidate at West Virginia University, is completing work on her dissertation "The Battleground of the Adolescent Body: Growing up Female in Contemporary American Novels," which looks at novels written by women during the past forty years. Other work includes essays on the works of Katherine Anne Porter and Laura Ingalls Wilder.

DEBORAH CADMAN, Visiting Assistant Professor at Skidmore College, is currently working on an essay for the anthology *Imagining Adoption: Essays on Literature and Culture*, ed. Marianne Novy. Other works include essays on Toni Morrison, Emily Dickinson, Randall Kenan, and Charles Chestnutt.

RENEE R. CURRY, Associate Professor of Literature and Writing, California State University, San Marcos, is editor of *Perspectives on Woody Allen* (Macmillan, 1996) and co-editor of *States of Rage: Emotional Eruption, Violence, and Social Change* (New York University Press, 1996). She has published articles on William Faulkner, Elizabeth Bishop, and May Sarton, as well as on film directors John Waters, Stephen Frears, Julie Dash, and Errol Morris.

BRENDA DALY, Professor of English and Women's Studies at Iowa State University, is currently working on a book called *Father-Daughter Incest: Narrative, Representation, and Reception in Contemporary American Culture*. She has written two other books, *Authoring a Life: Woman's Survival in and Through Literary Studies* (SUNY, 1998) and *Lavish Self-Divisions: The Novels of Joyce Carol Oates* (Mississippi, 1996), and is co-author of the edited collection, *Narrating Mothers: Theorizing Maternal Subjectives* (Tennessee, 1992).

ISABEL C. ANIEVAS GAMALLO, Associate Professor at University of Leon, is currently working on a study of Jean Rhys's *Wide Sargasso Sea*. She has published *Race and Displacement in Joan Riley's The Unbelonging*. Her scholarly interests include novels of bildungsroman and the possibilities of cultural resistance in textual colonialism.

ROSEMARY MARANGOLY GEORGE, Associate Professor in the literature department at the University of California, San Diego, has published *The*

Politics of Home: Postcolonial Relocations and Twentieth Century Fiction (Cambridge University Press, 1996) and edited *Burning Down the House: Recycling Domesticity* (Harper Collins/Westview Press, 1998). She has published articles in *differences, NOVEL, Cultural Critique, MELUS,* and *Diaspora.*

GINA HAUSKNECHT, Assistant Professor of English, Coe College, received her Ph.D. from the University of Michigan–Ann Arbor. Her dissertation and ongoing research are on gender and consent in Milton's prose and poetry and surrounding seventeenth-century popular print discourse about marriage and political theory.

RUTH O. SAXTON, Professor of English and Dean of Letters at Mills College, Oakland, California, edited the *Doris Lessing Newsletter* 1992-1998. She co-edited *Woolf and Lessing: Breaking the Mold* with Jean Tobin (St. Martin's Press, 1994). Her next book examines constructions of the older woman in fiction.

DIANE SIMMONS, an Assistant Professor at Borough of Manhattan Community College, City University of New York, has published *Jamaica Kincaid* (Twayne, 1994) and *Maxine Hong Kingston: A Ballad of Belonging* (Twayne/Macmillan, 1999). Her scholarship includes marginalized literatures and the narcissistic nature of colonial and postcolonial relationships.

ELINOR ANN WALKER received her Ph.D. from the University of North Carolina–Chapel Hill and has taught at Rockford College and at The University of the South. Her research interests include southern literature and culture, and she has published essays on Walker Percy, Josephine Humphreys, Jill McCorkle, and Richard Ford. She is currently working on an Author's Series volume on Richard Ford, and a manuscript on Josephine Humphreys, Jill McCorkle, and Kaye Gibbons.

Index